ENOUGH

DANIELLE NORMAN

ENOUGH

DANIELLE NORMAN

DEDICATION

To my own beta hero,
Can I keep you?

* * *

To the bad ass bitches: Arell, Jessica, Lisa, Sonnie, Sophia, and the baddest of them all Maria. Who would have thought on one hot day in North Carolina our lives would collide and never be the same?

* * *

To Eric and those brave enough to come out of the closet, thank you. That is no place for people, you take up too much room, and I have too many pairs of fucking fabulous shoes.

I've never met a strong person with an easy past.

— UNKNOWN

ARIEL

*M*oving to the happiest fucking place on Earth had nothing to do with fairy tales or finding my Prince Charming. Thanks to my daddy, I no longer believed in magic or happily ever afters. I landed in this city because this was the land of hotels, conventions, and destination weddings, which meant it was my best bet at becoming an event planner.

I didn't hate being a seamstress, but it wasn't my dream, it was my mama's. I never told her that I'd rather be on the other side, planning the events where people wore the fancy clothes, costumes, and uniforms.

I never got the chance.

During my freshman year of high school, she had her first stroke, spoke with a slur, and relied a little more on me. But just before my senior year, Mama had her second stroke, and someone needed to keep the business going to pay the bills, so I took over. Because Daddy was long gone, he had no use for an invalid wife, and no interest in raising a teenage daughter who hated him.

I told myself repeatedly that Mama would have wanted me to follow my dream, even if it meant hers was gone. Though, I doubted that included buying a motorcycle.

I BRUSHED the wetness away then strapped on my helmet and headed to my motorcycle. Ever since binge watching *Sons of Anarchy*, I wanted to be badass. Okay, not like crime badass. Just the I-look-cool-on-this-bike kind of badass. So, after I unpacked my last box, I went out and purchased a Harley Sportster. I couldn't wait to start the engine and let the wind whip across my face. It was cathartic. As the engine roared to life, I replayed the words my teacher said just a few weeks ago during motorcycle safety class.

Ease up on the throttle.

Hold steady.

Don't freak.

The bike will go where your eyes go.

I found myself twisting the throttle a little more than I should have, and a small smile pulled at my lips.

I shifted gears and headed to the service road around the Mall at Millennia, Orlando's version of Rodeo Drive. Since I lived in metro Orlando, finding somewhere to practice riding wasn't easy. There were always constant road improvements or tourists who drove like idiots reversing down the interstate because they missed the fucking exit. So, the rarely traversed area behind the mall was one of the best places to practice.

It was also one of the only places I'd practiced. I stayed within a five-mile radius of my home, but I needed to get comfortable and feel confident so I could take my bike out for a long ride, let the sun shine down on my face and forget the reality that was my life.

After a few laps around the mall, I pulled my bike into a parking spot, headed inside to grab a drink, and was walking back out to my bike when two men dressed all in black cut between two cars.

They reminded me of Crabbe and Goyle from the Harry Potter movies, and I was still watching them from the corner of my eye when they broke into a run. There was nothing oaf-like or klutzy about them. Maybe they had just robbed Tiffany's or Cartier? That didn't seem right, though. There were no security guards chasing them. No alarms going off or police cruisers peeling into the lot.

Eyebrows dipping, I paused. Watching.

The two men zigzagged through another section of cars, and the one on the left pointed in my direction. In that earth-shattering moment it connected—they were after me. I ran. Fuck. I had no clue what to do. I would never be able to start my bike and get away quick enough. Their footsteps got closer then stopped. I turned around just as the two men separated, one going left the other going right, moving in an arc around me. They were corralling me like a caged animal.

"Help!" I shouted just before a hand clamped over my mouth.

"Shut the fuck up, bitch," a husky voice commanded. I didn't. I continued to try to scream as I kicked and hit him. Biting. I raked my nails down his forearm, his face, his shoulder—wherever I could dig my nails. I wasn't going with these men willingly.

People say your life flashes before your eyes in times of crisis, when what they mean is that you replay your life in slow motion.

In those brief moments, it seemed as if I relived that day when everything seemed to unravel.

Mama sitting at her sewing table as she looked up and hollered, "Close that door. You weren't born in a barn."

And I'd had it, she kept forgiving him. "Why do you stay married to him? All day long Billie Sue Werner ran around school telling the entire freshman class that her mama saw Daddy parked by the railroad tracks with Ms. Kinney, and they were 'going at it.' It's the same thing Daddy does almost every night just with different women. You know it, I know it, the whole town knows it, Mama. And they're laughing at us."

I marched back through the house and slammed the door shut. This was just one of the many things I hated about living in a small town, everybody knew your business, and nothing ever changed.

"You go get your homework done, you hear me?"

"Yes, I hear you. But do you hear me? Mama, I'm serious. I'm leaving. I can take no more."

That was when Mama's face took on an ashen appearance and she collapsed.

I learned real fast how wrong I was, I could take more. In fact, it was shoved down my throat, heaped on my shoulders, and I was still taking it.

The brief flash from my past was shattered by the smell of days-old sweat on the man holding me. My body revolted, my mouth went watery, and my stomach lurched with the sour taste curdling on my tongue. I was going to vomit, and there was nothing I could do to stop it.

"Fucking watch it, man. We ain't supposed to hurt her, just scare her." The guy I nicknamed Crabbe had a Hispanic accent and seemed a bit uncomfortable about what they were doing.

I broke free from the Goyle-dude as he argued back.

Scare me? Scare me? What the fuck? "Help!" My shout rang out across the parking lot. "Fine. You scared me. Let me go!"

They came at me again, obviously not convinced that I was scared enough. They circled me, Crabbe in front and Goyle-dude at my back. The guy behind me wrapped his arms around my chest, restraining me and lifted me off the ground. The toes of my left shoe scraped the concrete, giving me just enough leverage to pull my leg back and aim for the fat guy's nuts.

"Help!" I shouted again and again until my throat burned

Someone had to hear me. There had to be someone! I refused to cry, not yet, not there, I needed to get a grip on at least one of these men. Anything. Anywhere. These bastards, whoever they were, were not going to get away with what they were trying to do. I had to break free long enough to pull off their damn masks, at least one of their masks. If I survived, I wanted to be able to identify these sons of bitches. I didn't get the chance, though.

Untrimmed nails bit into my ankles as the other thug grabbed my legs.

"Let's go," Goyle-dude ordered.

I bucked, twisted, and tried to get away as they carried me like a piece of furniture.

Then I heard it, a shout in the distance.

"Police! Freeze!"

In their haste to escape, the men dropped me, I scrambled to right myself and get my feet under me. My head snapped back, pain shot through my scalp as one of the men grabbed a fistful of my hair and slammed me forward. My face met the hood of a car with a sickening *crack*. The wet heat of my own blood and searing pain were the only things I registered before the man yanked back one more time. I didn't have time to put my hands up as my face barreled toward a window and I hit the car again, this time with enough force to knock me out.

I awoke on the ground, the burning hot pavement seared through my skin and deep down to my bones. Tiny pieces of gravel and sand pressed into my skin. I wasn't sure how long I'd been lying there, but I was hyperaware and could feel every single pebble and grain.

Gentle fingers wrapped around my wrist that rested at my side. I felt the brush of a watchband against my palm and scratch of calluses over my skin. Somehow, I was alert enough to process that this was a man's hand. He pressed two fingers to the underside of my wrist. It took a few more seconds to realize that he was checking for a pulse, and then the fear set in that my attackers were back.

I tried to get up, but I couldn't move, I ached too badly.

"Help," I begged, but my voice sounded like a gurgle, a sound that even I didn't recognize escaping my lips.

Lights flashed around me. I didn't understand where all the lights were coming from. My mind too clouded with fear, it took me several seconds to realize that they were prisms dancing in tiny shards of glass that surrounded me.

The hand on my wrist was gone, and a moment later, a man's face came into my field of vision.

"Can you hear me? I am Deputy Kayson Christakos; I'm here to rescue you. Paramedics are on the way. Don't try to move. You're safe."

Blink.

Our eyes locked.

Blink.

I saw stars. No . . . a star. Then I passed out, again.

KAYSON

"What?" I answered my cell phone for the third time in less than five minutes.

"Are you there yet?"

"Yes. I'm walking in right now," I snapped at Ian.

"Check it over and make sure they spelled our names correctly. Don't fuck it up."

"I won't fuck it up. Jesus Christ, I'm almost thirty." I hung up my phone without saying goodbye to yet another brother. If they were all so worried about it, they should have come to get it themselves. I'd argued about the gift, stating that our mother deserved the fucking Nobel Peace Prize, Congressional Medal of Honor, and a Star on Hollywood's Walk of Fame just for surviving us or at least not drowning one of us, but they squashed my ideas.

I waited for the lady at Neiman's to acknowledge me, when she did, "Hi, I'm here to pick up a bracelet under the name Christakos."

The woman smiled at me, but I was too tired to care that she was hot. I'd been on shift since six that morning and wanted nothing more than to be home where I didn't have to watch my back nonstop.

"Is this for your mother?" the woman behind the counter asked as she unbuttoned her top button. "Or are you buying it for your wife?"

The last question she directed to my crotch, but he wasn't much of a talker.

"Yes, it's Mother's Day weekend, after all."

"Do you need a gift for your wife?" She batted her eyelashes, and I wanted to tell her to stop. I didn't know one guy that found that sexy.

Really? I wasn't even going to answer her. What was it with women and men in uniform? It was as if they lost their minds. I stopped being a man and became an object, which was slightly ironic considering how most men thought about women. Most. Not me. It made me really freaking uncomfortable. Normally, I would have gone home and changed to avoid this shit, but the mall closed in ten minutes and this couldn't wait until tomorrow. My patience hung on by a thread, so I had no time for aspiring badge bunnies.

Finally, she turned over my bag and receipt, and I left, nodding to the two security guards as I passed them on my way out.

The automatic doors to the mall's west entrance slid open. I took my first step out, and my head snapped to the right. Listening.

"Help!"

I wasn't on shift, but that didn't matter. I raced toward the voice, cutting through aisle after aisle of parked cars before two men came into view. My blood boiled. They were carrying a woman between them—one holding her ankles and the other with his hands hooked under her arms. The woman, who seemed so tiny, was screaming and thrashing between them. I drew my sidearm without stopping and shouted, "Police! Freeze!"

They ignored me, they didn't freeze.

They never did. They slammed her against a car and took off. I had a choice: pursue them or help her.

"Fuck it." I pivoted toward the car, and radioed into dispatch.

"This is thirteen twelve." My badge number told dispatch exactly who I was. "Female down. Need backup and FD at Mall at Millenia west side perimeter road. Responding units, locate and hold two subjects wearing dark jeans, black T-shirts, and dark ski masks. On foot, heading south through the parking lot."

Keeping my gun at the low-ready, I scanned the nearby cars,

looking for witnesses or other accomplices as I neared the woman. I took a deep breath and slowly exhaled before returning my gun to its holster.

Her body lay splayed on the ground, her red hair spread out around her as if she were only asleep. Taking in her outer appearance as I bent down I noted her missing shoe and black leather biker vest. No patches or emblems. Her wrist was already blooming with purple and blue bruises, so I was as gentle as possible as I checked for her pulse, which was strong. My relief was short lived when I brushed her red hair away from her face. She was covered in blood, but it didn't look like any of the glass cut her. Then I lowered my eyes to hers and stared into piercing green eyes that seemed to hide years of worry in their depths.

"Can you hear me? I am Deputy Kayson Christakos; I'm here to rescue you. Paramedics are on the way. Don't try to move. You're safe."

Sirens wailed, getting louder the closer they came, and the lights swirled brightly in the twilight. The ambulance, fire truck, and two cruisers came screeching to a stop not too far away.

As a motorcycle deputy, my job involved traffic, crowds, and speeders. I didn't work crime scenes. So, when the two rookie deputies climbed out of their cruisers, I gave them the run-down and then stepped aside. I was free to go. I was off shift and they were there to secure the scene until a detective arrived. I should head to the station and fill out my statement but for some reason I didn't want to leave this woman. Her eyes spoke to me, and they begged me to keep her safe.

I needed to see her eyes, make contact one more time, but they'd covered her with a metallic insulated shock blanket and strapped a c-collar around her neck. Two EMT's knelt next to her body while a third held her head.

"On three—one, two, roll." As a unit, they all moved at the same time to roll her onto the backboard, and for the first time, I could see her entire face. Her lips were split and her forehead had a large gash.

In a flurry of movements that had her lifted and on a stretcher, someone called out, "Heading to ORMC," and I found myself nodding, even though anxiety twisted in my stomach.

Shit. Why were the paramedics taking this woman to Orlando Regional Medical Center when Sand Lake Hospital was closer? She was slammed into the car and hit the ground. The paramedics were obviously worried about spine or neck injury, both of which could be catastrophic.

The stretcher was loaded and locked, and before the doors swung closed, I edged around for one last glance wondering if the woman would survive.

Green eyes stared back at me.

Blink.

The doors slammed, and the paramedics were off.

"Hi, Sergeant Christakos." I ripped my attention from the fading taillights and turned to the two deputies that came to a stop next to me.

"Here's her other boot." Dean, a rookie announced as he held up a single black-and-red tooled cowboy boot. "Damn. Something 'bout a chick in cowboy boots that gets me hard."

"Let's hope she survives to wear them again," I said, cutting a severe glower at them both. Though, I wasn't quite thirty, I felt ancient compared to these callous dickheads. They may as well call me fucking Buddha with the wisdom I doled out nowadays.

"Ariel Louise Beaumont, twenty-seven years old. Five feet and two inches tall, red hair, green eyes—"

I grabbed her license from the other deputy for a brief second, I knew that I couldn't keep it but I wanted to learn what I could about this woman. When I looked down, her beautiful smile was shining back at me. It was those eyes, which were full of hope and questions, that stalled the breath in my lungs. They told my heart to inform my brain that everything in my life had just changed.

ARIEL

*W*ould someone please turn off that beeping sound? Reaching up, I grabbed my head and a tug on my arm pinched. The distinct smell of bleach and medicine filled my nose on a deep inhale. I was in a hospital.

I knew the smell all too well. I had practically lived in a hospital for the last ten years, taking Mama back and forth to physical therapy after her second stroke. Then after her final stroke, I had spent day and night with her, dreading having to make the choice that would end with Mama's life support being turned off. I didn't think I would be in one again anytime soon. Yet, there I was.

Opening my eyes to the realization that I was hooked to tubes. "Ariel. You awake?"

I turned my head to find a statuesque blonde in scrubs.

"Stahhwa." I swallowed.

My throat was dry, so she handed me a cup of water.

I took a swig and tried again, "Stella. What are you doing here?"

"I work here." She set the plastic cup on the rolling tray and turned back to me. "What I really want to know is why you're here. What the hell happened, girl?"

I closed my eyes and tried to think past the fear. "Two men. They

11

attacked me." I tried to reach for my head to stop the drumming of the marching band going through. The tubes tugged again, and I balled my hands into fists, fighting against the panic trying to bubble and spill over. The beeping was frantic, my pulse going haywire.

"Shhh. Calm down, Ariel. Take a deep breath." The next second Stella's hand squeezed mine, trying to get me to focus on her.

I shook my head, as if the action would erase the images flashing in front of my face, the attack, running, fighting.

"How long have I been in here?"

"Three hours." Her voice was soft and calming. "We've kept you pretty drugged to help with the pain so you've been out of it. You have some serious lacerations."

Lacerations. My mind fluttered around the terms.

"How did I get here . . . wait, a star. No, that isn't right, is it?" I rolled the blankets up under my chin, trying to cocoon myself against the images that were slowly coming back to me.

"You were brought in through the ER, so I'm assuming someone called nine-one-one. But I can find out for you if you want. My brother is a deputy, and he can look up the call record."

I pulled my lip in to bite it, a natural reaction of mine and let out a squeal at the pain.

"Careful. You have three stitches in your lower lip and fourteen across your forehead. No worries, they had a plastic surgeon do them, so the scar will be tiny." She picked up a pitcher, "Let me fill this with some water and send your doctor a message that you're awake. I'll be right back." Stella gave my hand another squeeze then strode from the room.

Closing my eyes, I took a deep breath, trying to relax. It was almost working too, until I heard the barely there squeal of the door swinging open. I jerked awake and was face to face with one of the most gorgeous men in the world.

"You must be my doctor," I said to the man with a fabulous smile wearing a white jacket.

"I'm a doctor. But I'm not your doctor."

Before I could ask why he was there, Stella pushed open my door.

"Hey, chickie, I sent a message—" Stella's face changed ten different shades of red before she continued, "Tristan, I mean, Doctor Christakos, what brings you here?"

"Hi, Stella. I was just getting ready to introduce myself to Ariel. Kayson asked me to stop by and check in on her."

"Kayson?" I whispered, drawing both their eyes to me.

"I'm Tristan Christakos," he clarified, stepping forward and wrapping both his hands around the rail of my bed. "I work in the NICU. My brother is a deputy for Orange County, and he was the one that found you. He's been concerned."

I stared at the doctor for a second, trying to absorb what he had just said, but my brain was still moving in slow motion while I took in his dark brown eyes, light brown hair, and olive skin.

"Will you tell him thank you?" I asked, my voice still scratchy.

"I will. Do you mind if he comes up and sees you?"

"I'd like that."

"I'm glad to see you're awake. You look much better. Is there anything I can get you?" Unless he was willing to break a few rules and get me some discharge papers, there wasn't anything I could think of that I needed. So, I just shook my head and gave him a weak smile.

Doctor Christakos left my room but not before stopping to give Stella a light squeeze on the arm. When I was sure he was out of hearing distance, I turned to her with a shocked look on my face.

"Holy shit. He's gorgeous."

"Tell me about it," Stella said in an ethereal voice. "Every nurse in the hospital throws herself at his feet."

"You included?"

"Bite me. Hey, I need to go clock out, want me to come sit with you for a while or are you sleepy?"

"No, come back please."

Stella and I got along great when we first met, but we hadn't spoken since, which was a few months ago. She'd been participating in a motorcycle challenge and needed a rush job on her funky costume. Luck had shoved her in my direction.

"Okay, now spill. Tell me what you remember about your hot rescue guy. I know Tristan and all three of his brothers, and believe me when I tell you that they are all fine." Stella curled one leg up under herself as she plopped into the only chair in my room.

"Honestly? I don't remember him, I mean, when the doctor came in he looked sorta familiar, but I didn't know that was why. If this Kayson is half as hot as his brother—"

"Oh no worries there, he is equally as hot just in an athletic way."

"Let me finish." I air smacked her and continued. "Look at me, I haven't even seen myself in a mirror yet, but if I go by what you've said and how I feel, I must look hideous."

Stella stood and settled her hands on my shoulders and squeezed. "Look at me, you're one kick ass woman. You may be short, but you're scrappy, I'll give you that. You kept two grown men off you until help could get there. Girl, you're ferocious. The only thing people are gonna see is someone that no one will want to fuck with. You hear me?"

Nodding to let Stella know I heard her words even if I didn't necessarily agree with them, "But what about the bruises on my face and my hair?"

Stella crossed her middle finger over her index, "No worries girl, I got you covered. Me and MAC go way back. Tomorrow, I'll bring you some good cover up shit when I come in."

KAYSON

"What's up?" my oldest brother Damon asked as I strode into the kitchen at my parents' house.

"Same ole, same ole." I gave Mana a kiss on her cheek and hugged Pop.

"Where's Ian?" He was the only one not there, and I was starving.

"He's on his way," Mana answered as she set the table. "How's the girl?"

I punched Tristan in the arm, "Really, asshole?"

You did not mention a girl in front of a Greek mother who had four bachelor sons.

The four of us boys—Damon, Tristan, Ian, and me—were only six years apart.

"What's her name? Have you gone up to see her? Have you talked to her?"

Mana continued, obviously having heard the question. There was no point in trying to answer because she wasn't out of breath, yet. Plus, if I waited, I would only have to answer the last question.

"Is she Greek? Have her parents been to the station? What exactly happened?"

"Mana, one question at a time. We all want to hear Kayson's answers," Tristan said as he raised one eyebrow.

"Fuck you," I mouthed. That was one word I wouldn't say in front of her.

"Is she a good girl, Kayson?" Damon jumped into the conversation before placing his folded hands under his chin and batting his eyelashes. It looked just as dumb when he did it as it had when the girl at the mall did.

Fuck it; they weren't going to let this go.

"No. Nothing like that," I ground out.

"She isn't a good girl?" Damon asked a little too innocently.

"Shut the hell up. I don't know whether she is a good girl." The last part I said using air quotes. "Tristan is just causing shit."

"You have a picture?" Mana asked hopefully. "Can I meet her?"

"Will all of you please stop?"

"What are we stopping?" Ian asked as he walked in.

"We're talking about whether or not Kayson found a good girl," Damon said.

"Oh, is this the one in the hospital?" Ian asked.

Tristan and Damon gave each other high fives and burst out laughing.

"Grow up." I stood. "I'm heading home."

"Sit." That was all Pop had to say to have me taking my seat again. "You're not going anywhere. Your mother worked all day to make this meal. The least you can do is show some respect and answer her questions. She has put up with the five of us guys for all these years. If she wants some girls, then you four best get on it, cause I already have one. The best of them all." Pop leaned and planted a giant kiss on my mother's lips.

When Pop spoke, we listened. The man had a temper, and the four of us had brought it out in him many times. But when it came to my mother, he was whooped. She knew how to work him.

I admired my parents, their marriage, and even though I got aggravated at my family, I wanted this. Family dinners around a giant table, children that grew up fighting but were still the best of friends, and a woman that I was madly in love with after forty years.

"Mana, don't listen to Tristan. I haven't even met her, not really. She was in an accident, and I was the first one on the scene. That's all."

I glared at my brothers, daring them to continue. I may be the baby in the family, but I could make their lives hell and sometimes needed to remind them.

"When's the last time any of you got a speeding ticket? I bet you'd hate to have to spend a day in court over some silly ticket that some pissed-off deputy wrote you. I'm sure he could add some more shit to those tickets like not coming to a complete stop or failing to signal."

Mana waved my threat away and kept on with her questions. "Accident? Is she going to be okay?"

I looked to Tristan, who just smirked and gestured for me to answer.

"She should be. She's still in the hospital."

"When does she go home?" Concern crinkled Mana's forehead.

"Not sure."

Mana looked at Tristan, expecting him to answer the question. "I work in NICU, that's babies. I'm not her doctor, and even if I were, I couldn't talk to you about her, not without her permission."

"Where does she live?" Her eyes landed back on me.

"Just up the road." Satisfaction flashed in her eyes and I bit back a groan. Yes, yes, I knew where the girl lived. I had her driver's license for crying out loud. No one at the table would believe that was the only reason, though.

Sometimes, I considered skipping family meals, but it wasn't as if I could use distance as an excuse. My parents lived just around the corner from me. And it wasn't exactly a hardship, either, because I always went home with tons of leftovers. Even when they picked on me, which seemed to be more often than not lately. I was the youngest, and sometimes I needed to remind myself that I loved my family even when they did stupid shit like this.

After dinner, Tristan pulled me to the side. "Hey, I wanted to talk

17

with you about Ariel. I spoke with her today. She looks good, well considering everything she's been through."

"Is she going to be okay? Does she remember anything?" For some screwy reason, I wanted to see her, I'd never visited any of the accident victims I'd helped, but she was unique.

"Yeah, from everything I can tell, she's going to be okay. I don't know what she remembers. I'm sure by now the hospital has called the detective in charge of her case and informed him that she's awake. You'll be able to find out that information faster than I will."

"I'll put a call in tomorrow and see what I can find out."

"I did ask her about you coming up to visit . . ."

"And? Fuck, don't keep me in suspense here." I was pacing a small corner of my parents' living room, torn between standing and listening to everything Tristan said and rushing off to the hospital to see for myself that she was awake and going to be okay.

"She wants to see you, too." Tristan let out a laugh as I pulled my keys out of my pocket. "Hold up there, Kayson. You need to relax, it's past visiting hours. She's being monitored due to head injury, and you aren't family. They aren't going to let you see her right now. You can go up tomorrow."

"Right. I'll get some flowers."

"Still going to try to claim she's just another call?"

I heaved a sigh and turned to face my brother.

"Not a word to Mana."

"Not a word," he agreed, and I nodded.

"Thanks." I leaned in and gave him a quick one-arm hug for getting the information for me.

* * *

I TOSSED and turned all night, anxious at the thought of seeing her. Were her eyes really that vibrant of a green, or was it a figment of my imagination? My adrenaline was pumped that night, so maybe I had imagined the whole thing—that whole instant connection.

Just before lunch, I headed over to the hospital, my heart pounding the entire time I stood in the gift shop trying to pick out a bouquet of flowers. Roses were no good, so I ended up grabbing some poofy things in bright colors instead. The elevator ride up was a test of restraint, and when the doors opened, I had to fight to keep my steps casual. They fought to match the rhythm of my heart. The nurses situated behind the desk waved as I passed, but when I got to her room, I stopped. She wasn't alone.

"Ariel. Darling."

I wasn't sure what else he said because the words were drowned out from the beating in my head that had been in my chest just moments ago. Ariel had a boyfriend, or maybe he was her fiancé, which wasn't something I had considered. For some stupid reason, I only remembered how I felt when our eyes locked.

Turning around, my feet heavier and my gait slower than it had been, I moved back toward the elevators, dropped the flowers in the trashcan, and pressed the button for the elevator to come back and get me.

ARIEL

 hree months later . . .

MY LIVING ROOM looked more like a Skittles factory had exploded than it did an actual apartment. With fabric in every color strewn throughout, I was working on another rush job of bridesmaid dresses, trying to catch up on work after the accident.

Why did bridesmaids wait until the week before the wedding to try on their dresses? I understood not wanting to put it on since the dress was god-awful, but someone needed to remind these bridesmaids that looking as if the dress were painted on their asses wasn't gonna do that atrocious fabric any favors. There was only so much seam I could let out.

My phone dinged to alert me of a text message. I plucked it out of my pocket and read.

Stella: Hey, bitch, we're going out tonight.

Me: Can't, I'm swamped.

Stella: And you'll still be swamped tomorrow. Pick you up at four.

That was in an hour.

Me: Not ready.
Stella: Get ready.
Me: Where?
Stella: Harley. Band, food, men.
Me: Not looking for a man.
Stella: Not man. MEN!!! Lots and lots. Ciao.

Laughing at Stella's one-track brain, I moved my foot to the pedal of my sewing machine and went back to work. During the two fucking days in ORMC after the attack, Stella and I went from acquaintances to friends. Like me, she loved riding, had a rocking sense of humor, loved all things leather, and was raised by a single mom. Our difference in the last one was that she still saw her dad after her parents split.

I finished the seam I'd been working on and started to shut everything down. One thing I'd learned about Stella was that she was never late, so when she said four, she meant four.

I was just dabbing concealer on the light pink scar that ran across my forehead when three sharp knocks sounded at my front door. When I pulled it open, Stella was standing there with a huge smile. She fit every description of a blonde bombshell, the hair, the blue eyes, the boobs, the hourglass figure, and the gorgeous smile. That was until she opened her mouth. When she spoke, she fit every description of a sailor or a truck driver. Stella was rocking the biker babe look.

"Is this all right?" I asked, looking down at my jeans, T-shirt, and cowboy boots. Biker chic wasn't in my closet, urban cowgirl? Yes. Rhinestone cowgirl? Yes. Midnight cowboy was probably as close as I got to the total biker look. Not wanting to get eaten alive by the state bird of Florida, I decided to wear a light-weight long-sleeve T-shirt. My auburn hair was down in long bouncy waves, which may or may not hold up in the humidity.

"You're a walking wet dream. If you don't get laid tonight, I might have to do you myself."

"Oh, you say the sweetest things." Laughing at her words, I leaned over and grabbed my keys to lock up. Stella only slightly raised an eyebrow as I pressed a piece of Scotch tape between the door and the frame. It wasn't obvious to the casual observer unless you knew where to look. But to me, that tiny piece of narrow tape acted as a security alarm. If I came home to a broken or bent piece of tape, then that meant someone other than me had opened my door. The police hadn't found my attackers, so I decided to get creative with my security system.

"Do you usually go to these events?" I asked as I climbed on my bright red Sportster, and she climbed on to her gold one.

"If I have the night off. But I requested tonight off. This one is for the Orange County Sheriff's Department. I told you about my brother, Carter, right?" Stella asked.

"The deputy?"

"Yup. Well, three deputies were killed earlier this year by a crazy motherfucker, I'm sure you heard about it, it was all over the news. All proceeds from tonight are going to the widow of one of the deputies who just so happened to work with my brother and Kayson Christakos as a motorcycle deputy, he was their sergeant."

"Let's not mention *that* name. Remember, he never showed up to the hospital, and I let you put all that shit on me even though it hurt like hell when you rubbed it on."

"I'm telling you, there had to be a good reason." Stella's defense of all things cop was bias in my opinion.

We strapped on our helmets and headed out to support the worthy cause. On my bike, I forgot about my fears: who attacked me, why they'd attacked me, and why it seemed to come out of nowhere. I wished that I could remember this feeling when I faced the daunting task of walking to my bike alone. But no, it took Stella being with me to give me the assurance that I needed.

Warm sunrays kissed my cheeks as I squeezed the clutch, shifted gears, and turned the throttle. Within seconds, the wind shook loose strands of hair from underneath my helmet, and I felt the stress start to ease. The ride was short but worth every second, and when we pulled into the parking lot of the Harley dealership, the scent of Bubbalou's Bodacious Bar-B-Que hit me.

Finding a spot to park was almost impossible. Cruisers and police bikes were mixed with regular partygoers, so we cut left and headed to the employee parking lot. Like all biker women, we had our priorities. First things first, we ripped off our helmets and attempted to resurrect our hair, but helmet head was its own hairstyle.

"Yo, Stella!" someone shouted.

I turned to face two women walking toward us. One looked as if she were a regular at these types of events, worn and faded jeans, Harley T-shirt, and black combat-style bike boots. The other woman had strawberry blonde hair and seemed to be in great shape, which was mostly hidden under a thick Kevlar vest and a God-awful polyester sheriff's uniform. Why law enforcement agencies hadn't switched from those uniforms to BDU's like the military or jeans was beyond me. They should save the seventies fabric for formal occasions like the military does.

"Yo, bitches!" Stella hollered back. "Ariel, that is Leo. She's a mechanic here at Harley, and that's Piper, she works with my brother."

"Hi!" I pasted on a giant smile and shook both their hands, and Leo turned to Stella.

"Speaking of your brother. We need to go find him. I just finished adjusting his clutch cable."

"He should already be inside." She gestured to the open gates, and we all headed that way. I hadn't met her brother, but I'd heard enough stories about him to know that he was just like Stella, and I couldn't wait to put a face with the name. Then the four of us moved toward the gates, passing a stage and a large black-and-orange tent for food and alcohol set up with several tables and chairs on the way.

"I need a drink." I groaned, wondering if they would let me detour to the bar.

"Shut up," Piper said with a smirk. "I'm on duty."

The officer, who was standing just outside the gate collecting money, nodded his agreement, and Piper sidled up next to him as I pulled my wallet out.

"Is there a cover charge?" I asked.

"Nope. Just donation." Stella dropped in a twenty.

I happily followed her lead.

On the inside of the gate, rows of new motorcycles were lining the walkway. It was like candy cane lane, all shiny and tempting. I didn't need a new bike, but like most people, I would walk over there and check out the gorgeous machinery.

"How many bikes do you own?" I asked Leo.

"Two. A Sportster and a Low Boy."

I turned to Piper. "You ride?"

"Yeah. And I'm hoping to start riding a lot more. There's an opening in motors, so I'm going to interview for the position." The excitement in her voice was unmistakable. "But I'm not holding my breath. They've never had a female."

I pointed at my temple, "You'll get it. I'm psycho that way."

She laughed. "You mean psychic."

"Either or."

She let out a laugh, and I decided right then that I liked Piper. She was the yin to Stella's yang. Her personality seemed opposite of Stella's, which was larger than life. Piper was calming, and I could picture her being the one called in if someone needed to be talked off a bridge.

"We can all start riding together," I said, hoping they'd agree since it would help me get out of my apartment.

"Great idea." Stella swung out her arms and announced. "All girls' biker club."

"That's not a bad idea. My boss wants to get more women involved." Leo gestured toward the Harley building as if her boss was still inside. "We could start a ladies' club and go for rides. We could even have some classes. I could show you how to do some basic servicing on your bike."

"I could teach some defensive maneuvers," Piper added.

"I can make patches or vests for the club. Sorry, sewing and event planning are my only talents."

"The bathroom wall said that you had way more talent than that." Stella's wit was quick, but laughter garbled her words. "Truthfully, though, since I'm a nurse, I could put together some small first aid kits."

"We can do this, we can so have a biker's club," I said.

"We got ourselves a gang. Now, we just need a name," Stella added.

"Not a gang," Leo, Piper, and I all said in unison, and Stella gave us all an annoyed look.

I missed having friends, people to do things with, I'd lost too much of my life over the last ten years. I needed friends, lots of friends.

Up until my senior year I had a small group of friends, hell I even had a boyfriend. But after Mama's second stroke, they were busy going to football games, out on Friday nights, and to school dances.

The girls and I walked past a few vendor trucks that were selling patches for vests and lights for bikes before heading under the tent. I looked up at the sky, this was my favorite time of day, late afternoon when the sun still shone as if it had no intention of going down. It wasn't sweltering hot, but there wasn't that oppressive heat, either. By the time I headed home, it would be cool, especially on the bike at sixty miles per hour.

The band was already on stage and playing a mix of soul, rock, and country. A few women swayed to the music, but no one was dancing, which was a shame. I loved to dance. That was when I spotted them.

"Holy shit, look at all those men in uniform. I've hit nirvana." I announced, admiring the well-built bodies in different outfits and gear. "Why are some in regular uniforms but you're in full gear?"

"Since this is a law enforcement charity event, the brotherhood comes out in full force."

"Brotherhood? Not a lot of sisters?" I wasn't trying to preach feminism, but if we could learn to stop calling flight attendants "stewardesses", then we could stop calling things the brotherhood.

"I work with several women. It's just always been called the brotherhood, and since they're like my brothers, I've never been offended."

I hated it when people made sense. I saw her point, and since I wasn't a deputy, maybe I should mind my own damn business. I could hear my mama's admonishment. "Aren't you a little Miss Busy Body? Got anyone else's business you want to get into?"

25

"It's wonderful. It's like FAO Schwartz for grown-ups," Stella whispered. "Except for that one." She pointed to a man, but all I noticed was the back of his blond head. He was with several other guys, who were all wearing dark green shirts that had OCSO on the back. "Thinking of him like that is just, blah-gag." She shook her head as if trying to erase the thought from her brain.

"Your brother?"

As confirmation, Stella took off running and jumped on the man's back. "Hey, bro."

"Hey, spider monkey. Where'd you come from?" Stella's brother had a deep voice full of brotherly humor. He turned as he shook his shoulders, trying to extricate himself from her grip.

Some of the men resembled linebackers, but others were lean, yet muscular at the same time. Where were all the doughnut-eating cops? The ones they show in movies and on COPS? These guys looked like Dolce and Gabbana models bred with Seal Team Six to have a bunch of love children. They were hot. I take that back—they were so gorgeous that they were erotic. I felt as if at any moment someone was going to tap me on the shoulder and ask, "Was it good for you?" And of course, the answer would be yes. A resounding yes.

"I want you to meet someone," Stella said to Carter, but in her usual loud fashion she caught everyone's attention, and they turned their gazes to me.

Spending almost half of my life secluded with just my mama, I was uncomfortable with the stares, but I tried to smile through it. I held my hand out to Carter, it was shaking, but I didn't have time to hope no one would notice before another voice cut in.

"Ariel?" My eyes darted left to the man who had spoken.

He had my attention even though he butchered my name. A smile spread across his face as if he knew me, and my stomach fluttered with a remembrance that clung to the outside of my memory. He resembled Theo James with the same golden-brown hair, chocolate eyes, and sun-kissed olive skin.

"It's R-E-L, not Ariel. Sounds just like you are saying the initials for Robert E. Lee. You know, rebel leader and all that," I repeated the same line I had heard my mama say when she corrected people on how to pronounce my name. But for some strange reason, when I did this, my voice became twangy. Or maybe that was twangier?

Several people gawked, but no one interrupted or even bothered to introduce themselves. Everyone focused on the Theo James look-a-like man moving toward me.

"How are you?" he asked, taking a step into my personal space.

"Fine?" My answer sounded more like a question as I stepped back. "Do I know you?"

"Yeah. Well, sort of. I'm Deputy Kayson Christakos."

Mother nature could have opened the gates of hell with thunder and lightning, and I wouldn't have heard another damn thing. Because when he said his name, the only thing I saw were stars, no a star. A single star.

I raised my hand in front of me to stop him from saying another word while I absorbed the fact this man was my rescuer. Him. Standing in front of me was the man who prevented those two guys from taking me. He quite possibly saved my life that day, and the magnitude of that threatened to drag me under.

Wrapping my arms around my stomach in a tight hug, I tried to find strength to do what needed to be done. I had prepared myself for this moment while I was still in the hospital. I'd had a thank you speech prepared. Every word had been chosen with care. Standing there in front of him . . . knowing he was flesh and blood and more handsome than my memory told me he was, my words were gone.

In between deep swallows, I managed to utter, "Thank you. Thank you. I don't know how I can ever thank you."

"I'm glad I was there," he assured me. "You're shaking, why don't you sit down." I nodded and let him guide me to the nearest table. The heat of his hand on my lower back was nothing but a soft hum of comfort and safety, and I couldn't remember another time a simple touch had felt like that. The others followed close behind as witnesses to my freak out in front of this gorgeous man, but I couldn't think about that. All I could think about was the man next to me.

Someone set a few bottles of beer in front of me. I wasn't sure who, but I appreciated it. I took a long pull of the Yuengling, and a few deep breaths later, my head stopped spinning enough for me to look at Kayson, who had taken a seat across from me. He was built like a brick shit-house. Being from Alabama, I knew football, and Kayson had the body of a running back, muscular but not engineered with testosterone injections.

"I can't believe you're here. How are you feeling?"

"Better." I lifted my bangs to show him my forehead and the scar, the worst of my evidence. "The plastic surgeon assured me that in no time it'll hardly be noticeable, I'm still waiting."

"I wouldn't have noticed it now unless you pointed it out." Kayson took a swig from his bottle of water. "Just you and Stella come?"

"Yeah. She forced me since I don't get out very often. I'm still jumpy after the attack," I explained.

"I can understand your fear, but I'm glad you came." The silence was heavy with all the things I wanted to say, but I didn't know where to start. I bit the corner of my lip as I looked to where his legs were stretched out, bracketing mine, and then took a deep breath.

"Can I ask you something?"

"Sure."

"I met your brother while I was in the hospital, and he mentioned that you might come up, did I miss you?" I tried to ask my question without sounding as though I had been anxiously awaiting his visit.

"I came up but you, umm, you had a visitor," he explained. "Well, it sounded like you were in the middle of something. I didn't want to interrupt."

Besides his brother and Stella, I only had one other visitor: Brandon. After moving to Orlando, I dated him for a few months. It hadn't ended well, and when he had shown up at the hospital, I had been shocked and annoyed. When I had broken things off with Brandon, I thought I had made it clear that I wanted nothing to do with him anymore.

"I wish you would have interrupted. It was just a guy I dated for a few months who thinks he is God's gift to women." I could still hear his words, and they grated on my nerves, he was a douche. Sure, he visited me in the hospital, but that didn't change how I felt about him.

"He's that cocky?"

"Ugh, don't even get me started. Do you know why he was at the hospital? To tell me that I should move in with him because I obviously can't take care of myself. Like getting attacked was somehow my fault. I mean, really? This asshole lied and cheated on me." I heaved a heavy sigh and pinched my lips together. Kayson didn't need to hear about my pathetic dating background I looked up and saw a smirk on his face. "What?" But I already knew what. Just thinking about Brandon and the way he had told me the world was too dangerous for a single woman had me seething.

"Nothing, Tiger." Kayson held up both hands in a gesture of surrender.

For the first time, I noticed Kayson's badge on his belt. I wanted to reach out and touch it, trace the star that had haunted my memory, but that would probably make me seem like a pervert or get me in handcuffs. The latter of which wasn't such a bad idea. It had been way too long since I'd had sex. I moved my hands under my thighs and sat on them to keep myself from doing something stupid. Like reaching out and running my hand up his thigh to the bulge in his pants.

I looked up and met his gaze. Fuck, the man was smirking again.

I cleared my throat. "I remember seeing your star badge during the accident."

"You do? What else do you remember?"

"Not much, just that there were two guys. I remember trying to fight them off and the smell. My goodness, one of them smelled so bad that I don't think I'll ever forget it. Everything else is blank space and panic."

"Yo, man of the hour." Stella squatted between Kayson and me, resting a hand on each of our knees. "I think you'd better go over and give your home fries the four-one-one on my girl here. They are acting like a bunch of teenagers trying to figure out what the two of you are talking about."

Both Kayson and I glanced in the direction Stella had indicated, and sure enough, there was a group of guys pretending not to watch us.

"Excuse me, I'll be right back," Kayson said as he stood and left the table. I watched him walk away, admiring the wide breadth of his shoulders and how his jeans hugged his nice firm ass.

"Fuck, you have the best luck in the world. Seriously? He's hot."

"Luck? I met him because some guys decided to beat the crap out of me."

"That's not what I meant, and you know it. That man couldn't take his eyes off you. I got hot just watching him look at you."

I narrowed my eyes at her. "What do you mean?"

"Girl, you can't be that clueless. When he saw you . . ." Stella lowered her chin and puffed out her chest. "He went all, me Tarzan, she Jane, no one else can talk to her, I'm staking my claim."

I turned to find him, doubtful that she'd read the situation correctly. Kayson didn't seem overly excited about meeting me. Running into someone he'd helped was probably something that happened to him all the time. When I finally spotted him, our eyes locked, but I looked away and my attention landed on a group of women trying to mingle with the guys Kayson was talking to.

"Ignore them." Stella grabbed my hand in hers. "They're badge bunnies. And the brunette is Gigi, queen whore, I mean hopper."

But I couldn't ignore them or him for that matter. Maybe it was because by that point, the number of beers I had drunk were equal to the number of women surrounding him.

Every time I raised my eyes, they flicked in his direction. Every time they did, he was still gazing at me. The girls were gorgeous and they all seemed comfortable around the deputies including Kayson, and as much as I hated to admit it, I felt a little possessive. Maybe I had staked as much of a claim on him as Stella thought he'd staked on me. The part of myself that was telling me that saving me was just part of his job wasn't loud enough to drown out the part that wanted him.

With a last name like Christakos, and olive skin, the man had to be Greek. I made a mental note to add "Sexy Greek Men" to my searches on Tumblr.

"Did you get a chance to meet everyone?" A deep voice asked from behind me. I hadn't noticed that he had moved while I was lost in thoughts of Tumblr porn.

"No."

"Max and Aiden are motors along with Carter and me." He pointed out two men standing near Stella's brother. "That's Eli. He's with DOJ, Special Response Team." Kayson pointed to another guy and said DOJ as if that meant something to me, but I was clueless.

He moved around to my front and kneeled at my side. Resting one hand on mine, he stretched across me to pick up his bottle of water, leaning in closer to me as he did so.

"You're beautiful," he whispered so only I could hear. "I've thought about you. How you were doing and all that. I wanted to contact you, but I was worried that you had a boyfriend or you might think I was a stalker. Fuck. Sorry. I must sound like an idiot. Let me start over, you're gorgeous, and I'm just happy to see you out and about."

My head was spinning from a combination of the drinks and his words and actions, he was saying all the sweet things any woman would want to hear, including me. He was also too good-looking for his own good, and I wasn't the only one who felt that way.

Just over Kayson's shoulder, I could see Gigi watching us through narrowed eyes. The saying "If looks could kill" seemed too passive. Maybe, if there were a saying more along the lines of "If looks could cut a bitch, piss down her throat, and burn down her house," then yes, that was the look she gave me.

Everything in me told me she was staking her own claim on this man, and I didn't want to draw a line in the sand, so I hastily stood and offered, "Thank you, and thank you for the drinks. I appreciate everything you've done for me. I really do."

He stood with me and took a tiny step closer. "Don't leave. Let's go over there and sit away from the stage. It's quieter." Kayson tilted his head toward the far side of the tent.

"Don't think your girlfriend would like that. She seems the jealous sort."

I cast my eyes over to where the badge bunnies stood, and Gigi was still burning me with her resting bitch face. Kayson didn't get a chance to respond because the steel guitar rang out with the first few notes of "Sweet Home Alabama" by Lynyrd Skynyrd. I think anyone from that state could sing the lyrics before they knew their own name.

My smile was bright as I swung it to Stella and Leo. "Let's go," I yelled, grabbing their hands and pulling them to the front of the stage area, not caring if they could or even wanted to dance with me. I had four beers in me, the right song playing, and friends, what could be better?

I moved in line, matching the beat. "Grapevine, cha cha," I shouted as I crossed my legs and moved my feet with the rhythm so that Leo and Stella could follow the line moves. As we danced, we sang—or more accurately, shouted the words at the top of our lungs.

"Are you going home with him?" Stella asked.

"No. I'm someone he rescued, just part of the job."

"Yeah right, maybe if he's playing naughty policeman and the nightstick." Stella squeezed my arms and spun me, forcing me out of sync with the line dance so I was facing Kayson. "See what I mean?" she asked. "That man can't take his eyes off you."

"Not looking for anything serious."

"Girl, that man is seriously hot and could probably do some serious shit with his body."

I smiled at him. He gave me that guy smile.

"How do guys make a smile look so seductive? You know, where they slightly raise just one corner of their mouth as if they have a secret and you're dying to know it?"

My eyes never left his lips and I ended up missing a whole chain of step transitions.

"Shake it, baby, make that man forget that there's another woman in this entire place," Stella's order pulled my stare away from Kayson and back to the music.

When the song ended and the next began, Leo and Stella returned to the group. But I remained on the floor with my eyes focused on the man to their left that hadn't taken his eyes off me, he moved slowly toward me. The first notes lulled in the air, pulling at my heart to keep dancing. I forgot about everyone else around me and let the music ebb through my muscles, bones, soul. It flowed through me, bending me to its beats. Captivated by the lights in the darkening summer sky, I stared up and twirled as the singer's gravelly voice sang "Kiss Me" by Ed Sheeran.

At that moment, I felt on fire, sexual, beautiful. The cadence of the song was like making love; each beat matched the pounding of a stroke. My hips swayed to the timing of the meter. The timbre of his voice reached my core. When I dreamed of being loved, this was what it felt like. I imagined just once in my life that I was enough for someone.

Dropping my head, I felt the tempo build one last time and reach its peak. Echoing pulses faded, the song ended, and I was surrounded.

Not by a ton of people, but by one tall Greek man, concentrating on my lips, as he moved with me. His hand cupping my chin as his thumb brushed against my cheek. I wanted to close my eyes, but I didn't dare look away. I wanted to make sure that he heard, truly heard the words to that song and was going to do what it said and kiss me.

It started in his eyes, the way he looked at me, the slight quiver at the corner of his lips. That was when I knew he'd heard every word.

He leaned in, his face close to mine, I felt the warmth from his breath as he whispered, "I don't have a girlfriend, at least not yet." With one finger under my chin tipping my face up until our mouths were almost touching. "I'm going to kiss you now."

There was no time for words, but for a brief—and I mean brief—moment, I thought about pulling back. Kayson could be very dangerous for my heart and that scared me.

His lips were soft, the kiss deep, and for the second time since I met him, I saw stars.

KAYSON

*F*or three fucking months, images of her face covered in glass filled my nightmares. I recounted every single blink and relived the memories of wondering whether or not, this time, she'd reopen her eyes. My dreams were ruled by the girl with green eyes and red hair, and she was there, tonight, right then, in front of me. Her lips soft, and her taste was everything. I wanted to devour her, but we were in the middle of a dance floor, undoubtedly the center of everyone's focus.

I was the first to break the connection, but I didn't let go of her. Tugging her hand, I pulled away from the bikers, who were still hypnotized by her dance, and away from my interfering friends, who were far too interested in the girl who'd caught my eye. I wanted her alone and in my arms.

"Go out with me?" My voice cracking with this need building inside me. I wanted to taste her again, to finish what we'd started. I knew I couldn't. I'd known Ariel for three months, but in reality, we'd just officially met. We were practically strangers. As much as I'd thought about her, I didn't know if she'd thought about me or even knew who had helped her that day. I had never expected to run into her. If shit happened for a reason, then there was a reason we were both there tonight. I wasn't letting this chance slip away.

"I don't think that's a good idea." She appeared less confident than she sounded.

"Why?"

"Listen, Kayson. I really appreciate everything you've done for me, and that kiss. Well, that kiss was great. It was more than great. It was . . ." She rubbed her lower lip as if trying to get the feeling of the kiss to return. A smile tugged at the corners of my mouth, and when she saw it, she pushed out a heavy breath. "Never mind what it was. I just don't think that going out with you is a good idea."

"Seems like the best one I've had in a while." Her eyes flicked away from me, and I could almost hear the no that was on the tip of her tongue. "Ariel. Have dinner with me. One night, that's all I'm asking. It's the least you could do, considering I saved you."

"You don't play fair, do you?"

"Not really. So, what do you say? One meal as friends?" I tucked a wayward strand of hair behind her ear.

"Just one?" I nodded at her words, her resolve slipping. There was no way I was going to be friend zoned, not after a kiss like that. If she came to dinner with me, I planned to charm myself right into her heart.

Again, she let out a deep breath. "One dinner, but that's it. I'm not ready for anything more."

The moment she acquiesced, I seized on it and pulled my phone from my pocket. I unlocked it and offered it to her. "Call your phone, that way you'll have my number as well."

Ariel hesitated for a second before taking my phone. Her fingers moved hesitantly over each number. When I heard the sound of a nearby phone ringing I relaxed, she pressed end call on my phone and handed it back to me. I just jumped a huge fucking hurdle, and I knew it.

"Do you need my address?" she asked.

"I'm a deputy. I can figure it out."

My hand rested perfectly at the curve in her lower back as I ushered her back to our group, Stella and Leo had fucking smirks on their faces, but by the looks on the guys' faces, they had a stockpile of jabs ready to let fly.

Ariel took a seat next to Stella, "I'll be right back, just going to talk with the guys." Namely three guys, who'd hadn't been here twenty minutes ago but were currently watching Ariel and me like we were some box office hit—my brothers. I sidestepped Eli, Carter, and the deputies and headed over.

"Is that her?" Damon asked. "She's beautiful, red hair is sexy."

"Someone care to explain where all you fuckers came from?"

"Kayson Michael Christakos."

I recoiled at the sound of my mother's voice. Meeting Ian's eyes, I followed his line of sight to a phone in Damon's hand. He had our mother on FaceTime.

"What are you doing?" I asked, the words sliding out through clenched teeth.

"You don't tell me anything. Carter, that sweet boy."

I looked over at Carter, and he was watching us with a grin on his face. I gave him a look that promised retribution.

"He texted your brother and informed him the girl was there. I sent them up to get pictures for me. You don't give me pictures. You don't bring her around to meet me. Are you embarrassed?"

I glared at them, but they cracked up.

Fuck, I was screwed. She piled on the infamous Greek guilt.

"No. Nothing like that, Mana. I haven't seen her or even spoken to her since her accident. I had no clue that she was going to be here."

"Yet, you were eating her face?"

"She just agreed to go out on a date with me. Okay. Give me a little breathing room. I will call you later. Love you. Bye."

I reached for Damon's phone and hit the button to end the call.

Really? I fucking needed new friends, new family. Fuck. Striding off, I heard Ian shout, "Thou doth protest too much."

I had my badge on and wore an OCSO shirt, but I flipped him off anyway. Let someone file a citizen's complaint. The satisfaction I got from raising my middle finger was worth any ass-reaming I'd get from my captain.

My gesture of love and appreciation was completely ignored, and they followed me over to the table. Thankfully, they didn't swarm Ariel, and Stella helped to act as a barrier. I would have to send her some flowers or something for her help.

Around midnight, Ariel moved around the group, saying goodbye to Piper, Leo, Carter and, even my brothers. When she got to me, I asked, "Humor me, let me escort you home. I won't press to come in, just see that you get there safely?"

She paused for a second before agreeing, "That'd be nice. I live off Conroy Windermere. Not far."

I didn't want to tell her that I knew exactly where she lived or that I drove past it every day on my way to and from work since I lived five miles past her.

Our bikes were parked on opposite sides of the building, so I followed her to her Sportster and then pushed her bike so that we could talk. It was bizarre to have her there, so close.

"How long have you lived in Orlando?" I asked.

"A year."

"What brought you here?" Even under the darkness of night, I could tell this was a bad memory. Her eyes glistened.

"Life just sort of went pear shape for me. I lost my mama. I needed a fresh start. Orlando seemed like the kind of place I could get lost in."

"Oh, sweet, I'm sorry for your loss." I wasn't sure what else to say, I still had my parents plus a large family that invaded my privacy and forced me to remember that they did it because they loved me. "Do you have any other family?"

"Nope. It was just the two of us."

We walked the rest of the way in silence, and when we were at my bike, I popped her kickstand to set the bike up. She watched me as I unclasped her helmet from her handlebars and fastened it on her head. The tears she'd fought so valiantly to hold back pooled in her eyes, and I swiped them away with the pads of my thumbs. She let out a tiny laugh that was probably meant to cover up how upset she was about her mother, so I didn't ask her if she was okay. Instead, I dropped my hands to her shoulders, offering silent support.

"I'll be right behind you, okay?"

She nodded. We started our engines and pulled out of the parking lot.

Following her was the worst idea I had ever had. I was hard as a rock. Concentrating on the way her legs splayed out around that big engine and each time she shifted, her back arched and her hips thrust. Holy fuck, I had seat envy.

We pulled into her apartment complex, and I couldn't rip my eyes away as she planted a foot on one peg, rested her weight on her right foot, and rotated. She moved like a dancer, her body spinning, her left leg came up and over the back of her bike until it rested on the ground and she faced me.

"Thanks for making sure I got home safe," she said, slipping her helmet off.

I got off my bike and stood next to her, my hand holding on to the back of her head.

"Blink your lights for me when you get in so I know that you're safe, okay?"

I was raised to be a gentleman, walk a lady to her door. But I didn't want to scare her or come across too pushy. Plus, I was so hard that I didn't think that I could walk. Before I let her go, I gave her a quick good night kiss.

Ariel had no clue, but she swaggered when she walked. It wasn't a lot, just enough that my eyes were naturally drawn to her hips and their side-to-side motion as she entered her building.

Her lights flashed, and I saw her in an upstairs window.

Pulling out my phone, I sent her a text.

Me: See you soon. Night, sweet.

I made it all of seven hours before I sent her another text.

Me: Morning, Ariel.

Ariel: Good morning.

Fourteen hours later.

Me: I'm just getting off shift. You still up?

Ariel: Yep.

Me: Hungry?

Ariel: Starving.

That was good, because I was sitting in her parking lot with a large pizza in my passenger seat. When I ordered it, I had every intention of bringing it home and eating it there. Apparently, my subconscious had a different idea, because I had driven to her place instead.

I made my way up to her apartment, but second-guessed myself before I could knock. What if I was moving too fast? But the fucking hot box of pizza from Antonio's smelled so good and I hadn't eaten since lunch. When my stomach made a gurgling sound that echoed through the hallway outside her apartment, I rapped on the door.

The smile on her face when she opened assured me that this was right.

"Dinner?" I strode into her tiny apartment and set the box on the counter. It wasn't hard to find my way around since everything was in plain sight. "Plates?"

"Is this our date?"

"No. I said go out, this is me coming in." I wasn't letting her get off the hook so easy. I had this planned out. I wanted her to get to know me, and if that meant me coming to her, us talking on the phone, and texting to get her caught up to where I was, then so be it.

"Semantics. Hmm, switching words around, are you sure you aren't a dirty cop?"

I lifted one brow at her question because that could be taken two different ways. No, I wasn't a crooked cop, but yes, I wanted to do dirty things with her, lots and lots of dirty things.

"Oh, shut up, you know what I'm talking about." Her face was brighter than her hair when she'd figured out where my mind went.

"Yes, I know what you meant. I'm not crooked or dishonest. I just want to get to know you." I'd been opening her cabinets as we bantered until I found her plates. After pulling down two, I opened the box to thick slices of Chicago style pizza and placed a slice on each plate.

"Want a bottle of water?" Ariel opened her fridge. "Or I have Cocola."

"Cocola?" She stuck out her tongue, my brain thought it was cute, my lower half thought something totally different.

"Coke Cola, don't make fun of my accent."

"I'll take a Coke." We carried our plates into the living room and she turned the volume down on the television. "What are we watching?"

"Real Housewives."

"How do you watch this shit? Carter's sister watches this crap."

"I know, who do you think got me hooked? But, oh my god, this one's husband is having an affair, which is so typical, right?"

I didn't respond to her comment, but it was a breadcrumb and I'd take it.

"And the blonde right there, she's the richest of all of them, and she's somehow related to the Kennedy's and has all of these connections." She took a bite of pizza without looking away from the hot mess happening on the screen. I had zero interest in what she was saying, but I would listen to her read the dictionary if it meant she would keep talking. I loved the sound of her voice.

By ten o'clock, the pizza was gone and Ariel was tucked against my side, passed out. I hated to wake her, but I needed to get up in eight hours for work. So, I slipped out from her hold, careful not to jostle her, and knelt in front of her. "Hey, Ariel." I whispered. When her eyes fluttered open, I continued, "Hey, I have to go. Will you follow me to the door and lock up?"

Slowly, she did as I asked, and after the door was closed tightly behind me, I stood until the clunking sound of a deadbolt twisted into position.

* * *

THE NEXT NIGHT, I didn't get off shift until late so I called her as I pulled back the covers and crawled into bed.

"How was your day?" I asked, wanting to hear her voice.

"I had to deal with some bridezilla who was pissed off because she ordered a wedding dress from a magazine and when it arrived it didn't look like the picture?"

"Was she scammed?" People got scammed all the time. Hell, Florida led the country on scammers, especially those that wanted to take advantage of all the snowbirds.

"No, it is the exact same dress. Her problem is that the model is nearly six feet tall and flat chested. My client is not much taller than me and gifted in the chest area, so the dress makes her look like a burrito." I let out a laugh at the image she painted.

"Did you calm her down?"

"Yes, but I wouldn't doubt it if she goes and gets a second opinion just to be sure. Enough about me, how was your day? You sound exhausted."

"I am. Today was a nightmare. I wish parents would sit their kids down and explain to them that there is a difference between an action movie and real life."

"You've lost me." She let out a yawn, and I chuckled.

"We had two college boys from UCF trying to reenact one of those street racing scenes down the interstate. Aiden, one of the guys on our squad saw them and called it in. There were so many cars around that it wasn't safe to do a high-speed chase, so we had to set up several road blocks, but they flew through us and refused to stop. When they passed me, I clocked them at over a hundred miles an hour."

"Holy shit."

"Holy shit is right. When we finally caught them, we had to pull them from their cars at gunpoint. They figured we were just going to give them speeding tickets, not arrest them and impound their cars." A soft hum vibrated into the phone, I didn't want to hang up even though she was asleep. Laying the phone against my ear I closed my eyes.

ARIEL

There were several ways to ensure that you wouldn't bring a man back to your apartment for sex. Don't shave your legs for weeks was one of them and the other was to not have a clue what to wear and leave your room looking like a tornado had whirled through.

I had already shaved my legs. So, it would definitely have to be the closet tornado.

With a huff, I snatched my phone and started typing.

Me: What should I wear?

Kayson: Anything or . . .

Me: Be honest.

Kayson: *I am.*

Me: Where are we going?

Kayson: Restaurant.

Me: Ugh, no help. Dressy?

Kayson: Sure, you can wear a dress.

Me: NO! I'm asking if it's dressy. Or are jeans okay?

Kayson: I'm wearing jeans.

Me: And . . .

Kayson: And what?

Me: What kind of shirt?

Kayson: Long sleeve button-down.

Me: Perfect. See you soon.

I didn't do dresses, so I wore jeans, killer shoes, and a sexy blouse. I had tried on six pairs of jeans before I settled on the perfect pair. The top was a bit more difficult. I continued adding to the pile of clothes stacked next to my closet doors, and then built a stack of shirts that were worth trying on. It had to be a blouse that didn't make me feel fat, because sometimes fat wasn't a look, it was a feeling. I chose my black tailored cropped top with fringe that hung from the hem to the floor, and my black leather ankle boots, with some chunky silver jewelry.

The subtle knock came a few minutes later, and I took several deep breaths, reminding myself not to put too much thought into the date. I wasn't looking for a boyfriend or husband, which was something I reminded myself of as I swung the door open. I didn't want a relationship, but I wouldn't mind a night of inappropriate thoughts and actions, okay maybe two nights.

Kayson was there, smiling back at me, and he was every bit as handsome as he was the other night. The breeze brought a rush of scent—a hint of Earl Grey tea and leather. I wanted to bury my nose against him and inhale, but I was afraid that I might get labeled as a whacko or lunatic. I didn't have to worry about that, though, because Kayson wrapped an arm around my waist and pulled me into him. I closed my eyes and took a whiff, allowing his scent to settle my nerves.

"I've been sitting outside your window waiting until I could come up and not appear too anxious," he said into my hair. "I've been dying to see you."

"Mmmmm." I let out a soft noise at his sweet words.

"Ready to go?" Kayson asked. "We can get a drink at the bar first."

I grabbed my handbag off the side table and locked my apartment. Kayson watched as I pressed the thin piece of tape in the corner, and when I turned, his eyebrows rose in question.

"It's my security, so I know if anyone's been in my apartment."

He nodded. "Have you always done this or just since . . ."

"Just since the attack." I answered for him.

He squeezed my hand, his fingers had calluses, but they soothed and comforted me. Kayson had the hands of a hardworking man. He only let go long enough to use his key fob and remotely start his engine and open my door for me. Leaning across, he pointed the air conditioning vents toward me, closed my door, and then walked around to his side. We drove the whole way with our fingers folded together, and I found I didn't want to let go when he pulled into a parking spot at Charlie's Steakhouse.

I had been there a few times with Brandon, but he came for their top-shelf scotch, which was more than a hundred dollars a glass. The last time we visited, Brandon returned from the restroom with his hair disheveled, the woman who walked out thirty seconds behind him was still fixing her top and her lipstick was smudged. I got a pit in my stomach over that memory.

Turning to face Kayson, I raised an eyebrow. "This isn't a restaurant friends go to."

"Why not?"

"Well, it's a date-date place to go. We aren't on a real date, this is just dinner."

"So, that means we should eat crappy food? Relax, Ariel. Let me take you to a nice dinner. It doesn't change anything," Kayson said, giving me a wink as he opened his door and came around to open mine.

It was strange, but his retort had the opposite effect on me. I thought I'd be relieved that he understood how I felt. He was giving me exactly what I asked for, but something inside me was throwing a tantrum. That tiny little part wanted him to insist this was a real date. I was not sure whether it was to provoke him or prove something to myself, but I pulled down on the hem of my blouse and revealed a little more cleavage.

Charlie's was one of those restaurants that if it were in a movie, there'd be a dress code. With its dark wood bar, brass finials, and high-back chairs, the place reeked of old money. I felt completely

44

underdressed, and ended up shifting uncomfortably as Kayson spoke to the hostess.

"They have a table, but we can still go to the bar for a drink first if you want?" His smile was sweet as he slipped his hand to the small of my back and pulled me a bit closer to him.

"No, a table would be good."

The hostess, who had been watching our exchange, gestured for us to follow her to our seats.

"Do you drink wine?" Kayson asked once we were alone again.

"I'm more of a Jack and diet girl."

Kayson nodded and ordered our drinks as well as calamari as an appetizer.

"Before moving here, I never tasted calamari, just the thought of eating fried squid gave me the heebie-jeebies, but now I love it." I was nervous and rambling. "Have you had it here before?"

"No, I haven't. I think this is only the second time I've eaten here. My parents like it. I eat at Sixes a lot."

"Sixes?"

"It's a bar slash restaurant. You know about the sergeant we lost earlier this year, the one we had the fundraiser for?"

"Yeah."

"He and his wife owned it. So, his widow is trying to keep it going. A bunch of us hang out there when we're off duty."

"Oh." I had no clue where it was and hadn't ever heard of it.

"You'll have to come with me sometime, it's a great place if you don't mind hanging out with a bunch of cops."

I laughed. I had no problem with having an overabundance of safety around me.

Just then, the server delivering our drinks, informed us that our appetizer would be up any moment, and Kayson reached for his phone, which was vibrating on the table.

"Sorry, sweet, this is work. I have to get it."

He stood and moved to take his call outside.

I sat there, waiting and wondering what was up with calling me "sweet." Not that I minded, but it seemed a bit presumptuous for him to give me a pet name. And while I waited even longer, I stared at him through the window and the way his fingers rested on his hip and strained the muscles in his forearms. He looked stressed, and I shifted in my seat, feeling more awkward the longer I sat. I decided that I didn't care what he called me or how he looked, he was taking an awful long time on the phone while we were supposed to be having a date, fuck, I mean dinner.

The calamari arrived, not wanting to start without him, I sipped my Jack and diet instead. After another few minutes, he strode back inside.

"I can't believe this," he said, slipping into his seat across from me. "I need you to understand something for me. In Florida, as law enforcement, we're technically always on duty. We're expected to have our badge and gun on us at all times and that also means we can get called in anytime." I rolled my eyes, I knew where this was headed even before he said the next line. "That was my captain on the phone. I have to go into the station."

"Now?" I asked, hoping that he would surprise me and say after dinner but who was I kidding?

"Yes. Apparently, the prosecutor on the Sello murder case, the man accused of killing the three deputies, is throwing a fit because he can't find the paperwork I filled out a month ago."

"And he needs it tonight? Right now?"

"My captain needs it to their office before nine p.m. I'm hoping it won't take long, but I still feel terrible. Let me get the bill, and I can take you home," Kayson offered.

"You don't have to do that. I'll just grab a cab."

"Please?" Kayson's words were soft and full of regret. But my mind was already racing off into another direction. How many times had Brandon canceled plans with me because he had to "work"? How many times had my father told my mother some lame excuse as to why he was late or didn't call not to mention come home? Too many to count. Sure, Kayson could have been called into work. He might really have paperwork that needed to be filled out again. There was nothing about him that screamed liar and cheater, but I'd yet to see a liar and cheater with the words tattooed on their forehead, they were more cunning. I needed to remember my motto: the only way to protect my heart was to pretend I didn't have one.

"May I stay? I can eat alone. Text me when you're finished."

He paused, seemingly torn between staying and going. After a beat, he said, "I will, promise. I'll hurry and try to make it back before you leave." Kayson waved down our waiter. "Can you run this, please? Whatever she orders is on this card and add twenty-five percent for a tip." The waiter took his card, and when he returned with the leather check presenter, Kayson signed the slip before setting two twenties on the table, "For the cab, just in case I'm not back in time." He gave me a questioning look. "You sure I can't take you home and get a do-over?"

"I'm fine. Really. I'm not mad. Not shocked. Not anything," I told him with all seriousness.

Our eyes locked, I tried to read something in them, something that would tell me that he was different. All I saw was the time Brandon came to my apartment smelling of perfume. When I had asked him why, he said it was because he had been at the mall trying to figure out which perfume I wore so he could buy me some. I didn't point out that he'd apparently been trying to find my shade of lipstick as well since there was a smudge behind his ear. That was the last time I went out with him.

Kayson leaned in to kiss me, but I wasn't in the mood for a kiss, so I turned and offered him my cheek.

"Ouch," he whispered as he walked off, releasing a low whistle.

Kayson was barely out the door when a shadow fell over the table.

"Ariel. What a lovely surprise."

"Brandon. Why am I not surprised?" I was disappointed that it was him standing there and not Kayson returning.

Brandon leaned in and kissed my cheek. "You alone?"

I wasn't in the mood to be kissed on the lips by a gorgeous Greek man, and I certainly wasn't in the mood to be kissed on the cheek by Brandon.

Looking at the empty chair across from me, I was sure he already knew the answer. Something in the back of my head told me that Brandon had witnessed the whole embarrassing thing.

"Yes."

He didn't wait for me to offer him a seat. He just took it—such a Brandon move. At some point in my head "Brandon move" and "dick move" had become synonymous.

"Was trying to enjoy my night out." I brought my hand up near my face and gave him a subtle go-the-fuck-away flick of the wrist, but he didn't get my hint.

"Let me help. I've wanted to see you. I've missed you." His words sounded genuine, which I knew wasn't the truth. Brandon was a master of manipulation, and I never knew whether he was telling the truth or spinning a lie.

"I'm shocked you've had time. You were always busy with so many 'just friends' dinners when we dated for those few months."

I was bitchy, but I was justified in my mind. My night had just gone from good to bad to crushingly disappointing in less than a handful of minutes.

He reached for my hand, but I pulled it back before he could grab it.

"Ariel, no reason to be jealous."

"Jealous? Not jealous, Brandon. Tired. Don't want to deal with you tonight. Just want to eat and go home."

He picked up the beer and my Jack and diet, "How are you getting home?"

"Cab."

"Let me take you."

"No, thank you."

"I'm staying until I know you get home safely. Ariel, please. I care about you. I've let too much time pass. I was wrong. I thought you just needed some space to realize how great we were together, but you haven't called. Do I need to prove it to you?"

"Brandon, there's no need. We aren't getting back together." Wow, that was a Taylor Swift song if ever there was one.

"Whose beer is that? You don't usually order beer."

"My date got called away," I replied.

"Were you here with Deputy Christakos? I saw him leaving."

I nodded.

"I know him, Ariel. Believe me, Christakos isn't someone who deserves your trust and faith. I know that you have trust issues and insecurities. Christakos is a cop. Cops are famous for sleeping around."

"Pot meet kettle," I retorted.

Brandon slammed his hands down on the table, causing me to jump. Snatching my purse, I stood and walked to the hostess and asked her to call me a taxi. Much to my annoyance, Brandon followed me.

"Ariel. Please. I'm sorry." I ignored him.

When she informed me that it would be about ten minutes, the thought of standing there with Brandon harassing me dropped heavy into my stomach.

"Fuck the taxi. I'll walk."

ARIEL

"*M*en suck" I held my glass up in front of me, and Stella and Leo followed suit, raising their glasses and joining in. My friends didn't suck. When I texted Stella the details from my night, she came and got me, we picked up Leo, and headed to her favorite hangout, Sixes. At first, I tried to talk her into another bar, but she was insistent. Apparently, it was the only place worth hanging out and we wouldn't have to deal with tourists. At least I didn't have to worry about running into Kayson since he was working, emergency paperwork if that was the real excuse.

"Enjoy the night. Don't let date ditching ruin the evening," Stella's smile was evil. I shook my head, knowing exactly how she thought I shouldn't let him ruin my night.

As if to punctuate her hidden meaning, she waved over a server and ordered three rounds of shots—blow jobs, panty droppers, and screaming orgasms.

Leo leaned forward to grab my attention and raised her eyebrows. "You know why I ride a Harley?"

I shook my head.

"Cause using a vibrator in public is frowned upon. You don't have to go home with a guy to have a good time."

I lost it and was thankful I hadn't just taken a sip of my drink.

When I finally got myself under control, I blurted, "I've never had drunk sex."

"We'll see if we can change that for you tonight," Stella offered. "I'm sure we can find someone."

"Well, unless Bob counts."

They laughed because, like most women, they were in on the joke. Guys may not know Bob, but women did. He was our insta-date, never broke his word, and always gave an orgasm. Our beloved, Battery Operated Boyfriend.

The server came back, setting all the shots in the middle of the table. Stella and Leo stood, so I followed their lead. I'd done enough shots but where I came from shots were whiskey, tequila, or vodka. I grew up in a dry county, we drove thirty minutes to cross the county line to buy booze at the Sip-N-Sak.

"Blow job," Stella and Leo shouted.

"Put your hands behind your back. You can only use your mouth. You have to swallow the entire shot," Stella instructed. "Ready, ladies?"

"Is this how you give a real blow job?" I wanted to know having never given one.

"What?" Leo's eyes narrowed on me, incredulous.

"Shit," some guy from across the bar said as he spewed his beer.

"You don't know?" Stella shook her head in disbelief.

"Never gave one." I'd only dated two guys, one when I was seventeen and the other was Brandon, who was dipping his wick in one too many places. I wasn't putting my mouth down there.

With a hundred assurances from Stella that this type tasted better, but the reward wasn't as great. She went first then slammed the empty shot glass onto the bar. I examined the mocha-colored drink in front of me with whipped cream piled on top before mimicking her movements. Holding my left wrist with my right hand behind my back, I leaned over opening my mouth wide, and wrapping my lips tightly around the rim of the glass. I used my teeth to hold it in place and then tossed my head back and swallowed the shot in one big gulp before taking the glass out of my mouth and setting it back on the bar.

"Did I do it right?"

"Now, that is how you swallow a mother-fucking blow job." Stella slammed her glass down and picked up the next.

"Do we do this one the same way?" I sniffed the next shot glass with its pinkish color.

"Nah," Leo assured me.

I downed the drink. "Very berry." It was a bit strange after the thick consistency of the first shot, and I puckered my lips. My stomach was already getting warm and my nose had the telltale tingles of a buzz.

"I'm gonna pass on the third," I announced. "Someone should be sober enough to drive."

I had been completely sober when I was attacked, and just the thought of being attacked when I wasn't in control of all my faculties set my nerves on edge. Since Stella showed no sign of slowing down, I had to drive or call a taxi.

"No. Piper's coming. She's taking us all home," Stella said.

The thought of Piper with a gun ensuring that I got home safe had me reaching for the final shot. Once all three shots started to work their magic, I no longer cared about being left in the restaurant, and I needed no coaxing to take over the dance floor.

I fist pumped the air, shouting, "Stronger! Stronger!" I bounced to the beat of the music, twirling, swinging to the rhythm.

"We need a name!" I hollered.

"For what?" Leo asked as she continued jumping to Kelly Clarkson.

"Our group. Gang." I pointed at Stella as I said the last word.

"It has to be sexy like us," Stella purred. "Show our feminine wiles."

"Fuck that, it needs to have something to do with motorcycles." Leo dismissed Stella's suggestion.

Hmm, sexy bikes. "Maybe we could put it together, like Steel Magnolias?"

"I'm Ouiser," Stella shouted. "That bitch was funny."

"Oh, Ouiser, I love you more than I do my luggage." Cracking up over that line from the movie, I had to try to get them to refocus. "We aren't using Steel Magnolias. It's just an idea starter. C'mon, think."

The music changed, and Charlie Puth sang fuck-me music. We swayed, okay, to be honest, we had no choice. The alcohol had taken effect, and we were solidly into too drunk to stand straight. Still, we did our best to be sexy and maintain our balance.

"Throttle. Iron. Engine. Motor," Leo spouted off words associated with bikes but sounded as if she were suffering Tourette's.

The gleam in Stella's eyes turned wicked. "Throttle Cats."

"Isn't there a cartoon with that name?" I asked, turning to her.

"That's *Thunder Cats.* Ours is Throttle Cats, for getting the pussy going."

My laugh bubbled up and wouldn't stop. I reached for Stella but made her wobble, which had her reaching for Leo, and the three of us tumbled to the floor. If I were sober, I would have been mortified to be spread out in the middle of everyone, giggling.

"Pussy Cats!" I yelled, pretending to hold a glass and cheer.

"No, Throttle Cats."

"I think we should use Orchids," I told them, my mind shifting back to magnolias during my few seconds of false sobriety.

"What the fuck does that have to do with pussy or bikes?" Stella asked.

"They're the flower of women. Aphrodite's flower. They mean sexual and beauty. They're Greek."

"Greek?" Stella turned her head to me and squinted, probably trying to bring me into focus. "Ah, shit, you liked him. Didn't you? Be honest, I hate the way things turned out."

"No. Men suck. I told you that already."

They did suck. I was sure of it. He'd ditched, but I didn't know why, which I think bothered me more than him actually leaving. Lord knew that Brandon fit every stereotypical jerk profile there was, but I didn't get that feeling from Kayson. He had this wholesome, boy-next-door vibe. Knowing that he was just like my ex made it hard to remember how fantastic his lips felt or how badly I wanted to know what was under his clothing. It didn't add up.

"Okay, ladies," a familiar man said as he helped to lift us up. "You have caused quite the show. How much have you had to drink?"

"You've got good hands, has anyone ever told you that you've got good hands?" I looked at him. I knew him but couldn't place him, he was muscular, square jawed, and tanned. He looked like he rode a motorcycle all day in the wind with the sun shining on his face. I tried to picture what his face would like against a pillow, my pillow, in my bed.

"I want more blow jobs." I sounded petulant.

"Don't we both. But we don't always get what we want, do we?" he asked.

Reaching up, I patted his cheek. "You look like Jax from *Sons of Anarchy*. I could so tap Charlie Hunnam."

"Me, too," Leo added. "I could tap Charlie Hunnam. You know who else I could tap?"

"I don't like Charlie Hunnam. But I could tap—"

"I've never given a blow job, you could be my first." I met his eyes and tried on a sexy smile. This was what Stella wanted me to do, right? I swiped at my head to clear away the buzzing sound or was that a growling sound?

"Enough. I don't want to hear this." He was glaring at Stella. "I'm Stella's brother, I don't ever . . . ever need to know about who she would or wouldn't 'tap'. I don't want to be your first blow job." When he turned to me, there was kindness in his eyes but frustration. "I'm Carter."

"Fuck. Fuck. Shoot. Poop." Seriously? This guy was Stella's brother? Mortification flooded me as soon as his features started to place themselves together. Yup. I'd met him before.

"Normally, people don't go from trash talk to second-grade vocabulary, but okay. I think it's time you ladies get some water and food."

"You got a girlfriend?" He probably did, but you didn't know unless you asked. I looked over at Stella to see if she minded me hitting on her brother.

"Shhh. Carter doesn't date girls," Stella whispered at a drunken decibel, which meant she screamed it so the whole bar could hear.

"Ahhh, now I understand why you turned down the blow job, you're gay."

"Fuck no. Kayson's one of my fucking best friends." In his ire Carter released his hold on me, and without the extra support, I stumbled and fell backward.

Before I hit the ground, large hands wrapped around my waist, and a deep voice whispered, "Careful, sweet, I've got you."

I looked over my shoulder and into velvety chocolate eyes, which were full of concern and passion. Drunken anger and hurt were pushed to the surface by life-long insecurities, and I straightened.

"Get your hands off me. Men suck. You aren't going to ruin our fun." Including Leo and Stella in my statement as I swatted his hands away from me made me feel better.

"That's right, asshat," Leo said, and we cracked up as if that was the funniest word in the entire world.

"Blow jobs!" Stella, Leo, and I shouted in unison, though I was pretty sure I shouldn't drink another drop . . . ever.

"If you hand over your keys, I'll keep the drinks coming."

"Deal!" Stella nodded.

"To the bar!" I ordered in a battle cry.

Stella, Leo, and I returned to our seats with help from Kayson and Carter, and we waved our server over. After ordering a few more rounds, well, pretty much one of everything on the bar menu, I was set for a forget-about-the-clusterfuck-that-was-my-night kind of night.

Food arrived at our table, and I looked over my shoulder to see Kayson making the universal sign for eating by acting as if he was shoveling something into his mouth.

"Where'd the food come from?" I wasn't sure whether Stella or Leo asked that because the words were jumbled and I didn't see anyone's mouth move.

Throwing my head on the table, "Is it bad that I still want him to do sexy things with me, really, really sexy things, all night long?"

"You all are shitfaced, what are we drinking to, and who are you talking about, Ariel?" Piper asked as she slid into the seat across from me.

"We know."

"Motherfuckers."

"Wanting to do sexy things with Kayson."

Leo, Stella, and I spoke at the same time, but it was my declaration that had everyone turning to stare.

"Men?" Piper asked.

Turning my head toward Piper. "You can't live with them and you can't shoot them."

"Well, you can't, I can if there's probable cause." She snagged a potato skin from the plate in front of us.

"Maybe I should become a deputy." But I didn't want to shoot men. I just wanted them to stop being assholes.

Leo gave Piper the Cliff-notes version of my night and then moved the conversation to safer water. "We're trying to come up with a name for our group. I suggested something to do with motorcycles and Ariel said Orchids."

"I was pulling for Throttle Cats, but these two"—Stella gestured drunkenly to Leo and me—"shot me down."

"Got it. Motorcycles. No cats," Piper replied.

We probably looked like a hot mess to her since she was the only sober person at the table.

"Drink up. You got some catching up to do. Provided you think men suck. Tonight is a bashing men, they all suck kind of night." I waved my finger in her face.

"Yeah. Men suck." Piper spread out three shot glasses, but she held firm with water. "But DUIs suck worse."

We cheered and then downed the blow job shots, sans hands, and sat back down.

"Would you forgive him if you knew he was actually at the station filling out paperwork? I got off shift an hour ago and he was in the captain's office getting chewed out."

I stared at my empty shot glass, her words bouncing around in my brain and trying to override my anger. "No. It wouldn't make me forgive him."

Piper was turned to face the other patrons. "That's a shame. He's been watching you since I got here."

"Good. Let him agonize." I meant every word of that. Okay. Not every word, but most of them. Crap. Okay. I meant like one of them. Okay, okay. I meant the period at the end. I glanced over at him, and he was watching me with an almost sad puppy-dog look in his eyes. I should give him a chance.

Wait a minute, I had, and he blew it. Somewhere in the back of my drunken mind, I knew it wasn't reasonable for me to demand he risk his job—or whatever case he needed to fill out paperwork for—for someone he hardly knew, but I shut that thought down. It was the same voice that told me to give Brandon the benefit of the doubt. Though, Brandon didn't have a coworker vouching for him . . .

"Got it," Piper said, slamming her hands on the table. "We could name our group Iron Orchids."

As easy as that, our group had a name. By one o'clock in the morning, Leo, Stella, and I were in no condition to drive let alone walk unaccompanied.

"I'll take Ariel," Kayson said to the others.

I should have turned him down. And if he had said that four shots ago, I would have. Instead, I stumbled and turned to the girls. "See you Iron Orchids later."

Kayson escorted me from the bar, and I was so hyper focused on the way his body moved, I hardly thought to care that I was about to be in his truck. There was something about alcohol that made me horny. I couldn't explain it. It was like, once the buzz wore off in my head, it settled down in my girly parts. He opened his truck door and helped me in.

I rested my head against his truck window while Kayson drove.

"Will you ever forgive me?"

"You don't get it. You have no idea what it's like to know." The flash of yellow and white stripes from the road as Kayson drove made my head spin. I fumbled with the air conditioner until the vents were blowing on my face. "It's not cool when you know what he's doing but there's nothing you can fucking do about it. I mean, you're powerless. So fucking powerless." I stopped talking as Kayson's warm hand found mine.

"Sweet, you have more power than you'll ever know, I just wished I had a clue what the fuck you were talking about."

When we arrived at my apartment, he didn't ask if he could come in, he just did.

"Go get changed, and I will grab you some water and Advil."

I nodded and headed down the hallway to my bedroom. I pulled on my favorite T-shirt and crawled into bed.

"Here you go." Kayson sat on the side of my bed and handed me the water and two Advil.

I took them, and he set two more on my nightstand.

"Keep drinking the water, okay?"

I nodded, but I was already halfway passed out.

"I'll lock up. You lie down." He tucked the covers around me. "Rest," he whispered.

I felt the wisp and heat from his breath next to my ear and then it was gone.

I awoke some time in the middle of the night with what felt like a mouth full of cotton, I drank the entire bottle of water, stumbled to the sink in my bathroom to refill it, and took the two remaining Advil on my nightstand. When I curled back in bed, memories of Kayson's warm breath tickling my neck lulled me back to sleep.

When next I woke, I was still thinking about the feel of Kayson's breath on my neck, only instead of lulling me back to sleep, it was doing much more interesting things to me. Without opening my eyes—no need to break a perfectly good fantasy—I opened the drawer of my nightstand and pulled out my coveted Womanizer, the best fucking vibrator in the entire world. That gorgeous man, his sexy olive skin, and steamy, sultry dark eyes had me all kinds of twisted as I thought about all the other places his warm breath could go.

Kayson's big hands spreading my thighs as he brought his head down between my legs. His velvety brown eyes with their laugh lines smiling at me before he went in to feast. What would his hair feel like as I ran my fingers through it, gripping his head to hold him in that perfect spot?

I wiggled out of my panties and pressed the rhinestone button to turn Bob on and . . . nothing.

Fuck.

The motherfucker was dead. I hurled it across the room. I'd forgotten to charge the damn thing. The thump it made as it hit the wall was loud, but I was too horny and frustrated to care.

At least until my door swung open.

Kayson stood there in a T-shirt and boxers. "You all right?"

I wanted to die.

Disappear.

Crawl under my bed and hide.

Because six inches in front of where he stood was my vibrator.

"Yeah, everything is just peachy." My voice was way too high, so I cleared my throat and tried again. "You're still here?"

"I didn't want to leave you. I had no way of locking your deadbolt or safety chain."

He was thinking about my safety, and my only thought was *don't look down*. And of course, fuck.

He fucking looked down.

My humiliation flared as he tilted his head, and a smirk curled the side of his perfect, perfect mouth.

Fuck. I was so busted.

"Is that what I think it is?" he asked as he bent down to pick up my leopard print sex toy.

Jumping from my bed, I snatched it out of his hand and shoved it back into my bedside drawer. "It's nothing."

"It looked like something to me."

"Well, it wasn't." I huffed, refusing to turn around and face him. He wasn't letting me off the hook that easily, though. I squeezed my eyes shut as he moved deeper into my room, and then I felt his forearm slide over my shoulder and rest there. I cracked my eyes open just enough to see that he was dangling my recently discarded panties in front of me.

You have to be kidding me. What made this whole situation worse? His free hand was on my hip. Warm and big and inviting. That hand promised all sorts of delicious things as it squeezed, pulling me back against the heat of his chest.

Forcing myself to slow my breathing down and regain control.

"You know," he whispered against the soft skin of my neck, "if you need help letting off some steam, I'm happy to oblige."

"I said it was nothing." Everything from my breathy words to the thundering pace of my heart told him that was a big, fat lie. I was so turned on that he could probably smell my arousal. I didn't want a relationship, just one or two times with this man. This man had me wound so tight that I was going to break at any moment.

"If by nothing, you mean sex toy, then okay." He moved back an inch, and I wanted to scream in frustration. Thankfully, he only did it so he could turn me around. I tilted my chin so I could look at him, which was a mistake because he took it as permission to drop a kiss to the corner of my mouth. He moved his lips along my cheek to my neck and kissed behind my ear.

"Stop that. I can't think if you're doing that." My words were worthless, because even as they were leaving my mouth, I was tilting my head to give him better access and pressing my body closer to his.

He slid his left hand up my arm, and I twitched as he left goose bumps in his wake.

"I need to go brush my teeth," I said as I pulled back, but he caught my hand, stopping my escape and pulling my back to his front.

"Mm-hm." His warm breath tickled the shell of my ear as he wrapped his arms around me and pressed his erection into me.

"I called you when I left the station, but you didn't answer, so I called the restaurant. They told me that you had left shortly after I did," he said, sliding one hand around the hem of my T-shirt. "Then I came by your apartment, but you weren't here." He inched his hand up under my shirt and paused at my hip, waiting for me to slap it away or tell him to leave. I didn't do either.

"Did you?" he asked.

"Did I what?"

"Come?"

"None of your business. Did you really look for me?"

"I told you that I would. And don't change the subject. I'm making it my business. Did you come?"

He traced the outline of the V between my legs with one finger. "I want this, but I need to know that you want this."

For some reason his words controlled my legs because when he said that my knees buckled. His gentle hands that seconds ago had been tracing the outline of my body were now pressing me back toward the bed.

"Do you want this?"

My breath faltered as his fingers traced a lazy path up to my breast before he cupped the weight of it, pinching my nipple between his thumb and forefinger. My only answer was a barely coherent moan as he dropped deep kisses along my shoulder.

"You never answered my question. Did you?"

"No. The damn thing was dead," I admitted.

His soft chuckle vibrated against the curve of my neck. "Lucky for me."

He caressed my skin with his large hands, and I felt pint-sized electrodes shoot through my body and race straight to my core.

"Would you like to come?"

"Obviously."

"Tell me you want me to make you come." Kayson's voice was deep and raspy.

"Yes. Damn it. I want you to make me come."

Kayson thrust his tongue inside my mouth and wicked thoughts filled my head, this wasn't all I wanted him thrusting inside me.

KAYSON

"*A*riel." I nudged her back onto the bed and dropped to my knees in front of her. My lips trailed a slow line from the inside of her knee to her core. I'd never thought much about eating a girl out. It was a good way to get a blow job. It was reciprocal. But Ariel, I wanted her. I wanted every bit of her. I wanted to taste her on my fingers, on my lips, and on my tongue.

"You're so beautiful," I whispered.

With one long stroke, I licked her slit.

I heard the slap of her hands as she smacked the bed, and I felt her body jerk from the sensations.

"Holy shit," she cried.

"Shhh, *sweet*. Lie back."

But she didn't lay back, she stayed propped up and watched me as I devoured her. I held her eyes as I swiped my tongue through her soft, pink folds. Her face tightened at the sensation. It was a look I wouldn't ever forget. The low, desperate sound she made was one I'd make sure to hear again.

"Please. Kayson. I'm gonna . . ."

Her words melted me. The more she begged for me, the harder I sucked, licked, and tugged. Her fingers gripped my head, holding me against her as I found that perfect spot. Once more, I lifted my eyes to meet hers, but her lids were closed and her head was tilted back in pleasure. I felt the moment of her release. Her thighs tightened, her ass rose off the bed, and her knees became weighted.

"Kayson!" she shouted, and my body tingled at the sound of my name escaping her lips.

I nibbled, she pulsed, her body releasing its satisfaction.

Slowly, I ran my tongue over her, easing her back down from the peak of pleasure. This was absolutely, positively the breakfast of champions, and my cock was so hard, it took every bit of my willpower not to strip off my clothes and bury myself deep inside her. I had to remind myself that I was working toward a bigger goal. I looked down at Ariel, satiated, flushed. Her chest rose and fell in little pants, and pride washed over me. I'd wrung this beautiful woman out. Maybe she'd accept my apology for having to leave her last night. A small grin crept across my face . . . maybe I'd apologize again later.

She was still in a lusty daze when I pulled myself to my feet and made my way to the bathroom to catch my breath. If I stayed there, kneeling in front of her with her spread like an offering, I would never have stopped.

Splashing cold water on my face helped, but it didn't stop the images of Ariel in twenty years, thirty years, and forty years. I wanted all the versions that flashed behind my eyelids. By the time I left her bathroom, I had one creed, and that was that I'd make love to her and it wasn't going to be a one-time thing.

I made my way to her kitchen and rummaged until I found her coffee and mugs. After I had that started, I riffled through her refrigerator and pulled out bacon, eggs, and cheese.

"That coffee smells like heaven." Her voice was soft, and I turned to find her standing in the doorway with a wary smile. Her hair was tousled, and she was still wearing that old Crimson Tide T-Shirt that hung mid-thigh.

"I'm making breakfast."

Wrap it, tap it, and go was the unspoken motto of most law enforcement officers. Relaxing enough to let down our guard and spend the night at a woman's house took some serious trust, but last night I didn't consider leaving, not once. Ariel needed me, maybe that was why I loved my job so much, I liked being needed.

Stretching out my arm, I invited her into the crook between my shoulder and chest, shocked and amazed when she took it.

"How are you feeling?"

"Confused."

"About?" I drew out the last part of the word.

"You. Me. What we're doing. We barely know each other. You're in my apartment, in your boxers, cooking breakfast. I woke up after having the hottest dream, and you were there. You . . . took care of me and didn't ask for anything in return. It's confusing," she said, her face turning almost as red as her hair.

"Was it a sex dream?"

She buried her face deeper into my chest. I moved just an inch so I could remove the bacon from the pan.

I felt her nod then mumble against me, "It was hot, you were on your knees."

"Weird, I had the same fucking dream."

I brought my mouth down to hers and kissed her deeply. She pushed up onto her tiptoes to kiss me back. If I pushed her back, propped her on the counter, and knelt for round two, she would let me. I didn't, though. I'd screw this up if I took too much too soon. Ariel claimed she didn't want a relationship, so I was making it my job to prove her wrong.

"Since you're in such a good mood, how about doing me a favor?" I asked.

"What?"

"I don't even know how to explain this, but the night of your attack, left me with this weird feeling as if I was supposed to know you." Leaning back, I rested my hips against her kitchen counter and continued trying to explain that I already felt something for her without freaking her the fuck out. "When the paramedics shouted they were taking you to ORMC, I called my brother Tristan and asked him to check on you, I was worried about you. Tristan protected your privacy and wouldn't tell me anything until you gave the all clear for me to come up. Unfortunately, he didn't feel the same way about protecting my privacy..." God, why was this so fucking hard to ask? "I'm Greek. I told you that, right?" A smile crossed her face. She could tell I was nervous. "Do you see where I'm going with all of this?"

Nodding her head Ariel said, "yes" --then in a swift sweeping motion she shook her head--"no."

"Let me try again, come to dinner with me at my parents' house?" And with those words the smile left her. "Don't freak. We get together every week. It's noisy and loud, but the food is always amazing. Plus, my brothers will be there, I saw them talking to you and Stella last week at the Harley event."

Ariel reluctantly asked, "What would your parents think of me tagging along?"

"Well, I'm Greek and that means there are no secrets. The first thing Tristan did was tell Mana that I asked him to check on you. I had to practically threaten to throw her in jail just to keep her from coming up to the hospital and sitting with you. So, she'd be ecstatic."

"Mana?"

"Greek for mom. There are always other people joining us. My brothers frequently bring friends, even Carter occasionally comes." What I wasn't saying was that none of us had ever brought a girl before. "If you say yes, I could pick you up around four. If not, you can expect an overbearing Greek woman with weeks full of food at your door any day, and she's hard to get rid of."

Ariel let out a laugh at the idea. "I'll come, but I can drive, just give me the address. I want to stop by a florist first. If I'm meeting your mom, I'm not showing up empty handed."

"Want me to run into Publix and grab some?"

"Uh, no. Flowers from the checkout lane at the grocery store aren't acceptable."

"I'll find us a flower shop."

"But, I can drive," she offered again. "Just in case you get called into work."

And there it was. The hurt she was trying to hide. I pulled her back into my arms and dropped my lips to her ear.

"I really am sorry for having to leave you last night."

"I believe you." It didn't escape my notice that she didn't say she forgave me.

"If I get called in, I will bring you home first or I'll give you the keys to my truck."

There was a brief pause before her body slowly relaxed and then she stepped back.

"Okay."

It was a small win, but it was still a win. I gave her my most charming smile. "Great. Now eat," I ordered in a gentle voice and pushed the plate in front of her.

"You aren't eating with me?"

"No. I have to run to the station and then get some errands done before dinner. I'll be here at four."

While I dressed, she ate, and then she walked me out. I stood on the other side of her door and listened as she secured the security chain. The thump of footsteps behind me raised the hairs on the back of my neck, and I turned, expecting someone to be there. The steps and walkway were deserted. I kept my hand on my gun as I made my way to my truck. There wasn't anyone getting in a vehicle, or walking across the parking lot, but I couldn't shake the strange feeling that someone had been watching me.

I picked up my phone and called the non-emergency line into the station.

"This is Sergeant Christakos. Let's put Coconut Bay apartments on signal eighty-seven."

It would ensure a steady flow of deputies doing an area check through her complex, just in case her attackers knew where she lived. Whoever they were, they hadn't sexually assaulted her or stolen money, jewelry, or her motorcycle. All signs led me to believe that her attackers knew her and for some reason it was personal.

ARIEL

*W*hat kind of outfit does one wear to meet the parents? Do I introduce myself as the girl that isn't in a relationship with their son but wouldn't mind sleeping with him? The girl who completely appreciates just how awesome his tongue skills were? I snorted. His mom would kick me out and his father would probably congratulate him.

No. He said that his parents knew of me because of the attack. I shook off the jitters and told myself that I was meeting them as just another person he'd helped. He probably did stuff like this all the time. Saved someone and then befriended them . . . wait. Did he save women and then seduce them? I froze, with one leg in the jeans I was pulling on. Did he?

My gut, which was right as often as it was wrong, told me he didn't. He had looked almost nervous about inviting me to dinner. Men who did something all the time didn't get nervous about it. When Brandon would lie to me, he had always been convincing. Calm.

Okay.

I kicked the jeans off—they were the wrong color anyway—and dove into the pile that was still next to my closet mirror from last night. I tried each pair on, again. But they didn't feel right, too tight, too loose, too dark, too light.

I finally decided on a chocolate-brown peasant shirt with tiny yellow flowers and yellow ribbons and my yellow denim shorts. It screamed happy and wholesome.

Then I cleaned up the rest of what remained of Hurricane Failed Date that turned into Awesome Oral with Hot Greek Guy before grabbing my brown cowboy boots and shutting my closet doors.

By the time Kayson arrived, my apartment was spotless and smelled of cinnamon and apples. Around noon, I'd decided that flowers weren't enough and had tossed my kitchen, looking for the ingredients to make . . . something . . . anything to bring with me. Thankfully, I had everything to make a pie. If it tasted half as good as it smelled, then it was going to be a hit.

"Did you cook?" Kayson asked with astonishment.

"Yes. Don't act so surprised. I'm a pretty good cook. But today I baked an apple pie to bring to your folks."

Speaking of desserts, Kayson looked delicious. He wore khaki cargo shorts and a navy T-shirt. His forearms stretched the fabric at the sleeves, making it seem as if the shirt was made just for his body. Ripping my eyes away from his biceps, I slipped my purse over my shoulder and nodded to the pie.

"Could you grab that for me?"

"Of course."

I locked my apartment and then went through my safety routine: lock the door, check the deadbolt, and fix the tape.

"Always the same way?" he asked.

"Always. My apartment doesn't allow the installation of security systems."

"Why the fuck not?"

"Because if the next tenant doesn't want it, then there are all these wires and the box. And to hardwire them, the techs have to crawl into space between apartments."

"That is fucked up."

He and I were in agreement on that point. There were new wireless systems for apartment renters, but the monthly monitoring fees were astronomical.

Kayson opened his truck door for me and helped me in, pressing the auto start on his key fob, then once again leaning over to make sure the air conditioner vents were directed toward me before closing the door. He placed the pie on the floorboard of the backseat and then moved a towel and what looked like a first-aid kit around it to keep it from sliding around. It was a sweet and thoughtful gesture.

"I wish I were a mind reader," Kayson said as he brushed my cheek with the back of his knuckles.

"Just thinking about how you take care of things, like putting stuff around the pie so it didn't slide and get all smashed."

Kayson put his truck in gear and pulled out of my apartment complex.

His eyes darkened, and his voice softened. "There are a lot of things that I want to take care of."

Red flares flashed in my brain, telling me to *abort, abort, abort*. I needed to pull this conversation back onto my safe ground.

"So, tell me about your mom. What's her first name? Are you sure she won't mind?" I picked at a loose thread at the hem of my shirt. "What about your daddy, will he care?" That damn thread bothered the hell out of me.

Kayson took his right hand off the steering wheel and gave my leg a quick squeeze. "Let me try to remember all those questions. My mom's name is Christine, she is nosy and will ask a million questions, but she is the kindest person I know. My dad, we call him Pop, will love having you there if for no other reason than Mana will be happy. That is all that man worries about."

"I'm sorry. I'm nervous. Thank you for this morning." I felt heat rise in my cheeks when I realized exactly what all I was thanking him for and not just breakfast. Well, not just my breakfast.

A smile titled at the corner of Kayson's mouth as he drove to a store that looked more like a head shop with its psychedelic spinners and lava lamps in the window displays. But they were set off by gorgeous floral arrangements, and the name Flower Power seemed to bring the whole look together. As we walked in, a lady greeted us by handing me a sheet of waxed paper to hold the buds and blooms that I pulled from the glass refrigerators.

"Each type of flower has a meaning." I wanted him to understand why I felt it was important to select each flower personally.

"Which ones mean sex?"

Typical.

I laughed and shook my head, pointedly ignoring his question as I selected three large flowers the color of port wine.

"What's that?" he asked.

"Dahlias, they represent kindness."

"And those?" he pointed to the white flowers I had just pulled from a bucket.

"Mini Calla Lilies, they mean beauty. And these are Zinnias." I added the fuchsia-colored flowers to the mix. "They symbolize thoughtful friend."

I arranged the flowers to see how they'd look bunched together and then fluffed the arrangement with a few sprigs of cotton stems and fern before declaring the bouquet complete.

"Are girls pulled aside and taught this flower language at some point in school?"

"Most of us know the basics, red roses for love, yellow for falling out of love or jealousy."

"What the fuck? There's a flower to say, 'I no longer love you'?"

"There's a flower to say just about anything."

"How about I'm horny?"

"Do you think about anything else?" I asked.

"Food. Football. You."

"Charming."

Kayson held out his hands as if asking for mercy, and I laughed. This man and his words melted my heart, but only a little. I had heard sweet talk before. Hell, my daddy was the king of it.

"To answer your question, coral-colored roses mean I'm horny. They're a cross between red and orange. Red is passion and orange is fantasy. It literally means passionate fantasy."

"So, if I say, 'I'm coral rosing,' a woman will understand me?"

"Hate to burst your bubble," I said between fits of laughter, "but probably not. I took a class on floral design, and we learned the meanings. I'm a rare breed."

"You're one of a kind." Kayson's words were soft, almost a whisper, but I still heard him. My heart had this way of flitting like a butterfly whenever he was around, which was very off-putting. I needed to work harder to steel myself against him.

I gave him a smile and handed over the bouquet to the cashier while I dug into my purse for my wallet. But Kayson beat me to the punch and forked over his card.

"These are from me; I want to pay," I said.

"Just because I paid doesn't mean they can't be from you. When you're with me, I'd like to do the paying."

"Neanderthal much?" He smiled as if I hadn't just insulted him.

He drove to his parents' house, and we chatted about the difference between Florida and Alabama. Kayson had traveled all over the world but had never been to Alabama. He wasn't missing much.

"Well, some parts of the state are nothing but suffering, and people are barely making ends meet. Then there are areas where you feel like you've stepped back to the antebellum time and everything there seems to move slower. Those are the towns where people sit and chat over a glass of lemonade on the porch for hours."

When he turned onto Pente Loop, Kayson took over the conversation and pointed out his house and each of his brothers' houses along the way.

"When we turned twenty-five, Mana and Pop gave each of us a house."

"Holy shit. Who the hell gives a house as a birthday gift?"

He laughed and gave me a sideways glance. "The type of people who want to keep their kids close. The houses are all on my parents' property. I think the only reason Pop went along with it was because Mana told him it would make her happy, and he would do just about anything to make her happy. Plus, he owns Christakos Construction, so it wasn't too much of a hardship."

Still, that was one hell of a gift.

"My mama always gave me embossed monogram linen stationary," I said with a cheeky grin, as if that was the same caliber as a house. "And the first thing she expected me to do with my stationary was to write thank-you notes to everyone who gave me a gift for my birthday."

Kayson gave me a sweet smile.

"Did you design your house?" I asked.

"Damon, my oldest brother, is an architect. He works with Pop. I picked out the style, but he did everything else."

"Can I see it?"

"We can go by after dinner if you want."

"I'd like that." Which was the truth.

Kayson pulled up to a sprawling ranch style home with a large wrap around porch. It was well kempt and the landscaping was envy inducing.

"This is the house you grew up in?"

"Yep. Pop renovated it a few years back, but it's still home. What about your parents' house? Did you live in the same house all of your life?" Kayson asked me.

"Yeah. It was just Mama and me, though." I held my breath, praying he didn't ask about my daddy. Thankfully, he didn't.

"You miss it?"

"I miss my mama. But, no I don't miss the house. It didn't hold a ton of great memories."

"Then we'll just have to find some ways to make great memories," Kayson said as he got out of his truck and strode around to open my door for me.

"Are you sure I'm dressed okay?"

Self-doubt hit me, this whole meet the family had a strange, we-are-in-a-relationship feel to it and it had me fidgeting nervously with the hem of my top.

"You look stunning."

I nodded. "Thank you. I have to admit I'm really nervous right now."

"Growing up did you ever have dinner at your friend's houses?"

"Not the same."

"Why?" Kayson asked. "Why isn't it the same, Ariel?"

"It just isn't, all right?"

Kayson's hand touched my cheek before sliding to cup my chin.

"Admit it. You know it and so do I. There's something between us. I can't put words to it, yet, but I will—soon. There's something about you that's familiar, like I've known you forever."

"It's because you got to play my knight in shining armor for a few minutes when you rescued me." A few minutes were all I'd ever get, if I got a lifelong knight, he'd probably look more like Mr. Bean wrapped in aluminum foil than he did Kayson Christakos.

"Whatever you say." Kayson chuckled as he grabbed the pie from the floor of the backseat while I hopped down from the truck.

With his free hand resting on my back, we walked up to the front door and wandered in.

The smell of lemon filled the air, and I could sense the laughter and love that radiated from the walls giving the house its homey feeling. This house epitomized family. Kayson led me through the enormous house and into a beautiful family room that had photos hanging in four columns on the wall, one for each son. I stopped, running my eyes over the column that was all Kayson. He looked just like his dad.

"These your parents?" I asked, gesturing to a group photo taken when Kayson was probably in his teens.

"Yep. We were cruising around Crete."

They were all on a boat together, but it was the look in the dad's eyes that made me swoon. He was looking at Kayson's mom with what I could only describe as absolute adoration.

"Does he always look at your mother like that?"

"Like they're ready to get a room any moment?" Kayson asked, shaking his head in mock horror.

"Yeah, just like that."

"Always."

At that, he guided me away from the pictures, through the dining room, past a parlor—or at least that was what we called it in Alabama

—and into the kitchen. His mother was there, and as soon as she spotted us, she grabbed a towel to dry off her manicured hands. Her smile matched the house, big and bright.

"Mana, I'd like you to mee—"

"Ariel," Kayson's mother said as if she knew me. She had a slight accent to her voice, but I found it soothing.

"Hello, Mrs. Christakos. It is lovely to meet you. These are for you," I said, and handed her the bouquet of flowers while Kayson set the pie on the counter. "You have a lovely home."

She didn't inhale their beautiful fragrance like most people would have. Instead, she focused on me.

"You call me Christine. I want to look at you." Handing the flowers to Kayson, she reached for my hands and held them in hers. "You're so beautiful. No wonder my boy is smitten."

Smitten? I looked to Kayson, but he wasn't saying a word. I couldn't even read anything in his eyes.

"Would you like some help? I love to cook."

"Please."

"What are you making?"

"Avgolemono. It is chicken with a lemon sauce."

"Tell me what I need to do. I'd love to learn."

"Go. Leave us be." Christine flittered her fingers, shooing Kayson away.

Kayson grabbed a beer, turned and kissed his mother's cheek before dropping one on mine. As he walked through the sliding glass door that lead to a pool with a built in waterfall, he stopped and turned to look at me, my heart fluttered. My eyes flashed back toward the wall where that photo of his father hung, that look. My heart raced, shit, I was too young to be having a heart attack.

"Smitten." Christine's lilt penetrated my panic attack.

Maybe I was wrong. Maybe he was that elusive *one*. Maybe I should grab hold before he was gone.

KAYSON

*D*amon and Ian were down by the lake shooting the shit with Pop when I got out there.

"About time you got here, I'm starved," Damon bitched. "Now if Tristan would hurry his ass, we could eat."

"Sorry, I was talking to Ariel."

"Ooooh." Damon had a shit-eating grin on his face. "Is that where you were last night? I came by, but you weren't home, came by this morning and you still weren't home. Too 'hard' to leave her."

"Ha-ha, very funny." He thought he was hysterical.

"Come to think of it," Ian piped in. "I came by the other night, and you weren't home. It was close to ten."

"What? Can't I have a life that you don't know about?"

"Admit it, Kayson; It's that girl. You're whipped," Damon said.

"Let's don't go there, I'm not whipped. Hell, it's only been a week."

"Any clues on who attacked her?" Pop asked, trying to intercept the conversation before we were back to being ten years old and rolling on the ground fighting.

"Not yet."

Un-fuckin-fortunately my peace didn't last long because we were interrupted when the door opened. "Mana's in heaven!" Tristan shouted.

"Why's that?" Damon and Ian asked in unison.

"Ah shit," I said in an undertone. "Wait," I hollered.

But Tristan didn't listen to me.

"Kayson didn't tell you? There's a smoking hot redhead inside. Her name is Ariel."

Damon, Ian, and Pop jumped up and ran for the door. "Don't be a bunch of asses," I called out after them. "You'll scare her off."

It was too late. I turned to Tristan and glared.

"Thanks a fuckin' lot."

"How was I supposed to know you didn't tell them you brought her?"

When I got inside, I took a seat at the bar and listened as my brothers peppered Ariel with questions. Thankfully, she handled them like a champ.

"Do you have a sister?"

"Nope. Just me."

"You and Kayson are just friends, right?"

"Yes, we're friends."

"Then why not go out with me, I'm the best looking," said Damon.

"How about me? I have brains and looks," said Ian.

"Excuse me?" Tristan added. "I don't think either of you has 'doctor' by your name."

"You're not a rocket scientist, either," Ian cut back.

"And we wonder why they're still single?" Pop added. "Ariel, I'm George. You can call me Pop."

"Hi, Pop." I was surprised that Ariel came around the kitchen counter and gave my father a giant hug. I wasn't surprised when all three of my brothers turned and checked out Ariel's legs.

There was something about a woman in cowboy boots that drove men nuts.

Damon turned to me and mouthed, "Damn."

"Shut the fuck up," I mouthed back.

Dinners were always loud at our house, but for the first time in my life, I realized it was also calming. This was home, family, what I wanted. We sat watching as Mana and Ariel worked in the kitchen. Ariel had no trouble making herself at home. She wore a spare apron and tasted everything Mana put in front of her mouth.

"She looks good," Pop said. I looked up and over my shoulder to meet his eyes. "Your girl, she looks good with your mother in the kitchen. They get along like family."

Pop supported Mana in whatever she wanted or didn't want to do. But he liked the fact that she stayed home to raise us and that he came home every night to dinner on the table and a beautiful wife. Pop calling Ariel family was like him asking me what I was waiting for and then telling me to get a ring and get to making babies for Mana to spoil. Ariel had the George Christakos seal of approval mainly because she made Mana happy.

My family forgot one big thing—to them, I had known her for months because they had heard me talk about her for months. To Ariel, we had known each other for just over a week. She said that she didn't want a relationship, and I was trying to change her mind by hook, crook, or lick.

After dinner, Mana pulled out a tub of sweet cream ice cream and Ariel sliced apple pie on to plates that we carried outside and sat by the pool. The sound of the trickling from the water fountain added the perfect peace to the night.

* * *

"I LIKED BEING with your family tonight. Your mother is lovely," Ariel said as she clicked her seatbelt.

"They liked you. You know that we get together every week. The day changes depending on my and Tristan's schedules, though. You are always welcome. My mother would love it."

Ariel avoided answering me by changing the subject. "Will you still show me your home?"

Trying to figure her out was like putting together a five-hundred-piece jigsaw puzzle. She said one thing, acted one way, reacted a totally different, then when she didn't think anyone was watching she would let down her guard and show me an entirely different person.

Until I figured out which was the real Ariel, I would give her what she said she wanted. Right then, she wanted to see my house. I drove up my driveway and pushed the garage door opener so I could pull in.

I led her inside and up the stairwell, figuring starting upstairs and circling back down would be best.

"Holy cow, this place is large."

"You've met my parents. Need I say more?"

I made fun of them, but they were the best. We were raised in a house where we were expected to make mistakes provided three things: we learned from them, we didn't make the same mistake twice, and we said sorry.

We were respectful to our parents, which was evident since we all still had our teeth. If we had been disrespectful, Pop would have kindly removed them for us. And we were always gentlemen. Other than that, our house was a zoo, and on any given day, there were at least five or six friends over.

"Both sides are identical," I said, pointing to the left and right side of the second-floor landing.

Heading left where three doors sat closed in this part of the house. "Straight ahead is the linen closet, and to the left and right are bedrooms." I led her through the first room, which was empty, and showed her the Jack-n-Jill bathroom, which led to the second bedroom that held my childhood bedroom furniture.

"I grew up on reruns of *The Brady Bunch*. I thought it was horrid that all those kids had to share a bathroom. I especially felt sorry for the girls. I remember the fights we used to have as kids about who had the poor aim on the toilet seat."

"Eww." Ariel groaned. I laughed as we walked back into the hallway and to the right side of the landing.

"There's my room, it has an en suite bathroom." I pointed but didn't take her in there. I needed to get her back downstairs. The mere thought of this woman being feet away from my bed had me ready to jump her. Think, Kayson, think—paper cuts, those pitiful Sarah

McLachlan commercials, YiaYia. Yeah, my Greek grandmother, that was so fucked up, but it worked, my erection wasn't as noticeable.

When we hit the landing and turned the corner, I felt a bit less like a caveman. "So, that's the living room, kitchen, dining room," I said as we walked through each room respectively.

She had moved her hand into mine, and I loved it. Her hand was so small that it fit entirely in my palm. Maybe I wasn't as firm in the friend zone as I thought I was.

"These two rooms are his and her offices, and finally, we have the pool bath that leads to the outside for if I ever want to add a pool."

"Are you planning to install a pool?"

"Some day. I just haven't been able to justify the cost since I hardly have time to swim."

"Are your brothers' houses just like yours?"

"They are all different styles but, yes, they are around the same size. She calls it her insurance policy," I said as I laughed.

"What do you mean?"

"Family sized houses encourage . . ." I let that last word dangle in the air unsaid.

Ariel caught my meaning. "Grandbabies."

"Bingo. The woman is unrelenting."

She was still laughing as we climbed back into my truck and headed to her house. Outside her door, I rubbed my thumb against her lower lip before leaning in and giving her a gentle kiss. It was difficult to pull away, but I had to be up for work at six in the morning, and one more breath of her perfume would have me carrying her to bed and ravaging her the entire night.

Not a bad idea, if I were to be honest. That wasn't my plan, though. I wanted more from her, and I wouldn't get that if I proved I was just every other guy in the damn world. I had to find that fucking door hidden in those walls she had built. Once I did? I wasn't going to leave.

ARIEL

J had taken a step inside, hoping that he would follow, but he didn't cross the threshold. All I got was a kiss. He left me with a kiss? That man wanted me, I could tell. Hell, I'd seen it, several times.

God, I was so fucked up, this was my fault. I'd been giving him mixed signals. Somehow I needed to show this man that I wanted more, well I wanted sex. I didn't want a relationship, did I? Men were asses. They cheated, lied, and left you when you needed them the most. Fuck. Now, even I was confused. I needed help, serious help. Grabbing my phone I sent Stella a text.

Me: I need help.

Stella: Are we talking bail you out of jail help or bring a shovel and hide a body kind of help?

Me: Love you.

Stella: Ditto. Now, whatcha need?

Me: I want to have sex with Kayson.

Stella: Fuck yeah. But why are you telling me and not him?

Me: I need to go shopping for sexy stuff.

Stella: Then go.

I stared at the blank oval space where I could type a response. How did I ask for moral support? I didn't want to go to the mall alone. Should I just admit I was afraid?

Stella: Fuck. Sorry, A. I'm off on Wednesday. Let me text and see who else is off, and we can all head out together. Maybe have some drinks to celebrate you getting some.

Me: Not getting any, yet. Just thinking about it.

Stella: Admitting it is half the battle.

Me: Bite me.

Stella: Pick you up around lunch on Wednesday. Ciao.

* * *

STELLA WAS ON MY LEFT, her fingers woven between mine. On my right, Piper was scanning the area as we walked, it was her day off, but she was a deputy to the bone.

"What color do you think Kayson would like best?" Stella asked, diligently trying to take my mind off the fact that we were in the same parking lot of my attack.

"You know, just the thought of helping you buy sexy lingerie to have sex with Kayson kind of weirds me out." Piper shot me a tight smile. "If I get the motors position, he will be my boss."

"What do you mean 'if'? You're going to get it," I assured her.

"Even if Ariel has to use sexual favors to secure your promotion." Stella bumped her shoulder against mine and smiled playfully.

"By the way, I never said that the lingerie was for Kayson."

"You have met Stella, right?" Piper gave me this dumbfounded look as she asked the question. "You put it in a text. It became part of a group message to see who was available today."

Stella let out a snort. "You said you wanted to jump his bones, ride his heat seeking love missile . . ." I punched her in the arm.

"That's not what I said either."

"Well, not verbatim. But you did text that you wanted to have sex with him."

I needed to keep reminding myself that when Stella was around,

81

this wasn't fight club, there were no secrets, and everything was discussed and shared.

"Just a few more steps," I whispered, looking up at the giant glass doors.

"We've got you," Stella whispered back.

I was at the mall, I wasn't alone, it was daylight, and Piper was a cop for fuck's sake. But still I was doing it. My hands shook and a cold sweat broke out over my skin. Memories flashed across my mind of two masked men when the sound of flip-flops flopping behind me echoed like thundering hooves. I ripped my hands out of Stella's and Piper's, I needed to move, not be restrained. I suddenly felt caged. A doorman opened the large glass doors, and I rushed past him and slowed after I was sure I was safely inside.

"Let's eat first," Piper said, linking her elbow loosely with mine and steering me toward the Cheesecake Factory. "It will give us a chance to plot our strategy for shopping."

We were quickly seated and ordered appetizers and dessert, they were the best things on the menu anyway.

I lost my appetite the second Brandon was seated at the table next to us. I had no clue what the fuck was up with him lately, but he was showing up everywhere. And let's be honest, Cheesecake Factory didn't exactly sound like his kind of restaurant.

I slid down in my seat, trying to crawl under the table before he noticed me. But as my luck would have it, I wasn't fast enough.

"Ariel Beaumont, you look lovely. I'm a lucky man to get to see you again so soon."

Brandon's smooth words grated on my nerves. Why had I never noticed how smarmy he always sounded? When we first met, I found him eloquent, which clearly wasn't the case anymore. Piper cleared her throat and shifted. Obviously, I wasn't the only one picking up on his bullshit vibe.

"Hi, Brandon. It's definitely a surprise." See? I could have manners. "This is Stella and Piper," I said, gesturing to each in turn.

"We've met," Piper said as she extended a hand, and Brandon ignored it.

"Oh yes. Deputy DuPont. Ariel, it seems as if you've been busy making new friends. How did all of you meet?"

"How do you and Ariel know each other?" Piper asked, avoiding his question.

"Who are you?" Stella's eyes were narrowed as she skipped over all the bullshit.

"Brandon used to be a friend. We went out a few times."

"Oh, I would say we were more than friends." He turned to Stella. "Ariel and I dated for a few months. We were very happy."

Fuck. Shit. Fuck.

"If you were happy, why does Ariel look as if she'd rather chew on poison ivy than talk to you?" God, I loved Stella. Too bad Brandon didn't take the very obvious hint that he wasn't wanted there and slid into the seat next to me.

"We're having a girl's day out." I glared at his glass, which he had set next to mine, and then back at his abandoned table. He didn't get the hint. I always set my expectations way too high.

"Then let me pay for your lunch," he offered.

"Let me order a bottle of their best wine," Stella replied as the server delivered our appetizers of Thai wraps, buffalo blasts, and pot stickers. "Since you're such a good friend of Ariel's and all."

I kicked her under the table because, although she was being a smart-ass, he would do it as a way to flaunt his money, and a bottle of wine would force us to sit there with him longer.

"Where are you headed after this?" Brandon asked as he slipped an arm around me.

I did that wave-sorta-thing with my shoulders to get his arm off.

"Shopping," I said at the same time Stella said, "Sex toys."

Brandon raised one eyebrow and gave me a disapproving look.

"I think you would need to go closer to where you work for those," Brandon retorted, giving Stella an icy glare.

"Excuse me?" I narrowed my eyes at Brandon. "That was rude."

"Stella. She's a nurse at ORMC, correct?" All the faked innocence in his voice made me want to punch him.

"Yes," I said, drawing out the word, finding a little discomfort at how he knew where Stella worked.

"ORMC is a great hospital, but let's be honest, it isn't in the most respectable of areas. You can buy just about anything or anyone around there," Brandon explained. "That was all I meant. Isn't that the area you grew up in, Piper?"

"No, I grew up in Tangelo Park."

"Brandon what's your problem? What are you doing here?"

"No problem, Deputy DuPont and I graduated together, just mistaken on where she grew up. I came to get my watch repaired."

I would buy that excuse if I hadn't already known that he only wore Patek Phillippe watches, and the authorized service store was on Park Avenue on the other side of town. A tiny knot of unease settled into my stomach at his lie and comments to my friends. His frequent appearances in my life were getting a little too . . . well . . . frequent. I'd gone months and hadn't run into him once.

"Well, if you don't mind, we're going to eat and enjoy our girls' day," I told him.

"No worries. It was lovely seeing you again, Ariel. We need to catch up." Brandon kissed my cheek, stood, and left without saying goodbye to Piper or Stella or ordering a single thing to eat.

"He fucking weirds me out," Stella said. "I can't believe you ever dated that douche. Who is he?"

"District Attorney Brandon Fagan," Piper said without lifting her head from whatever she was typing on her phone.

"Don't judge. I had just moved here, and I had been lonely. I forgot that men were asses. Brief lapse in memory."

Stella picked up her fork. "Politician. Makes so much sense now." She started eating, and that was the last any of us said about Brandon.

She was right, Brandon was a politician through and through. After lunch, we officially launched Operation Seduce Kayson. The name was Stella's idea. After I told her about my mixed signals, she advised that I make the first move and jump his bones so we headed to Victoria's Secret.

"This one," Stella said to the first woman in a black jacket she found, "has caught a fucking hot man and needs some lingerie."

The clerk accepted Stella's brash behavior as if it were nothing at all and turned to me.

"I'd be happy to help. Do you know your sizes?"

I rambled them off as Stella and Piper decided that if a piece looked the least bit sexy, then I had to try it on. If it shouted it that was guaranteed to get me laid, then I needed it in two colors. This, of course, included garters, thigh highs, and corsets, none of which I'd ever worn before.

Our day went from comic relief to comic ruination when Piper mentioned the spa and waxing. I was more awed by the fact that the store employees permitted us to stay.

"If I had a hot number wanting in my panties, then I'd be at the spa getting all that down there," Piper said as she moved her hands over her privates, "buffed and waxed."

"Spa. We need to get you waxed," Stella agreed.

"Excuse me? Do I look like I signed up to be on your reality show? This is not *Ariel's Bush Makeover*."

"You have a bush?" The completely appalled look on Stella face was hilarious.

"Shut up."

"You said bush. Is it landing strip or jungle love?"

Piper hugged her middle while busting a gut laughing, and I tried to be the adult there, but it wasn't working.

"Just so you know, I am well groomed, thank you very much. We can skip the spa."

"Really? So, Brazilian not the jungles of Brazil?"

"Ignore her," I said to the clerk as I followed the sales lady to the back of the store.

"You go into the dressing room, and we will bring you stuff," Piper offered.

"Why don't I just try on what I have here?" As it was, we would be there for at least an hour before I got through all the items.

"Come on, Ariel. We want to see you and Kayson make cute Kay-Riel babies."

"No, just no. There are so many things wrong with that, not to mention, no one combines names anymore. How old are you?" Stella shrugged as I shut the door behind me.

I tried on bra after bra, nightgowns that the sales clerk called negligees. I couldn't reconcile paying three hundred dollars for something that I would wear for ten minutes or a hundred dollars for thigh-highs when I didn't even wear skirts or dresses.

Finally, I settled on five gorgeous matching bra and panty sets, two sexy nightgowns, one corset with garters, and several pairs of thigh-high stockings.

"Exactly what is Victoria's secret? Has anyone figured it out?" I asked.

"No clue. But whatever it is, it must be top secret. That bitch has it locked up tighter than Piper's legs," Stella added.

Piper punched Stella in the arm.

"Do y'all ever ponder stupid shit like that?" I asked. "I'll never understand why random thoughts like, what is Victoria's secret, will enter my head just as I try to fall asleep. Then, BAM. I can't fall asleep until I finally get up and google it."

"Can't say that has ever happened to me. Usually after working a twelve-hour shift, I'm either too hyped up on adrenaline to sleep or so exhausted that I fall asleep half dressed. There's no in-between at my house."

"You know, come to think of it, I'd like to know who let the dogs out?" Stella scratched behind her ear like she had a flea. "Or why in the fuck they let those dogs out in the first place."

"Let's go to happy hour. I know the perfect spot, not a lot of cops go there but a lot of local hot guys hang out there." I had to give her credit she was working hard at ignoring the two of us and our bizarre thread of conversation. "I need a drink after dealing with the two of you." Her smile gave it away that she wasn't really mad.

"It's Wednesday, there is no happy hour." At least I had never heard of happy hour on any day other than Friday.

"First, any hour that we are drinking is happy hour, and second, this is Florida." Stella thought that explained everything, so I looked to Piper for clarity.

"It's always happy hour here. Tourists like to party."

I looked at my phone to check the time and as much as I hated to admit it, I wanted to see if I had any missed texts. "Where we going?" I wasn't familiar with the area.

"Rocco's Tacos." The name was echoed in unison.

When we walked in, it was instant love. I'd never been impressed by a wine room but an alcohol room, there was definite value. Rocco's Tacos had three bars—one in the front room, one in the main room, and one in back with seating that overlooked a lake. Each one of them was stocked with top-shelf liquor.

Stella waved at a few people.

"Who's that?" I asked.

"My old neighbor. She was awesome, but the bitch went and got engaged and moved in with her fiancé."

"The place next to you is available?"

"Yep. She has it priced right. She'll sell it quickly."

"I want to see it. I hate living in an apartment."

"Why? You'll move in with Kayson and make little Kay—"

I threw my hand over her mouth to shut her up.

"Shut up, shut up, shut up."

Okay, that sounded more like a temper tantrum, but seriously, enough already.

We grabbed seats. "You ought to invite Kayson. Maybe you can begin operation Kinky Kayson tonight." Stella had a one-track mind.

I pulled out my phone and sent him a text.

Me: Stella, Piper and I are at Rocco's Tacos. You're welcome to come.

No bubbles telling me that he was texting back immediately appeared so I scrolled up to our previous messages. We hadn't seen each other since the night at his parents' house, but every morning and night he'd sent me a message. I cracked a smile as I scrolled through all the random photos he'd sent me.

"What are those?" Stella, who had been peeking at my screen, pressed the phone down on the table so Piper could see as well. "Apples at the grocery store, cherries, red Jeep, an FSU shirt. Don't get it? Okay, maybe I can understand the cherry, wait? You aren't . . ."

"No. Nothing like that." I laughed. "He has this game where he sends me different pictures every day of red things until he can find the exact shade of the color of my hair. He said it was impossible because I'm one of a kind. I reminded him that most people were grateful that there weren't more than one of me around."

"Ahhh." Piper and Stella put their heads together in mock cuteness.

When the waiter came around, Stella and I ordered a round of margaritas. Piper, who had to work later, opted for a coffee. No matter how many times I got on Stella about her ribbing me about Kayson, I still grabbed my phone almost as soon as the text beeped.

Kayson: I love that place. Sorry, sweet, I'm working late, or I'd come crash girls' day.

When I looked back up, the disappointment must have been painted across my face.

"Kayson?" Piper asked.

"Yep. He's working late, again. Do you always work past your twelve-hour shift or get called in all of the time?"

"You have no idea. Don't be so hard on him. He likes you. But things are hard right now, he's the interim sergeant, and it isn't even like he was taught the ropes. He's trying to figure it all out and discover where the previous motors sergeant kept everything."

"There wasn't a passing of the torch, so to speak?" I always thought that was how things were done, at least on television they were, whoever got promoted taught the person who took their place.

"But it's different, the sergeant was Haines, one of the deputies killed earlier this year. There's an entire pomp and circumstance of protocol. Haines' motorcycle is on display for one year, for that year, his position is left open, but someone still has to do the work. There isn't the budget for another deputy but that leaves us a deputy short as well. So, technically Kayson is doing his old job and the new one. I know the other guys on the squad, Carter, Aiden, and Max, are trying to pick up some of his workload, but there is only so much that they can do. When the year is up, they will fill Kayson's old position, which is what I want to interview for, and Kayson will be the official sergeant."

Well, damn. I felt like a total jerk for being annoyed that he seemed to work all the time. The guy was putting in the hours of two men.

After our round of drinks, we headed home, and I had a plan formed in my head. I was going to take Kayson out on a date.

Stella dropped me off, and as I walked to the main door, my mind was so consumed with ideas for my date that I didn't see Brandon until I was almost right next to him.

"I want to talk with you," Brandon said from his spot in the shadows.

I narrowed my eyes and clutched my keys tighter. "What are you doing here? Talk about what?"

"Ariel, I'm concerned."

"It isn't your place to be concerned about anything that deals with me. Or have you forgotten that we broke up."

He reached for me, and I wasn't fast enough to dodge his hands before they landed on my shoulders.

"Ariel, I care about you. I want us. I'm willing to prove that to you."

"There's no point. I gave you a chance. You blew it, Brandon."

"But you jumped to conclusions," he said.

"One time okay, but a second time? The third time? I doubt it."

"You need me. I can take care of you. I have money. We make a great team. I adore you. My friends adore you."

He rummaged in his suit jacket pocket.

"I've been carrying this around with me since before we broke up."

He pulled out a red velvet box. A small square box. It was Cartier. Brandon didn't do Robin's egg blue. No, you'd never see him holding that famous shade that could only mean one thing: Tiffany's. It was too common. Everyone else did Tiffany's. Brandon had to be different, stand out.

My mind tried to process what I saw, and one word rang out over and over—no, no, no. NO. There was no fucking way. Brandon and I only dated a couple of months, and he couldn't even be faithful in that short period of time.

"Brandon, don't."

"Give me one good reason why not?"

The anger leaked out in my words as I spoke to him. Lately, Brandon had a creep factor, but he'd never hurt me. He was just spoiled and wanted what he couldn't have. I was probably the first girl that didn't fall at his feet, so I became his biggest challenge. I knew that was all I was. Men always had an ulterior motive, Brandon just tried to hide his a little better.

"Besides the fact that we come from different worlds? How about the fact that we don't love each other."

"It doesn't matter that you come from hillbilly Alabama or that you're poor. In fact, the public loves a good rags-to-riches story. As for love? It grows. You can learn to love me," he said this as though he thought I wouldn't take offense.

What. The. Hell.

Hillbilly?

Okay, Red Bay, Alabama was tiny, but that didn't make us hillbillies. And, I wasn't poor. I wasn't rich, but I had enough money to take care of myself and buy what I needed.

"Contrary to what you just implied, my mama was not my cousin. I think it's best for you to leave. Like, now," I said as I pointed toward his car.

"Okay. I'm sorry. What I said was out of line. I'm sorry." He had the balls to hold the red box a little higher. "I'm in love with you. You challenge me. You intrigue me."

"What you mean is that you want me because you can't have me. It's the chase you want, Brandon, not me."

"That isn't it. You know how we were together. People used to comment on how great we looked together. I saw the way men looked at you, but you were mine. I'm sorry, I didn't handle you right."

"Handle? I'm not a dog!" I squared my shoulders. "I'm not taking the ring." The idiot tried to hand it to me.

"Think about it. Really think about this. What do you know about that sheriff you've been hanging around with? Nothing. You are better than that. You deserve better than that. How much do cops make? Not nearly as much as I do. I'll be able to give you more. You can't trust him."

My laugh was cold and incredulous. "Is that what this is really about? Someone else is playing with a toy you threw away? Get over yourself, Brandon. I'm not marrying you—not now, not ever. Now, leave before I call the cops."

Yanking open the outer door to my complex, I left him standing outside holding his God damned ring.

KAYSON

"This is getting ridiculous," I shouted to whoever was in listening range.

"Deputy, do you know what I find ridiculous? The way some law enforcement officers can't do their jobs right the first time." I turned to see DA Fagan walking into my office holding a stack of papers. "I have a murderer sitting in jail, a cop killer, and guess what my biggest issue is?"

"That it wasn't me he killed?" I couldn't restrain my sarcasm.

Brandon gave me a scornful look. "No. My biggest issue is that the man might get off on a technicality because some incompetent deputy doesn't know how to fill out paperwork correctly." Fagan's ire leaked out in a calm and executed tone.

"Wait a fucking minute. I filled out all of the forms, twice. What you mean to say is that you've lost them—again."

Some of the deputies from Bravo shift, the one after mine, gathered outside my office. Obviously, Brandon and I were louder than I realized. I couldn't believe that I had to deal with his petty bullshit when I should have been out of there two hours ago.

"What the fuck is going on in here? Either pull each other's hair or throw a punch but this shit has got to stop," Captain Getty announced as he pushed through the onlookers.

"The DA's office is accusing me, again, of not turning in my paperwork for the case against Erskine Sello.

"Bullshit. I witnessed it. I even called your assistant and confirmed receipt," Captain said to Fagan.

"Oh, Deputy. See. Right there, that is part of the problem. Exaggeration."

I felt someone's hand grip my bicep. I turned to glare, but it was Piper. She didn't say anything, just shook her head and tried to silently tell me something. Brandon was goading me.

Brandon seemed a little too happy about Piper's presence. "Oh. Don't let me and justice stop you from flirting with your girlfriend."

Piper's hand tightened around my arm. I wanted to deck Fagan. Fuck being a civil servant. I could work for my family's construction company.

"Enough," Getty ordered. "Exactly what was wrong with the paperwork? I looked it over myself. Christakos is highly respected and extremely detailed."

"Perhaps that is why you're a cop and not an attorney. Let alone the District Attorney."

"All right, Skippy." Getty's face turned stoic and any moment I was expecting him to order some fava beans to go with a nice chianti.

I crossed my arms but couldn't hold back my smile. Brandon Fagan had done the one thing we all go out of our way to avoid. He pissed off the captain. Mark Getty was like a rapier, one of those well-honed, extremely pointed swords that you'd have no clue you'd been stabbed with until you saw your blood.

"I'm the captain. I've earned my title. It wasn't a popularity contest; it was service work. Something you should try doing. Until you do, I suggest you go and sort your office out, because it seems like that is where you will find the weak link. Not here. Not in my station."

Brandon didn't say another word before Getty stormed from my office. At least the man knew when he'd been bested. Unfortunately, he had no issue with waiting until my office had cleared out with the exception of Piper before turning his venom on me, again.

"Just remember, Deputy, you are a civil servant, and as such, you fall under a code of ethics. I don't think fraternization with a subordinate constitutes ethical behavior."

"I am not fraternizing with my subordinates, and if you feel like I am, you're free to file a complaint with IA. What I find most interesting is that the DA is in my office threatening me when he's supposed to be helping us get the criminals off the street."

"I'd advise you to watch your step, Deputy Christakos. Especially if you value your livelihood." I ignored Brandon's threat.

"DA, you know Kayson's girlfriend, right?" she asked him, her smile sharp.

Brandon got to the door of my office and froze at Piper's words. "Don't believe that I do."

"Hmmm," Piper said, but she didn't elaborate.

He left my office, slamming the outer door as he exited. He was good and pissed.

"Care to tell me what that was all about?" I asked Piper.

"No. Just something that's been bothering me. I don't want to jump to conclusions. Need to look into it a little more," she explained. "By the way, Ariel and Stella should never be allowed alone together."

"Noted. Will you look over this report if I print it out again?" I asked Piper as I pulled up the file on my computer and printed off another fucking copy. Piper reviewed it and then the captain reviewed it before signing off on it, again. With a cover letter that read:

Attention: Brandon Fagan. Here is the report for the *third* time.

I left off his title on purpose, and as soon as the fax went through, I sent it out again but changed the cover page to say the fourth time. I continued this until it had been sent a total of twenty times.

"Feel better?" Captain asked from his spot against my doorframe.

"Much."

"Go home. It is almost eleven, and you will be back here at six."

Fuck. I had lost track of time. I pulled out my phone and sent Ariel a text.

Me: Hi, sweet.

Ariel: *Hey.*

Me: Sorry. Just leaving the station.

Ariel: I'm already in bed. Talk tomorrow?

Me: Sure. Night, sweet.

Ariel: Night. Oh, I thought about something today while I was out.

Me: You did?

Ariel: Yeah. You'll have to wait until tomorrow to find out. . .

ARIEL

*T*he sound of someone rattling the lock on my front door had me wide awake in less than a second. I grabbed my phone and saw it was only midnight Jumping from my bed, not wanting to turn on a light, and searching for a weapon. Fuck I didn't have anything, I was a seamstress. Gripping the only thing I could find– a knitting needle for lace–it would have to do. At least the mother fucker was sharp. Moving out of my bedroom, I tried to slow my breathing, maybe it was just one of my neighbors, drunk and they accidentally hit my door. Nope, not a neighbor, the rattling sound was at my door definitely coming from my apartment doorknob. Clutching the knitting needle tight in my hand, I slid against my wall trying not to cast any shadows with the moon light that peered in through my few windows. Looking down I realized that my phone was still in my hand so I sent a quick text off to Kayson with one word: Help. Would he come, was he already asleep?

Then dialed nine-one-one.

"Nine-one-one. Police, fire, or medical?"

"Police."

"Can you tell me your location?"

"I live at the Coconut Bay Apartments off Conroy, unit 214."

96

"Can you tell me your name?"

"Ariel Beaumont."

"Okay Ariel, can you tell me what's going on?"

"Someone is trying to break into my apartment. Hurry."

"Ariel, I need you to find a safe place to hide, can you do that? I'll stay on the phone. We have deputies on their way. They should be there any second."

My phone vibrated and made a loud ding sound to alert me of an incoming call. I flipped the silence button. The call came in again, this time the phone vibrated but even on vibrate it made a sound, I looked and saw Kayson's name appear on the screen. The nine-one-one operator was talking to me, and I could hear her even though the phone wasn't against my head. Shit. Fuck. I was so fucking confused, Kayson kept calling, the nine-one-one operator was still talking, and I needed everyone to just be quiet so I could think and hide. I powered off the phone to keep anyone from calling back or the hum of vibration making a rumbling sound and giving away my hiding spot.

Escape.

Hide.

Fight.

The words ran through my mind, first I needed to try to escape. If I couldn't, then I had to hide. My last resort—I would fight. It was what you were supposed to do in a dangerous situation. Escape was out of the question unless I wanted to climb out a window and drop two stories to the ground.

Hide. Shit. My apartment was small. They would check my bedroom first, so that was out of the question. Not the fucking bathroom, which would be the second place they checked. Even in horror movies, the slasher opened the shower curtains. Fuck, images from the movie *Psycho* flashed across my mind. That left the living room, which was full of sewing stuff. I raked my hands through my hair, trying to find a place to hide. Panic bubbling, threatening to spill over, as I searched. Finally, desperate and on the verge of tears, my eyes fell on my garbage can. It was huge. Between sewing scraps and household trash, I had gotten tired of constantly emptying normal size cans, so I had bought an industrial can. I grabbed the plastic bag liner and pulled it out before jumping in and pulling the bag back over me.

A grunt and a clank was followed by someone mumbling, "Fuck" just as my door opened and I settled the lid back into place.

I heard them, two men talking.

"Fuck. This time we won't get paid if we don't grab her," one man said.

This time? Grab me? Ice slid down my spine. Were they the same guys who attacked me the first time? Why were they looking for me? I thought of Kayson, great, I was still trying to figure out whether he was one of the rare good guys of the world, and if these guys found me, I may not ever have the chance to find out. I wanted that date, the one I concocted in my brain, the one I wanted to take him on to show him that I was willing to try, not totally commit, but I was willing to try to see if we had something.

My mind was everywhere, bouncing through every thought that I'd had over the last forty-eight hours. Every sound amplified, punctuated by the rapid thumping of my frantic heart. I couldn't see anything. Whoever was in my apartment moved across the room, I felt the vibration from their heavy footsteps.

I jerked at the sound of sirens and then clamped my hands over my mouth.

"We gotta go, man. The cops."

"I need that fucking money."

"Just tell him we will try again. No clue why we're doing this in the first place. Just supposed to scare the bitch. I can't even touch her. Have you seen her?"

The floor shook again as they ran. I heard my door open and slam shut. Something about his words, "Just supposed to scare her" echoed in my head. I'd heard that voice before saying those same words.

It seemed like the two men ran out hours ago, but in all actuality, it was probably only a minute or two. The silence was heavy, suffocating. Still, I left my hands over my mouth and tried to ignore the way my pulse violently thundered through my ears. As much as I wanted to be left alone, I needed to hear something, anything. I needed to know what was going on, was I alone?

Shouts rang out; my front door banged open, I felt the quake as a herd of elephants trampled into my tiny apartment.

"Police!" someone shouted.

"Anything?" a male voice asked.

I waited, slowly moving my trembling hands away from mouth so I could wipe the tears from my eyes. Then I heard Kayson.

"Where is she?"

"Sir, the apartment is empt—"

"Fucking find her now!"

"Here," I said. My voice came out as a croak. "I'm in here," I said a little louder. "I'm in the garbage can." I didn't finish the last word because the lid was off, the bag pulled free, and fresh cold air rushed over me as I locked on to chocolate eyes.

"Beautiful." That single word came from Kayson's mouth as he let out a whoosh of breath.

Gut wrenching sobs overtook me as I realized that he had rescued me, again. Between heaves, I repeated, "Escape, hide, fight," as I raised my arms, silently asking him to help me out.

He placed his hands under my arms, lifted me out of the can, set me on my feet, and cradled me close to his chest. My back rested against his forearm, his hand holding my neck. With no other option, I met his gaze, and then his mouth captured mine, commanding my lips to let him lead. I handed over the control and invited him to deepen the kiss. All I had said was "help" and he came, ready to fight for me, rescue me. Slowly, Kayson pulled away from the kiss and dropped his forehead to mine before moving his hands to cup my cheeks.

"You okay?" I nodded. "What happened?"

"Bedroom's clear," a voice called from the back of my apartment a moment before another deputy stepped into my living room.

"Not sure. I woke, I think it was from the rattling sound I heard at my door, so I called nine-one-one and hid."

"Do you have any idea who it was? Did you see them?"

I bit my lips and shook my head. "No, I didn't see who it was. It was two men, though. I heard them talking." Burying my face into my hands, I tried to erase the memories of the night I ran through the parking lot, and for the first time I pictured Crabbe and Goyle from the Harry Potter movies. "You're going to think this sounds bizarre, but I think they were the same guys that attacked me, and for some reason, I think they looked like characters from a Harry Potter movie."

"Could you describe them if we got a sketch artist?" Carter wanted to solve this mystery as much as Kayson.

"No. I really picture Crabbe and Goyle from the movies. But one of them had a Hispanic accent."

"We're going to find out who's behind all of this," Kayson assured me. He moved to the couch and settled me next to him, his arm wrapped around my shoulders, keeping me held tight.

My apartment was flooded with cops, which probably wasn't standard, but I didn't complain. Cabinets opened, doors closed, men and women moved through my tiny space, searching for any evidence. Piper came in, and as she moved toward me, her radio made a loud static sound. Everyone froze, and the room fell silent. Kayson placed his finger against my lips. Not knowing what was happening, I watched with wide eyes as she unhooked her radio and moved it around the area. When she got closer to my couch, the static turned to a screech. Kayson stood, pulling me with him so Piper could move her radio around the couch. Into my ear, he whispered, "Don't say a word."

After pulling on a pair of gloves, Piper slid her hands between the cushions of my couch, underneath the base, and unzipped each pillow. Eventually, she stood and held out what looked like an old Junior Mint candy. The closer the candy got to the radio, the louder the screech, she placed it in an evidence bag and left my apartment. But still, no one said a word. Carter held his finger against his lips, telling everyone to remain quiet.

Kayson settled back down on the couch and positioned me on his lap. Piper returned a few minutes later with a handheld device that looked like a giant television clicker. She swept it from corner to corner of my apartment, moved it under my bed, in my closet, and even inside my shoes. When she finished, Kayson relaxed.

"All clear?" Kayson asked.

"Seems like that was the only one," Piper said as she turned to me. "Do you remember the static from my radio when I walked in?"

"How could I not?"

"That was a bug. Thankfully, it appeared to be only audio. We'll turn it over to our forensics division, and they will get the FBI involved to see what they can trace as far as signal or how far the range was."

I took a deep, shaking breath. "You're serious? Someone bugged my apartment. FBI?"

"Ariel, don't freak. FBI involvement is normal, we don't have that kind of equipment." Piper looked at Kayson and Carter. "Maybe one of you can give Eli a heads up." They both nodded.

"Who's been in your apartment lately?" Kayson tightened his grip around me as he asked.

"That's easy until recently, I haven't had a life. So no one other than you and Stella, not even Leo and Piper have been in my apartment. I haven't even had workers here, I installed the new deadbolt and security chain."

"How about before Stella and me?" Kayson was fishing for something. I could hear it in his voice. "Let's say before your attack. Since you moved in."

"My landlord. My ex, but I only dated him a few months."

"No one else?" Kayson tilted his head to the side as if asking me to think harder.

"No. I don't know anyone else. Will you tell me what's going on?"

"Was it the ex we met today at lunch?"

"Yeah, why?"

"Stay calm, Kayson," Piper instructed him. "Have you seen him other than at lunch today?"

"Yeah. Which, to be honest, has started freaking me out, then tonight he was outside my apartment waiting for me, but I told him to get lost."

"Wait a fucking minute? Who is this boyfriend, is it the same one that came to the hospital when I was coming up?"

"Yeah, that's the one and only, his name is Brandon, he's a district attorney."

"Wait. A. Fucking. Minute. Your ex is Brandon Fagan? The guy whose new mission in life was to make me miserable, that Brandon Fagan?"

"I'm taking it you know him?" I guess it wasn't that big of a stretch that they would know each other.

"Yeah. I know him. And now it all makes sense," Kayson said.

"What does?"

"That was what you were referring to today in my office, wasn't it? Ariel is why he keeps mysteriously not having paperwork." He looked over at Piper as he said the last part, and she nodded.

"It makes sense, so much fucking sense, un-fucking-believable."

"Wait." They both turned to me. "You guys don't think that he bugged my apartment, do you? He's the DA."

"It appears that whoever planted the bug knew about everything going on in here," Piper explained.

Kayson reminded me of a wolf, with teeth bared and the scent of blood in his nose.

"Ariel, I will tell you what's going on with Brandon later." He kissed my temple. "Promise."

"If it was him . . ." Carter was careful with his wording since he obviously knew just how close to the edge Kayson was. "That doesn't explain the break in." Carter focused on me. "What did you hear, did they say anything, anything that might give us a clue of their identity besides the fact one had a Hispanic accent?"

I shook my head and stood. I needed something to drink, and I needed breathing room. My God, I couldn't remember ever being so thirsty in my entire life. I pressed my tongue against the roof of my mouth, trying to form saliva. Kayson stood and reached for my hand, but I pulled it away.

"Don't," I ordered Kayson and moved to the kitchen for a bottle of water. I wasn't trying to be mean, but right then, everything was bothering me. Even the seams of my clothes bothered me. They were rubbing my skin raw. Kayson followed me but kept two steps behind.

I took a long swig, water dribbling down my chin as my hands shook. "One of them said that they wouldn't get paid this time if they didn't grab me. But the other guy said he didn't understand why they were doing this since they were only supposed to scare me." I took another long drink. "It was the same thing the guy said the night I was attacked." I had this panicky feeling deep in my stomach. I didn't want to relive that night. I just wanted them to catch the bad guys and put them behind bars, I didn't want this.

Kayson rubbed my back and asked, "Did they say anything else?"

"They said that if they didn't find me they'd try again."

"Fuck. You can't stay here alone, Ariel. Stay with me for a bit? Just until we figure out who's behind this?" Kayson pleaded. "They're gonna see what they can get from the bug. Maybe they'll be able to trace it."

Brandon may be a douche but he was a concerned douche. I didn't think he had anything to do with the break-in or my attack, intelligent people didn't risk careers for this shit, they just didn't. But I had a pesky thought in the back of my head, masterminds were just that, they were smart, they had a master mind.

Those niggling thoughts helped me make a speedy decision. "Let me pack some stuff." I raced back to my bedroom.

KAYSON

"Which room do you want me in?" Ariel was standing at the top of the stairs, looking every bit as nervous as I felt.

"Mine."

"Kayson."

"Don't go there. I have fewer than four hours until I have to be back on shift. We can talk about this tomorrow. Tonight, just let me hold you."

She had packed only enough for the night, but I refused to let her go back to her apartment. Something in my gut told me that Brandon was involved, but until we figured out exactly what was going on, I needed to know that she was safe. I needed her near me.

"Where do those go?" she asked about the two doors, one on either side of the king size bed.

"His and her closets."

"Oh."

To the right was my en suite bathroom. But she didn't go there. Instead, she headed straight back to the other side of the bed to the French doors.

"Can I?" she asked.

I hit a switch next to the doors and turned on the lights for the balcony. It was the middle of the night, but the view of the lake was still breathtaking. At night, Florida's orchestra played. The buzzing of cicadas and the deep, throaty croaks of what most people thought were bullfrogs when in reality they were alligators. New Yorkers liked their street noise; this was mine. It could be just as loud at times, but peaceful in a weird sort of way.

"What does this overlook?"

I slid a small bar on a light switch panel to bring on several flood-lights and my backyard lit up like noon on a sunny summer day.

"Ahhhh. Gorgeous." Ariel's voice had an awestruck sound.

"Yes, she is," I agreed.

She touched her cheeks to mask the slight blush, but I couldn't take my eyes off her. She was beautiful and having her next to me seemed right. Four years ago when my parents gave me the property, Pop sat me down for a talk that I've never forgotten. He told me that this would be the house that I'd bring my wife home to and raise my kids in. Before I brought a woman home, whether it be a one-night stand or a girlfriend, I needed to remember this house would be filled with memories that my wife and me would keep for the rest of our lives. He'd warned me not to taint it or give her a reason to wonder if someone else had slept in her bedroom.

"Is this part of the Butler Chain of Lakes?"

"I'm sorry, what?" I asked, interrupted in thought.

"I asked if this was part of the Butler Chain of Lakes?"

"Yeah." I gripped her shoulders and rested my face next to hers. Pointing out so that she could follow the line of my finger. "That's my parents' house. And that's Damon's, Tristan's, and Ian's," I said as I bobbed my finger from house to house.

"All five of you are on this lake?"

"It's more of a canal, but yes. Just the five of us, which is why my address is Pente Loop."

"I don't get it."

"Pente is Greek for five." I turned off the outside lights. "Let's go to sleep. I'm exhausted."

105

She followed me inside, and I shut and locked the door as she grabbed her bag. She pulled out her toothbrush and something red. My mind went a million miles a minute as I thought about her in red as she headed off to the bathroom, and I decided I really liked the color on her.

"Care if I change in there?"

"Makes no difference." I couldn't help but chuckle.

My bathroom was an open floor plan. Except for the toilet, everything was open. There weren't doors to separate the bathroom and bedroom, just an archway. I wondered if she'd sit at the vanity, which Mana had insisted I have because all women needed a vanity.

The sound of rushing water turned on, off, on, and back off. She must have been brushing her teeth. I changed into pajama bottoms instead of my usual boxers. I was trying something different with Ariel. She wasn't a one-night stand. She wasn't in a position to feel that connection that I had three months ago. I needed to take this slow. I wanted her to fall in love with me.

I pulled back the covers and fluffed the pillows to give her more alone time. When I figured that enough time had passed, I asked, "Can I come in?"

"Sure, I can come out or move to another bathroom if you want me to."

She started to move toward the archway, but I was faster. She was in a long red silky nightgown. It dipped down in front, showing off her cleavage. Looking over her shoulder, I saw the back, or more specifically, what little there was of a back. Two little straps crossed from the top to the low-dipping back just above her firm gorgeous ass. I'd always considered Ariel a red head, but in the vivid red nightgown, her hair looked more like a chocolate cherry.

"Something wrong?" she asked as I continued to stare at her.

"Nope."

I wrapped her hand in mine and pulled her with me as I moved to the sink so I could brush my own teeth.

"Which side?" she asked once we were back in the bedroom.

"Doesn't matter." As if I would let her stay on a side, I intended to pull her into me as soon we were in bed. She'd had a scary night. I lost ten years after I saw her text and couldn't reach her. I'd hit over one hundred miles per hour in my truck, while I called Carter. There was no fucking way we were staying on *sides*. But she saw my phone on the nightstand and crawled in on the other side. I slid in and didn't hesitate to move my right arm under the arch of her neck before bending it up around her chest. My left arm wrapped around her waist. With a soft tug, I nestled her against me. Nothing had ever felt so right in my entire life.

"I've never spooned," she whispered.

"Shhh. Sleep."

"Kayson?"

"What?"

"Thank you." Her words were soft, but my heartbeat was loud. I could hear it echoing in the still of the room. I lay there not sleeping. Instead, I took in everything going on in my life and where I wanted it to go. I wasn't sure when I drifted off, but the last things I remembered was of her hand resting on top of my fingers as they caressed her stomach. Her breathing slowed, and the fucking cutest whistle came out with each exhale.

* * *

Four a.m. came too soon. I'd gotten all of two hours of sleep. But I'd wanted to check in on her apartment before shift and grab more of her clothes so she didn't have to return. Stacking several boxes into the back of my truck, I headed the few miles to her apartment.

I wasn't sure exactly what she wanted, so I decided to grab as much as I could. I second-guessed myself several times when I realized that all of her clothes, including her shoes, would fit into the boxes. So, instead of trying to figure out what to leave, I packed it all for her. Before leaving, I reached into her nightstand drawer and grabbed the leopard print toy that she apparently enjoyed. She wouldn't need it with me around, but it might be a fun addition.

When I got back to my place, I left the boxes in the truck for later and headed inside to scribble out a note to Ariel and leave it on the kitchen counter. I grabbed my bike keys and pressed the Bluetooth on my helmet that connected my radio.

Straddling my sheriff's bike, I called into dispatch as I pulled out of my driveway, "Thirteen-twelve, ten-eight."

"Orange County copies. 05:58 hours." Dispatch confirmed that I was logged in and on duty.

ARIEL

*H*oney was one of those smells that I would never forget; it was sort of like maple syrup. It warmed me from the inside out and made my tummy rumble with hunger pains just from the smell. I think that was what woke me, the smell of honey wafting into the bedroom. Several things occurred to me at once, I was hungry for something smothered in honey, I wasn't in my bedroom, and Kayson wasn't next to me.

I lay back and stared at the ceiling fan circling, listening to the light swishing sound. What was I doing in his bed? I kept saying I didn't want a relationship, but last night, he was the first person I thought of, no one else even crossed my mind. I didn't know if that was because I trusted him more or because I knew he would come and bring the cavalry. Maybe somewhere deep down in my subconscious I knew Kayson Christakos would keep me safe.

I had a sudden urge to see him, wrap my arms around him, and let him hold and assure me that I was safe. By the smell of things, he was in the kitchen. My stomach let out a growl, so I got out of the bed, tossed on the clothes I'd brought to wear today, and headed downstairs.

I rounded the corner to the kitchen, aware of the clink and scrape of someone working, and found Mrs. Christakos cooking.

"*Kalimera koritsi*" Her voice was extremely cheery.

No clue what she just said, but since it was early, I went with, "Good morning, Mrs. Christakos."

"Christine, darling. Just call me Christine."

"Sorry, I'll try to remember. Is Kayson here?"

"He's at work. He left you a note," she said through a smile as she tilted her head toward a piece of paper on the counter.

Picking up the note, I stifled a yawn before asking, "What time did you get here?"

"Seven thirty. From the sound of it"—she pointed at the letter —"you have a good reason to be exhausted."

So, she was either referring to my sleeping in her son's bed or the events from the night before. To save myself from embarrassment, I pretended she meant the latter.

Morning Sweet,

I hope you slept in. I added my extra set of house keys and truck keys to your key ring. Alarm code is zero-six-two-six if you have to go somewhere, but please don't. Carter is helping me bring your motorcycle over later today. Will check that all is secured from last night's break-in and grab you some more clothes. Before you get any ideas, I liked having you here; it feels right. Think about it.

K

I reread his letter, and if his mother weren't there, I would pitch a royal hissy fit. Damn it, why did the man have to be so arghhh infuriating? Damn know-it-all, it did feel right. I liked being there, too, I felt safe, which was something I hadn't felt in over three months.

"You feel it, too," Christine stated. She didn't ask.

"Feel what?" That was it, Ariel, play stupid, real smooth.

"You feel what my boy is feeling. Never seen him act like this. Never brought a girl home before. None of my boys have."

I folded the note and put it in my back pocket and looked to the stove. "What are you making?"

"*Galatopita*, it's Kayson's favorite. It's a honey custard."

"It smells fabulous." I opened cabinets until I found some mugs and stuff for coffee, "Want some coffee?"

"That'd be nice."

"How do you take it?"

"Cream please."

I fixed our mugs and sat at the kitchen island before pulling my plate toward me and taking a small bite of the wiggly food.

"Mmmm." I moaned at the creamy sweet taste.

"Good, isn't it?"

"Mm-hmm. You'll have to give me the recipe."

Before Christine could answer me, though, the telltale noise of a garage door lifting sounded through the house.

Kayson was back.

"What time is it?" I asked.

"Eleven," Christine answered.

"*Kalimera*, Mana," Kayson said as he walked in. He put a grocery bag in the fridge then turned and hugged his mother. "Good morning, sweet," he said and gave me a light kiss on the lips.

"*Kalimera*," Christine replied. "Sit, I made your favorite."

Finally, I felt as if I could repeat that word and only semi-slaughter it enough that they might understand me. "What does *kalimera* mean?"

"*Kali* is good, *mera* is morning," Kayson explained.

I took another bite. "This is the best stuff in the world. When I woke up smelling honey, my stomach started growling." I stopped talking as I watched a silent conversation between mother and son. "What's up? Did I do something wrong?"

"Of course not." Christine was quick to assure me.

"You said you woke to the smell? Mana was here when you woke?" He raised one eyebrow at his mother but was trying to hold back a smirk. "She couldn't have been; she doesn't have a key. Unless she broke into my house."

Christine had the whole raising one eyebrow thing that guys did down to a science, and mirrored Kayson's stare. The two of them went back and forth like a tennis match, no words, just this silent exchange.

"*Trelos eisai?* I used the key you gave me."

"Translate," I whispered to Kayson.

"She asked if I was crazy," he explained. "I didn't give you a key. You mean you used the secret emergency spare key?"

"No. I have my own."

"And how did you get your own?"

Kayson was up to something. I felt like this was how a cat played with a mouse just before it attacked. He was cornering her. Deep down, I rooted for Christine to turn the tables on him just to see him sweat. But I enjoyed this playfulness between the two of them.

"Tristan gave it to me," Christine said.

"Tristan doesn't have a key."

"Would you like some more, Ariel?" Christine asked.

Oh no, you didn't. No way was I being brought into this. I kept my mouth shut and held back a laugh.

"Mana?" Kayson drawled.

"Fine, I sent him up to Ace hardware with your emergency key," she said the last word with air quotes, "and told him to have five copies made."

"That was what I thought."

"Well, I wouldn't have to if you'd been considerate enough to do it in the first place."

Kayson reached over and wrapped his arm around his mother's shoulders. "But why, when it's funnier watching you squirm?"

Christine looked up to the heavens, made the sign of the cross, and then smacked her son upside his head. I choked as coffee went down the wrong pipe from laughing.

"I'm gonna go change," Kayson said since he still wore his uniform.

"You're already off shift?" I asked.

"I was so tired, I asked if I could take part of a vacation day. I am off 'til Monday."

"No work Friday, Saturday, or Sunday?" I was doubtful. He seemed to always to get called in.

"It's my regular off weekend."

"Let me get out of your hair," Christine said to Kayson before turning to me and placing a kiss on my head. "Lovely seeing you, *koritsi*." Christine's voice was kind, but it was Kayson's reaction that puzzled me. He and his mother had another one of those silent conversations with their eyes. This time the look on her face was like she was challenging him.

I'd ask him about what she said later instead I was thinking that tomorrow would be the perfect day for a date.

"I'm gonna go change," Kayson said as his mother closed the door behind her.

"Okay, let me grab my phone before you close the door. I need to text Stella."

Kayson hadn't waited for me to find my phone. He hadn't even closed the doors. He was standing in his closet pulling his shirt off when I walked in. I hadn't noticed his bare back last night or the way his olive skin, which looked perpetually sun kissed, enhanced his muscles. He laid his vest on the top shelf and turned toward me when he realized that I was there.

"Come here," he ordered.

And at that moment, I was telling all the voices in my head that reminded me, men were asses, men couldn't be trusted, and men will leave you once they thought they owned you, to shut the fuck up, and I went to him. As I got closer, I felt him, he reminded me of a stuffed animal that I'd had as a child. Puffy was my security, he comforted me, and made me forget all the bad nightmares, like this shit about me that had gathered in my head over the last thirteen years.

A rush of air escaped my lungs as he pressed me against the wall. "How'd you sleep?" His words sounded like a lullaby . . . soothing . . . I listened to the cadence of his breathing, it was so fucking relaxing. I felt his hand slide up my chest, the 'L' of his open left hand resting just above my breastbone, holding me firm.

"Fine." I curled my fingers around his shoulders, sliding my hands down his biceps, and immersed myself in the heat that radiated from his body.

"Can I tell you something?"

"Sure." But I wasn't listening. I was too busy studying the difference in our skin tones. My pale white against his golden warmth.

"I like this," Kayson whispered.

Okay, maybe I wasn't as hypnotized as I originally thought because I couldn't refuse the joke. "Being in the closet?" I tried not to laugh. "It's okay to come out. I won't judge."

One side of Kayson's mouth rose in a smirk. "You know what I mean. I like you being here. In my bed. I liked kissing your shoulder as I unwrapped you from my arms and got up for work, listening to the soft sounds you made as you slept while I got dressed. I liked knowing that you were going to be here when I got home from work."

What was I doing? I wanted this man more than I ever imagined wanting anyone. Kayson could break my heart if I let him. I couldn't let him erase the years it had taken me to get to this point, this spot of security where I could pretend that I didn't give a fuck.

"And you've shut the door," Kayson said as he pulled away from me.

"What are you talking about?" I snapped.

"You. You have these walls built up to protect yourself. I'm trying to find the door. I thought after last night that you had opened it, but I saw you. You just slammed it in my face."

I needed to retreat. "I have no clue what you're talking about. I need to text Stella, and I still haven't got to look around your house or be nosy."

"Thank God you're cute. Make your call or text or whatever and then snoop all you want."

Kayson kissed the tip of my nose and turned around, but I heard the distinct sound of his zipper before I left.

"Kayson?" I really wanted to just grab my phone and go, but I had to know something first.

"Yes?"

"What did your mother say?"

"When?"

"Don't play dumb."

He let out a long sigh, clearly not wanting to tell me. "She called you *koritsi*."

I waited for a second to see if he was going to offer up the translation but he didn't so I had to ask. "What does that mean?"

"My daughter."

I turned to face him at those words. "And that upset you?"

"Only because it would have upset you if you had known. You've made it clear that you don't want a relationship. I don't want to scare you or push you too fast. We have all the time you need."

I nodded and headed downstairs, and the entire way I was second-guessing my idea for a date. Sure, we'd spent a lot of time together, but we haven't had a date. Not a real one. Opening my phone, I found Stella's name and decided to call her instead.

"How's it hanging?" Her greeting threw me off and I giggled. "Okay, while you remember whatever it was that led you to call me, I will tell you that we have our first girl gang outing."

No matter how many times we corrected her, Stella was going to call Iron Orchids a gang. I think she just liked the badassness vibe of the word, which was kind of ironic since none of us were badass. Okay, well maybe Piper and Leo were, but Stella and I definitely weren't.

"We're going to Bananas on Sunday. A friend of Piper's is joining us, and she got a reservation. Plus she rides, add her with Vivian, the owner of Sixes, and we are up to six badass motherfuckers."

"Do I dare ask, what's Bananas?"

"Never fear, little one, we got you covered. Dress casual, like you are going out for a normal bike ride. Now, why did you call me? Cherries?"

"Shut up, no. Okay, maybe, but not cherry. I mean, I don't know.

I'm so confused. I want him, but I'm scared, and he's moving so fast that just when I think I can swim he dumps another five gallons of water on my head. And then I have all this shit from the attack. Part of me thinks that I need to get my life in order before I even look at Kayson, then there's the part of me that says what if he's gone when I'm finally ready, and then there's the third that says just have sex and don't worry about the other shit."

"Well, you know what I'm going to say?"

"Just have sex?"

"Actually, no, believe it or not I don't think that there is any possibility of him moving on to someone else if he's the right person. Soul mates are soul mates for a reason."

"Soul mates? Wow, Stella that is deep, you should grab a bucket and help Kayson with the water."

"Ha, ha, Ariel. Seriously, though. Go talk to him. We'll pick you up on Sunday morning around eight, we're riding there."

Disconnecting, I let my shoulders drop. She hadn't been helpful at all. I tossed my phone onto the counter and turned to see Kayson standing behind me, watching me.

"I picked up some steaks to grill tonight." Relief rushed through me. If he had heard what I said, he was going to let it drop. I did the same.

"Sounds good. Were you by chance able to grab clothes from my apartment?"

"I did, they're in the garage. I was going to bring them upstairs. I also grabbed several pairs of boots."

"Perfect. I should have something to wear. I just need to get my bike before Sunday."

"It's already here. Carter and I brought it over this morning."

I had a hard time comprehending Kayson's thoughtfulness as I headed to his garage to grab my clothing. He followed. The consideration he offered was foreign and made me a bit uncomfortable. Not because I didn't like it or appreciate it, but the men in my life always seemed to think about themselves first. My daddy never did anything for Mama or me, and Brandon became kinder only after I stopped seeing him. I told Kayson about my plans with the girls for Sunday, he seemed happy for me, not possessive. The brief time I was with Brandon, he expected me to be at my apartment if he wasn't with me.

"Didn't you take your bike to work?"

"Of course I did," he replied.

"Then why are my clothes in the truck? I just assumed you stuck a few in your saddle bags or in a backpack."

"I left early and got as much as I could before coming back for my bike." His words shocked me. He got very little sleep because of me and then got up early for me? I nearly choked as he unlocked his truck, and I saw all the boxes piled in the back. I jumped up in the bed of his truck and opened the first one—it was all the clothes from my dresser. The second and the third were what looked like all the clothes from my closet, and the last three were all shoes and boots.

"You pretty much moved me into your house when this is only temporary," I said, my voice an octave or two higher than normal. "Kayson, I only needed a few outfits, not my entire wardrobe. This is ridiculous."

He just shrugged, grabbed a box, and carried it upstairs into his bedroom.

"This is ridiculous. Absurd. Have you lost your ever-loving mind? I'm just gonna have to pack all this back up. I'll be lucky if I don't lose something."

Kayson headed back to his truck and came back with a few more boxes.

"My God, where the hell are we going to put all of this stuff? I'm gonna be living out of boxes. I need my space. I need my apartment."

It took two more trips for him to unload his truck, and I was the one left out of breath.

"Kayson, have you heard a damn thing I've said?"

"You done?" he asked.

"Don't even," I started up, but he stopped me.

"No. You told me everything that you needed. Well, actually you screamed it. But I heard you nonetheless. Now, please just listen to me. I want to give you everything that you need. All I ask is for one thing, just one."

"What's that?"

"Until we find out who is after you, you let me keep you safe. I need this. I need to know you're safe. Then I will help you move your clothes wherever you want. Hell, I will move them myself, and you can sit and eat fuckin' bonbons while I do it or you can shout at me again. Just give me that one thing. Okay?"

Uh, crap. He was just trying to protect me. Of all the things he could ask for, he asked for something for me. Really? Fuck.

"By the way," he said interrupting my self-degradation. "I didn't mean to pack everything. I took boxes intending to grab a variety for you. But you don't have much. Most of the boxes were full of boots."

I let out a small laugh. I didn't have a ton of clothes, but I did have at least twenty pairs of cowboy boots. "What if I pile my stuff up in one of the spare rooms?" I hated crowding his bedroom, and he had four spare bedrooms.

Lifting a stack of clothes still on the hangers, he opened the other closet—the hers side—and stepped back so I could peek around him.

"I'm in love," I told him in a dreamy voice. I hadn't actually looked in the closet when I got there.

Kayson stopped dead in his tracks and looked at me. I replayed my words. Shit. I had to finish that train of thought, we weren't at that point, we weren't in love, this wasn't love.

"I'm in love with this closet. It's like *Sex in the City*. This is a Carrie Bradshaw worthy closet."

"Don't care about Carrie. Are you okay with it?" he asked but his voice sounded a little disheartened.

"As if any woman would say no. It's every woman's dream closet."

"I don't care about every woman, only you."

After hanging up the first stack of clothes, he moved back to the bed and grabbed more. When we were finished, only one-fourth of the closet was full.

"What about your girly shit?"

"What girly shit?" I asked.

"You know, stuff you put on your face and you use on your hair." He mimicked the back and forth movement of spraying hair.

"Most of it I packed since I use that girly shit every day." His easy assurance that I belonged there and his name for my toiletries somehow seemed to relax me, and I forgot that just an hour or so ago I was furious. I didn't forget about asking him out on a date, though. No, for that I just chickened out.

KAYSON

At five o'clock, the sizzle of two steaks on the grill wasn't the only hot thing outside, the subtle sway of Ariel's hips as she walked toward me to hand me a beer was smoking. I snaked an arm around her waist and pulled her close.

She tilted her head back, and I licked her neck. Okay, weird I know, but damn, I couldn't help it. "You look so fucking edible and your scent is intoxicating." I wanted to discover if her skin was just as arousing.

"I need to go make a salad," Ariel said with a laugh as she extricated herself from my hold.

"Baby." I groaned.

I was stuck outside watching the steaks, but as soon as they were done, I flipped off the grill and headed inside.

"We make a great team," I told her as I set the steaks on the table and nodded to the corn on the cob and salad in front of her.

She nodded and the smile she gave me didn't quite reach her eyes. All through dinner, she didn't talk, we ate in silence and cleaned the kitchen in silence.

"What's up, sweet? You're awful quiet?" I met her eyes just as a tear rolled down her cheeks. "Ariel, what's wrong?" She didn't answer me.

She just flicked the drop away as if crying was no big deal. "What happened?"

"Nothing," she said before standing and striding toward the stairs.

I went after her, but she wasn't in our bedroom and she wasn't answering as I called her name. I found her lying on my old bed in the spare room.

"What's up?" I sat down next to her totally lost over what just happened as I ran my fingers through her hair.

"If it's okay with you, I thought that I'd move in here." Her words were muffled as she spoke them face first into a pillow.

"I'm okay with you moving into the house." Misunderstanding her words on purpose.

"No, I meant in here, this room, I can sleep on this bed."

"But our bed is in there." I pointed back toward the master bedroom.

"That's *your* bed."

"Last night, it became our bed, and today, that became your closet."

"No, it didn't, Kayson. We're friends. We aren't a team, and those shouldn't be *our* anything."

"What's your fucking point, Ariel? I'm missing something. You promised that you would let me keep you safe." She reached over for the second pillow and piled it on top of her head. "This is utter bullshit, I don't know what happened or what changed. Whatever it was, please change it back. I don't want games, Ariel. I never have and never will. If you'll just talk to me, tell me where this is coming from, then I'll try to help. But you have to talk to me."

"Don't you get it?" she asked, turning her tear-streaked face toward me. "This is your wife's house."

"What wife?" I nearly shouted, exasperated by this freakish conversation.

"Your wife, the one you will someday have. The one that will give you babies." She took a deep breath, trying to gain control. "She'll set the table and watch your kids play in the yard. You'll tell her that you 'make a great team'. That'll be her closet." Ariel pointed back toward the bedroom. "And one day you'll carry her boxes

121

upstairs. She deserves better. She doesn't need a second-hand house or a used closet, a bedroom where you've slept with another woman."

"So, you're mad because of some hypothetical one day?" Finally, I understood, and it was the most fucked-up reasoning I had ever heard.

Her tears slowed, and she studied me like she expected me to tell her that she made total sense. Instead, I couldn't contain the grin, which at least lightened her mood.

"What are you smiling about? Stop that," she demanded. "This isn't funny. I'm serious."

"That's what's funny. You're serious—seriously crazy and seriously adorable."

She let out a huff as if I exasperated her, but it was her, this was all her.

"Sweet, I've been telling you since the Harley event that there's something between us." I rubbed my thumbs across the apples of her cheeks to wipe away her remaining tears. "Stop fighting it, we're not in a rush, just enjoy the ride." Standing up, I held out one hand. "Okay, that's twice today you have gone batshit crazy. I have to ask. You by chance aren't on your—"

I didn't finish the question because Ariel smacked my back with a resounding slap, and her eyes were no longer red and teary. They were angry.

"Don't you even finish that sentence, Kayson Christakos." She pursed her lips. My grin was as charming as I could make it as I grabbed her hand.

"Come on, *Laila Ali*," I said, pulling her up from the bed. "Let's go watch a movie."

I didn't want to give her time to analyze her thoughts any longer or we might be facing World War three. Ariel and I, we were doing this. I'd figured it out. My mother had figured it out. I just had to wait for Ariel to figure it out. Her little freak out over some hypothetical woman meant she was jealous. She wasn't ready to admit that she wanted to be that woman, but I saw it, and it was enough.

"Fine." She sighed and then gave me the most adorable pout. "But you better have Netflix."

"Sure." I figured that I'd better leave it with that, telling her that I had more than three hundred cable channels, Hulu, Netflix, and AppleTV, somehow made me sound like a pitiful bachelor with no life.

I handed her my remote control, and she scrolled through the list until she found what she'd been searching for. "This movie makes everything feel right as rain. Have you ever seen it before?"

"Is it a chick flick?" From the picture, it looked like a chick flick.

"Yep. *Sweet Home Alabama* is absolutely a chick flick, but it's the best one ever made. It's about a little girl and boy that from the time they were little they were destined to be together—"

"Does it make you happy?" I asked, interrupting her full synopsis of the story.

"Yep."

"Then I don't mind. You fix us some drinks, and I'll make the popcorn before we start it."

Racing downstairs, we moved around each other in the kitchen.

She held a glass under the ice dispenser, and as I moved to stand near her, I shot my hip out to bump hers.

"If I don't watch the movie and just kiss your neck, will that be okay?"

"You'll watch it, it's a good movie."

"Is there sex in it?" I asked.

"It's not a porn."

Her words made my dick twitch. I backed away and then tossed a bag of Jiffy-Time into the microwave.

"Do you want to watch the movie upstairs or downstairs?"

"Let's watch it upstairs," I told her as I pulled the popcorn from the microwave and poured it into a bowl. Once we were settled on the bed, I leaned against the headboard and moved Ariel between my legs. I pushed play and discovered that Ariel was a movie talker.

"You ever find sea glass in the sand?" she asked. "It's made from lightning."

"When we go down to the Keys, but sea glass is different. When lightning hits sand it makes quartz, the different colored stones that wash up onto shore, that's sea glass.

"Either way, I love this opening. The way the little boy proposes to her."

As the movie progressed, I felt like Alabama was a foreign country.

"I've heard you say that things went pear shape. But since you used it in context, I understood the meaning. But I have no clue what that woman was talking about when she said, puttin' on the dog?"

"Well, I've never heard anyone say it, either, but I know what she meant. It means she would have fancied everything up or put out a lavish spread of food. You know, all the things you do when you're expecting company."

"It sounds like she's going to cook the dog, put him on the grill."

She was silent for a beat and then tilted her head to look at me. "Guess what?"

"What?" I couldn't help but share in her enthusiasm. "Please don't tell me you've eaten a dog."

"What? No!" She smacked my arm and gave me a disgusted face. "I was going to tell you that I've been to the Coon dog cemetery. Up until my senior year, we'd go and drink after football games."

"Why didn't you go your senior year? My senior year of high school was the most fun."

"I couldn't." Ariel stared down at her toes.

Part of me was afraid of the answer but she was finally opening up. "Why not?"

"When I was fourteen, my mama had a stroke, and it left her with a limp and she couldn't say some words. But just before my senior year, she had her second stroke, well . . . that one was a lot worse. She couldn't walk or talk. She was wheelchair bound after that one. I had to work full-time and take care of Mama."

"What about your father, didn't he help?"

"Yeah, right. He ran off as soon as Mama had her first stroke." I tightened my arms around her as if I could protect her from the memory.

"How about aunts or uncles, wasn't there anyone around?"

I paused the movie so she could keep talking.

"We had no other family. And if my daddy had still been around, he wouldn't have helped Mama with those things anyway." She stared off in the distance, as if she were lost in a memory. "I would still have had to finish my senior year via virtual school and get my degree online."

"Do you still talk to him?"

"No. He sent some money for the first year or so, but I never heard from him again once the checks stopped. The only thing my daddy did right was, he kept us on his insurance until Mama died. Our house was paid off, so after she passed away, I used the money to pay off the rest of her medical bills, you know, the shit that wasn't covered by insurance."

"Where's your dad now?" I asked, already hating this man.

"Not sure. Last I knew he worked at a factory a town over from where I grew up. I assume he's still there."

"You know that your dad was the loser here, right? He lost you."

Ariel turned her head, still leaning back against me as she gazed out the doors to the balcony. Rehashing old memories took its toll on both of us. I wanted to beat the shit out of the man for leaving a four-teen-year-old and his wife with such responsibility.

I needed to see her smile, erase the bad thoughts. So, I pressed play and turned back to the movie. Playing air drum on her thighs when the song "Sweet Home Alabama" came on, Ariel sang every word—off key. Just like that, she was back to being happy and laughing. I couldn't remember ever having so much fun doing absolutely nothing. No one was there, we were watching some screwed-up love story while sitting in bed, and I wouldn't exchange tonight for tickets to front-row seats on the fifty-yard line at a Tampa Bay Buccaneers game

"Oh, here it is again." She tapped my arm. "Remember when they were little and he proposed? Watch, watch,"

"I'm trying," I told her. Trying not to laugh was more like it.

"Isn't that the most romantic thing ever? They switched it, this time he wants to know why she wants to get married, and she says so she could kiss him anytime she wants. Did you hear me?" She sounded a little perturbed at the thought that I hadn't been listening.

"Yes. Yes. I heard every word."

"Then what'd I say?" She titled her head up to face me.

For a moment I second-guessed myself, was this the right move or not, was she ready to enjoy the ride and see where this took us?

"You said." I pressed my lips down to hers. "Fuck me. Fuck me right now."

Tiny goose bumps popped up along Ariel's skin as I traced the lines of her neck with my index finger. Skimming the exposed skin on her arms, I heard her as she let out a soft moan, and I chased the shiver that rolled down her spine with my fingertips.

Bringing my legs together, I shifted her so she was sitting on my lap and pulled her lips to mine. She melted against me, letting out a soft, soft moan as I swept my tongue into her mouth and sank my fingers into her hair. God, I wanted her more than I wanted my next breath, but I knew . . . I knew that I needed to slow down. So, I pulled away, resting my forehead against hers and forcing my heart to slow. I held her for a few minutes, neither of us saying a word. We just stared at each other. I held back all the unspoken words that said, 'I was holding my future in my arms'. I needed to find those words in her eyes.

I rolled off the bed, pulling her with me, and spun her around. Her back to my front. I grabbed the hem of her shirt and lifted it and tossed it to the floor.

"Do you feel how much I want you?" I asked.

She nodded.

Bending, I kissed each shoulder as I removed the straps of her bra and then unsnapped it, letting it fall to the floor.

Pressing my thumbs into the base of her spine, I worked my fingers in small circles massaging, still holding her firmly against my erection. Shifting my hands to her front, and paused.

"Is this okay?"

"Yes." The single word was nothing but a breath, but I heard it like a thunderclap rolling through my body. I unfastened her jeans and eased them off her, laving her skin with slow kisses as I did so.

She tried to turn around, but I held her firm. "No." I didn't want her to see but anticipate my next touch. I wanted her to relax. Enjoy. Trust.

Sliding my hands into the back of her black panties, I cupped her ass so the tips of my fingers kissed between her legs. "You're so fucking wet."

I slid her panties off and with one hand placed between her shoulder blades I gently pressed her forward so that she rested on the bed, her hair resembling flickering flames against the beige color of my sheets. Reveling in Ariel's beauty, my hunger for her and my thirst to drink her in took over.

I skated my hands up her body and stretched her arms high above her head. "Stay."

My clothes rapidly joined hers. I paused and took a few slow, methodical breaths. I was like a prisoner begging for a stay of execution. I didn't want to end the night too soon.

After pulling her up onto her knees, I moved behind her onto the bed, my knees on either side of hers. She had to feel my erection pressing into her back; it was throbbing for release.

I wrapped my arms around her chest, holding her firmly, and leaned down, whispering, "You're so fucking beautiful."

I was falling in love with this woman, with her aversion to relationships, and her crazy rants, I wanted every part of her. I'd been falling in love with her for over three months, and every kiss . . . every swipe of my tongue against her skin and soft keening noise I pulled from her, I fell a little deeper. My kisses followed the curve of her neck, across her right shoulder, and down her arm. Bringing my lips back up to the center of her neck, I started again this time going down the left side, each kiss following her sensual curve.

Sweeping one hand down her soft skin to her smoothed shaved center. My index finger slid between her folds, her wetness coating my finger. But I was lost. I had to taste her. Bringing my hand to my mouth, I licked, the taste even sweeter than the other morning. I ached for this feisty, crazy, emotional woman.

"Please, Kayson. I want to touch you."

She turned around, but our eyes never met because she was focused below my waist.

"Can I taste you?" she asked.

"You're killing me. You're so fucking hot, so perfect."

"Lie back." Ariel followed me and pushed up on to an elbow, sinking her free hand into the back of my hair before pulling my mouth to hers. When her tongue swept against mine, I groaned, kissing her harder.

"I've never . . . before," she whispered.

That was it, those words. Knowing that she had never, "Ariel. I'm so fucking close."

"Just a taste," she pleaded.

I watched as she gathered her hair over one shoulder so it would be out of the way. Every nerve in my body ready to ignite, it was the anticipation, just knowing that any moment her warm wet lips were going to wrap around me. Her tongue darted out, making my cock jerk, but it was just a tease, she licked her lips instead. I held my breath as her tongue swept out and tasted my tip.

"Holy fuck, Ariel."

"Is that sensitive?" she asked, repeating the movement.

"Yes."

"Where's the most sensitive spot?"

"That. All of it. Holy shit. Under the head." I couldn't think straight with the warmth of her breath on me.

She swirled her tongue around the head of my cock, once, twice.

"That's enough," I said, pulling her up and rolling so I had her tucked under me. "I want to come inside you."

Then my mouth was on hers again, tasting and controlling and taking. I needed all of her. When she body was arching against mine, her hips shifting, searching for me, I moved lower. Inching my way down her neck and chest to her nipples, sucking, biting, tugging on the tips, first on her left then her right until they were both hard nubs.

"Oh, God. Kayson."

I kissed lower, down her ribs, her belly, her hips until I tasted her desire for me.

"Spread your legs."

Teasing, lightly touching, I kissed around her center.

"Please. Right there," she said, trying to urge me to clutch on to her center. "I need you now." Her words were a pleading command.

"Uh-uh. Not yet. Relax. You got to taste, it's only fair I do, too." I told her as I positioned myself between her legs and rubbed my day old stubble against her inner thigh. She spread her legs wider, tempting me. I just gave her a single, long lick with the flat of my tongue before trailing kisses from her center down her calf, to the bottom of her foot. Licking a line around the top of her ankle. She flexed her foot, the sensation causing her to lift her butt off of the bed.

The sight of her spread out in front of me almost undid me. I couldn't tease anymore. I needed her. I pulled my legs up under me and reached for the box of condoms from my nightstand and tore one packet off the sleeve. Using my teeth, I ripped open the wrapper. She sat up and enveloped my hands in hers, echoing each movement as I rolled the condom down my shaft.

Holding myself up on one forearm, I positioned myself between her legs. Squeezing the base, I flicked my length against her, tapping, teasing. Each tap had the condom glistening more with her wetness. I wanted her slick and ready. I wouldn't last long, and I wanted her to go with me.

"Kayson, please."

It was all I needed. I thrust forward and buried myself to the hilt, her nails biting into my back. I stayed still, trying to wrap my brain around the fact that I had her in my bed, in my arms, and I wasn't going to let her go—ever. This felt right, so fucking right. The way the top of her head rested perfectly under my chin, the way she said my name, the way I felt buried deep inside her. Nothing had ever felt this way before. I couldn't feel where I ended and she began.

I drew out to the tip and plunged back in, loving the way her moans echoed my movements. I wasn't falling in love with her. I was in love. Gone, do not pass go, do not collect two hundred, gone.

Each thrust became my way of asking her, "Are you in love with me?" And when I was all the way in, I gave an extra push to drive even deeper. It was that cherry on top, that last word to my question. Was she in love with me, "Yet?" Because I had no doubt that she would be, I would work to make her fall in love with me. I just wanted it to be sooner rather than later.

"Look at me, baby," I told her.

I wrapped my hands around her and stretched her arms above her head, pinning her beneath me, forcing our eyes to lock.

"You're so fucking gorgeous," I told her as she let out a soft moan.

"Give it to me. Give me that release." Her legs wrapped around my waist, holding me tight, forcing me deeper inside her.

"I'm yours," I whispered as her body tightened.

I wanted to make love to her for the rest of my life. I pulled out and sank back in. I wanted to ask her if she was in love with me. Again, I pushed deep, making sure to hit that perfect spot.

"Do you hear my heart?" I asked her.

"No," she panted. "I hear mine. It's pounding, thumping."

"What's your heart saying, Ariel? Tell me, you know it. Tell me, sweet."

"You, Kayson, it's saying your name."

Her answer brought out a deep guttural groan from me. I reached between us and found her clit. Circling it, I teased her for just a second before pressing my thumb against it. Her entire body tightened, her legs clamped around my hips, her back arched, and I pulled my face back just in time to watch her lips take shape as she mouthed my name. Her release sent me over, every drop pulsating inside her.

We were spent, she held on tight as I rolled over and pulled her with me. I didn't want this feeling to end, holding her in place, our bodies still joined, I held her, and she let me.

I was just about to drift off when she spoke, her voice a sleepy content sound.

"Kayson?"

"Yes, sweet?"

"I read that there's a town about two hours away that's all Greek. The reviewers said, it's as close to Greece as people can get without leaving the United States. Do you know where I'm talking about?"

"Tarpon Springs. Yeah, divers still take their boats out every day and go sponge diving. Pretty much everything from the shops to the restaurants, grocery stores, pastry shops are all owned by Greek families."

"Will you take me? I've never been anywhere. I'd like to see a hint of Greece."

"You want to go to Tarpon Springs?"

She nodded.

"Tomorrow?"

She nodded.

I pulled her head down to my chest. "Then we better get some sleep."

ARIEL

*K*ayson and I headed to Tarpon Springs by nine, and I felt like a kid.

"You're bouncing, why so excited? It's just a town?"

"You don't get it. I've only left my home town one time in my entire life other than moving here and that was to visit the Grand Ole Opry in Nashville."

"Why the Grand Ole Opry? Weren't there more exciting things to do?"

"Uh no, Tammy Wynette was performing and she grew up in my town, she's sort of a legend. When I was about five, I was addicted to her song 'Stand By Your Man.' Don't say a word, I know, I'm a walking contradiction. Anyway, Mama took me and out comes Tammy, when she finally gets to that song and starts singing, there was nothing my mama could do to shut me up. I sang to the crowd around me about how it was to be a woman and told them to stand by their man. Before the song ended, so many people were staring at me because some thought it was funny and some probably just wanted me to shut the hell up."

Kayson laughed, "Well, your singing voice is something, I'll give you that."

"Hey! I'd been singing at the top of my five-year-old lungs. Well, next thing I knew, there was this bright light on me and someone was escorting me up on stage. I was standing next to Tammy Wynette herself. She started the song all over, and we sang it together." Looking over at Kayson, he had the widest grin on his face. "What? Don't look so smug.

"No, I can just imagine it. And, I'm wondering if I could find it on YouTube. Don't they record those shows?"

"Seriously, this happened way before YouTube was even a thing." I smacked his arm. "Besides, I have a VHS copy of it anyway, and I'm not telling you where."

"Shit. Who has a VHS player? We'll get it moved over to a DVD. I'm not worried, I have my ways. I'm sure that I can get it out of you."

He squeezed my hand before grabbing the steering wheel and turning left onto Dodecanese Boulevard. "Is that the name of a Greek god?"

"No, a group of islands in the middle of the Aegean Sea. Where did you learn geography?"

I stuck out my tongue, "Sorry but they didn't exactly teach the Greek islands in Alabama." Kayson parked on a side street, and we got out and walked down the main thoroughfare. It was very touristy, but I loved seeing the women in dresses that were obviously Greek attire. Kayson greeted them, and their faces lit up to have someone speak with them in their native language.

"What are these?" I held up a scratchy brown porous looking thing.

"They're sponges."

"Like you use in the shower?"

"Yeah. You can use them in the shower. The divers find them and dry them out before selling them. They are supposed to be great for the skin."

I picked up two and headed inside to pay, but Kayson continued speaking with the lady and before I was aware, he had paid, the thoughtful Neanderthal.

Back outside, we walked along the road, he always took the edge near the road. He held my bag in his right hand, I took a deep breath and reached out and grabbed his left. He gave me a light squeeze. Yeah, that was the right thing to do, I felt it in my heart. Damn, I forgot I had one of those.

We walked for a while, and then Kayson led me into a restaurant named Hellas.

"*Kalispera*," he greeted the people as we walked in, leaning over he whispered. "Means Good day."

We sat in a booth, and to my shock, Kayson sat on the same side as me. I read down the list of foods on the laminated menu.

"What's good?" I flipped the menu and read the back. "I have no clue what half of these things are. What do grape leaves taste like? I'm not sure I've ever tasted lamb."

"Trust me?" He raised one brow, daring me to say I didn't.

"Fine, order for me." I wasn't going to answer the trust part.

When the server returned Kayson ordered, "*E thelo saganaki, spaniópita kai tous kououmpiédes gia epidórpio.*"

I stared at him wide eyed, my mouth gaping open, "Huh?"

"I like that look." He smirked. "You agreed to trust me, I ordered an appetizer, entree, and dessert."

Our server returned with water, tea, and a few minutes later, a man came out carrying a pan. He struck a match and lit what was in the pan on fire. Everyone around us shouted "*opa*," then he squeezed a lemon over the top to douse the flame before setting the whole thing onto a hot pad in the middle of the table.

Kayson picked up a piece of warm pita bread from the basket they'd sat in front of us and dipped it into the gooey stuff in the sizzling pan.

"What is that?" It was creamy colored but also had the brown coloring from the fire.

"It's melted cheese." I gave him a questioning look. "Kasseri cheese. It's made from sheep's milk. Don't give me that look. You eat tons of cattle, cow milk, cow cheese. In Greece we eat lamb and use sheep's milk."

I shrugged, grabbed a pita round from the basket, tore off a piece, and dipped it in the melted cheese. It was delicious! "Oh my God, I don't care if it is chicken milk, okay, I know they don't milk chickens, but you get my point. I don't care what the hell it is made from; we have to get some of this cheese. Can we make this flaming stuff?"

"We'll go by the grocer before we leave. Kayson placed his hand on mine as I reached for another piece of bread. "Great idea, this was a great idea."

"What was a great idea?"

"Coming here, us getting away. Don't get me wrong, I loved last night. I fucking loved last night. But I also like this."

"Me, too."

Changing the subject, I pointed to woman that had just stood up from a booth in front of us wearing hot pink sweat pants. "What does that mean?" I asked. "I don't get it. Why would someone have the word 'Swing' printed on the seat of their pants?" Kayson and I watched as she kicked her legs, first her left, her right, she jiggled, then reached behind herself and pulled out a wedgie. I felt his hand whip across my mouth before I said anything.

"Don't say a word. Just don't fucking move," he whispered.

I felt his stomach shake as he fought to hold back his own outburst. When the lady finally was out of hearing range, I threw my head on the table and hooted, "Holy fuck, I did not expect that. Who'd have thought all those letters would have been up there?" I looked over at Kayson, who was still trying to catch his breath after laughing so hard. "Sweet Thing, her pants said, 'Sweet Thing.'"

Our server interrupted our laughter by bringing out our meals, small salads with giant olives, and potato salad in the middle, which was kind of weird.

Kayson must have noticed me examining the salad.

"It's a Greek thing, eat it."

And a piece of pie made of flaky phyllo dough filled with spinach and cheese. When I decided that I couldn't eat another bite, the server brought more. Small cups of coffee and powdered sugar cookies.

"What are these?"

"*Kourampiedes*, powdered butter cookies."

When our lunch was over, we continued our walk down Dodecanese Boulevard, stopping at the different shops until we made our way to the grocery store. Kayson grabbed a buggy and we piled in cheeses and spices. He picked up a jar of olives and turned to me with a quirky smile as he dropped them into the buggy.

"Olive in Orlando."

"I know, Olive with you."

We finished our day at National Bakery, filling boxes with baklava, those powdered butter cookies, and breads.

When we finally made our way back to his truck, it was after seven. We'd snacked through the day and didn't stop for dinner so we decided that we'd pick something up on the way home.

"Thank you for today. I know that I don't always show my appreciation, but I am grateful to you. I feel safe when I'm with you." Leaning up on my tippy toes, I gave him a kiss for all the things I haven't said.

"You are safe. I'd never let anything happen to you.

The two-hour drive back to his house seemed to go much faster.

"What time are you meeting the girls tomorrow?"

"They'll be at your house at eight. Oh shit, I didn't even ask if that was okay. Do you mind them meeting me there? I should've asked first."

"It's fine. Make yourself at home for as long as you want."

"By chance, you didn't grab my leather vest when you got my bike did you? I was working on a surprise for the girls and had it in the pocket."

"Got your vest and your helmet." He took his eyes off the road for just a quick second to give me a wink.

Curling against him, I shut my eyes, and within seconds, I was lulled to sleep by the humming sound of his truck tires on pavement, the low beat of the radio, and Kayson's hand lightly rubbing my arm.

I opened my eyes as Kayson laid me down on his bed. I didn't protest when his hands worked my jeans off me.

"Raise your arms, sweet," he whispered.

I did as he asked, and he lifted my shirt off and unclasped my bra. I would have been perfectly happy sleeping naked, but a second later, the silky feel of my nightgown kissed my skin as he slipped it over me.

"I'm so sleepy."

"I know, sweet. Slide under the covers."

The bed dipped, and Kayson pulled me against him, wrapping his arms securely around me.

ARIEL

*H*eat shot up my spine, and my core tightened, it was Kayson. He was filling my days, nights, and my dreams. My soft cries and moans were in agreement with everything he said.

"This morning is going to be rough and fast because you have to get up and get ready. But I don't want you to leave without feeling me all day, okay?"

"Yes. Yes. Just give it to me," I begged.

Two fingers slipped inside my opening, curling and straightening.

"God, you're so fucking wet. You ready for me?"

"Now, Yes. Now. I want to come."

"Look at me."

I opened my eyes and realized this wasn't a dream. I was getting it fast and dirty from Kayson, and I was enjoying it. There was nothing soft about him or his need at that moment. It was pure desire.

"Fuck, Ariel. You drive me mad."

"Please, Kayson."

He tore open the condom wrapper, but I wanted to do this. I took the latex band from him and placed it on the tip, squeezing his shaft, I drummed my fingers against his hard length as I inched the condom down.

"Hurry." Kayson's voice was all growl, and I forced my hands to move faster so that the condom was completely on.

With one fast, hard thrust he was in me. He was on his knees, hands wrapped around my hips. He lifted me off the bed and shoved me down on his thick erection, up and down.

"Fuck, sweet. I've never. Oh, my God. Baby. Ariel."

It was a mixture of his words, the hunger I saw in his eyes, and the raw need raging through him that had me tightening my legs around him, urging him to move faster, harder. He gave me everything.

When I felt his release, I was gone. I joined him. As our hearts raged against one another, I lay there, panting, and evaluating how this man had just turned my world upside down.

He rested back on his legs, me still impaled, his hands still gripping my hips. "Don't move. I'll turn on the shower and get the water warmed up for you." He pulled out of me.

I hoped that no matter what happened in my life, I never took for granted the little things that he always seemed to do.

When I got out of the shower, Kayson was standing there with a cup of coffee for me. While I dressed, he rested one hip on the counter, and we talked about his day's plans.

"I need to do some personal office work, pay bills, balance check-book, shit like that. And if possible, I want to get some mowing done today."

I felt guilty at the thought that he was doing all of that while I was with the girls.

"I'll go to the grocery store after breakfast with the girls," I offered, trying to do my part to pitch in.

"No. We can do that together. We'll plan out our week of meals."

His words didn't scare me quite as much as they would have even just a week ago. Sure, they were so domesticated—so *we*. But a part of me wanted to see the we that Kayson and I could be.

"Meet you downstairs." Kayson leaned over and kissed my cheek before leaving the bedroom as I gathered my essentials: credit card, license, and lipstick.

When I got downstairs, I didn't see Kayson anywhere, so I headed to the garage. The little things just kept shocking the hell out of me, they made my heart beat a tad faster, and the first crack in my resolve to avoid a relationship fractured.

Kayson had opened the garage door and was already turning my bike around for me, All I had to do was put on my helmet and go. The man was thoughtful; it was those damn little things. Looking up at the first roar from engines, I headed over to my bike and grabbed my helmet. But Kayson stopped me by winding his fingers through the back of my hair and pulling me in for a kiss.

"Be safe, I mean it," he said against my lips.

"Aye aye, Captain," I replied and gave him a weak salute. Then fastened my helmet and started my engine. Stella and Leo pulled up and turned their bikes around next to mine. Kayson walked over and hugged each one.

"Keep my girl safe. Okay?"

"We got her." Leo gave him the reassurance he needed.

We rode off, I wasn't sure where we were headed, but it was fun riding with a group of women. On this crystal Sunday morning, the roads were relatively deserted, and tourist traffic was down since most kids were back in school. We stopped at Piper's house to pick up her, and I was introduced to Everly, a paramedic, and Vivian, the owner of Sixes and the widow of Sergeant Haines who was killed earlier in the year.

The six of us left and headed downtown. The old brick road portion of Mills Avenue made my teeth rattle, and the roar of our engines probably pissed off the neighbors in the Lake Lawson area, but hopefully, they had excellent insulation. Falling into a two by two formation, Stella and Piper turned into a parking lot at the back of a restaurant.

I loved this area of Orlando. It was old, original, and one of the most diverse districts. Within a two-mile radius, there was VietVille, filled with Vietnamese restaurants and spice stores and an area full of biker bars and tattoo shops. There was also Highland Park, a school where you had to have your child's name on the list while they were still a pollywog in their daddy's nuts just to have a hope of getting in.

Last but not least, there was this area, where we were, this was where Orlando encouraged you to let your freak flag fly.

Passing by gawkers, who were all busy staring at a group of biker women, who dressed for the slide, not for the ride. We all had to contain Stella, who tried to sound like she was dishing out gang slang instead of medical terms.

"Stop with the gang shit." Everly wrapped her hands over Stella's mouth as if that would stop her. "There's probably several nurses and doctors back there who understood every word you just said and are scratching their heads at why bikers are talking about enemas."

"Well, at least they aren't scratching their balls."

I held out my hands palm up in a what-gives gesture, because really, how could these women, who had known Stella longer than I had, give her such great ammunition.

A harmony of sweet voices rang out, and the sound of an organ wafted in the air that was heavy with the smell of breakfast foods— bacon and maple syrup.

"Why are some people in their Sunday finest?" I wondered looking around at the women dressed in pastels with matching hats and gloves. We were a stark contrast to them.

"You hear that?" Everly pointed to the sky. "We're about to attend a whole different type of church."

Walking into the restaurant, we were greeted by a woman with a beehive hairdo wearing a fifties-style waitress outfit, and a name tag that read Alice.

Everly checked us in. Thank goodness we had a reservation, this place was the bomb, and the looky-loos that stared at us were going to be in line for a long, long time. The line wrapped around the building.

A group of women with bouffant hair, and wearing gospel choir robes, and fabulous five-inch stiletto heels walked across the stage. How they didn't break their necks in those heels was beyond me.

"Now you, honey child." I looked around to see who the gorgeous blonde with mocha skin was talking to. "Yes you, with the red hair."

"He's talking to you Ariel," Leo whispered in my ear.

"He?"

"Yes, he. This is a drag show."

"No fucking way. They have better bodies than we do." They did indeed know how to flaunt what the good Lord gave them.

"You know what they say about red hair?" the blonde asked me.

I thought for a second, do I let my smartass mouth loose or do I play innocent? Fuck it, "Redheads are only for men brave enough to play with fire?"

I heard a few snickers, and one person said, "You tell her, honey!" Of course, the Iron Orchids were cheering loudly.

"Come here, child. I like you. We must baptize you. Red hair is a sign of evil. You're a daywalker. Can I get an amen?"

Shouts of amen rang out from people in the audience. Every time the blonde said something, people were on their knees, crossing themselves and shouting it. But when it dawned on me that they weren't shouting "amen" but "hey men," I lost it. I had found my favorite place to hang out.

Blonde Beauty continued talking about my red hair, but it didn't bother me, I loved my hair. I was a real red, so I had heard just about every jab there was. Daywalker—that was so Cartman on *South Park* like ten years ago. And I grew up dreaming of someday being called Carrots by a boy that looked like Gilbert Blythe from *Anne of Green Gables*. Hell, I wanted to be Anne and cause that much mischief.

"You know what time it is?" the blonde asked.

"Time for breakfast," I replied.

"Oh, no, child. We're gonna . . ." And then he started singing. "We're gonna wash that sin right out of your hair."

I sang along since I knew the words from the musical *South Pacific*. But they had replaced the word "man" with the word "sin." He ran his fingers through my hair and massaged my scalp with his long red nails.

When the song was over, and I was permitted to rejoin my group, our food was being served. You didn't order, your table just got everything served family style. It was a real southern-style breakfast with grits, eggs, pancakes, biscuits and gravy. The only thing not on the table was bacon and sausage.

Servers walked around and enjoyed asking diners raunchy questions like, "Would you like to taste my sausage?" or "Would you like some meat?"

Best of all no one threw a hissy fit when I asked for iced tea for breakfast. Did I already say how much I loved this place?

The choir queens sang along to old hymnal songs that I grew up listening to on Mama's old record player. If a table was too quiet, the choir doused them in holy water then returned to singing. Since none of us particularly cared for riding wet, we stomped our feet and clapped our hands. I had given so many profound shouts of 'hey men,' that I either had a one-way ticket to heaven or hell. I wasn't quite sure which. It depended on semantics.

"That's right, you little daywalker, feel his spirit, let his spirit in," the blonde preached.

"I'm betting five bucks, she already let him this morning," Stella announced to the crowd.

I went to grab something sharp, Piper beat me to it and slid the knife out of my reach. "I won't kill her, just maim her." My plea sounded entirely rational to me.

"Well, we got a new song today, and I'm gonna dedicate it to our daywalker, who got a little sumthin', sumthin' this morning."

I laughed because, who wouldn't? Then I held my hands up in surrender. "Okay. If y'all are gonna discuss this at least get your facts straight. It ain't little."

Leo gave her loud, "Whoop, whoop."

While Piper covered her ears, trying to block out the words. Of course, I received high fives all around, until Stella pretended to send a text and blast the news all over the internet.

"Well, I want you all to know that I've worked real hard. Okay, not that hard," the blonde said into the microphone with a laugh. "Anyway, today's debut song is sure to get those juices flowing. Which always sounds good to me. How does that sound to you?" he asked the other singers with him. The organist hit the first keys, and a remake of the classic "Bringing in the Sheaves" got a whole new meaning.

There wasn't a lot that I could tell you about the song, but at least I knew that we all will *come* rejoicing.

After he had sung the last song, the gorgeous mocha blonde came over and sat with us. He introduced himself as Ringo.

"Girlies, look at you, bringing that eighties biker chic back in style."

"Damn right." I smiled at him. "Actually, we rode our bikes over here."

"All you ride motorcycles?"

We all nodded.

"Aren't you just a bunch of bad ass bitches. Look out. Meow. All of you need to come back during the week and watch my fabulous ass perform. I make a killer Whitney." Ringo swore that only two people could sing "One Moment in Time" and Whitney was the other one. Since that was my favorite song from her, I promised we'd return and see him perform.

An evening full of queen impersonators would be a hoot. Ringo got up to mingle with the rest of the audience, leaving the girls and I to have some talk time.

"Let's talk Iron Orchids," Leo said.

"Well, I have a surprise for y'all. I unzipped my pocket and brought out a piece of nylon fabric that I had sewn. "Kayson always wears his wings and says, 'No motor deputy rides without them,' so I added wings, of course I put a few orchids, and since we are in Florida, I had to put that as well. What do you think?" No one said a word. They just stared at the damn fabric. I thought it looked fucking cool as a patch, but maybe I'd misjudged. "I can make something different, it's just an idea for a patch. We don't have to use it."

"Fuck. I know what it is." Stella grabbed the fabric. "I want to know how the hell you made it? It is fucking wicked. We need this thing on our vests. You've been holding out on us, chickie." I smiled, finally understanding that they were admiring my handy work not judging. "Let's give Ariel our vests, we've got ourselves a gang."

"We're not a gang." All of us shouted, but by this point, Stella was just saying that shit to rile us.

"Harley is always having rallies, and it would be a great way to find more women to join, I can check with my boss." Leo offered. "Or we could sign up for one of their charity rides?"

"How about an all ladies motorcycle class? I was sort of intimidated by all the guys that were trying to show off on the bikes while I was just trying to stay upright. Not to mention I'd just moved here, I didn't know the roads to practice on, having women who were learning at the same time to ride would've been great."

"Enough with the evasive tactic, how big is he?" Stella asked. "I always assumed all four of those boys were probably demigods and they should be sculpted for some museum."

"Or just to help other men aspire," Leo added.

"What the fuck?" Stella had never kept it a secret that she thought Kayson and his brothers were hot, but Leo? "Are you crushing on one of the brothers?"

Leo's face turned flame red. "No. I just think that they're all hot."

"Whatever you say. But I'm calling bullshit on that lie," I whispered into her ear.

She turned to stare into my eyes, almost a pleading to let it drop, so I did.

"We aren't discussing the size of Kayson's pecker. Let's pay the tab." I could feel the heat burning in my chest, it was a strange feeling of comfort. Everyone knew and accepted that Kayson and I were together, a team, a we. Now I needed to admit it to myself and then to Kayson.

We stood, and I waved to Ringo, and then headed out to my bike. The rest of the girls had no choice but to follow.

* * *

WHEN I PULLED into Kayson's garage, he was waiting for me with a smile on his face. It was comforting and frightening at the same time. When I looked at him, I saw home.

"Did you have fun today?" he asked.

"Mm-hm."

He swept me up into his arms. "Where'd you go?"

"A restaurant called Bananas. Heard of it?"

Kayson let out a throaty laugh. "Yeah, I've heard of it."

"How about you? What'd you do?"

"Went to your apartment. Just wanted to check on it and grab some more of your girly shit."

"My girly shit?"

"Yeah. The good-smelling girly shit."

"Ooh."

Wrapping one strong hand on either side of my hips, he pushed me toward the stairs, hustling me up and through the open double doors.

"Ohh," I whimpered. He had set out a few photos on the dresser of my mama and me.

"That's 'Ohh, Kayson' to you," he said and tossed me into the middle of the bed.

KAYSON

I had the best night of sleep in my entire life, which ended at five Monday morning when my phone dinged.

Reading the message I sighed.

Captain Getty: Need you to come straight into the station.

Studying Ariel's body as she slept, I admired her smooth skin, a flawless canvas begging to be painted. I refused to wake her and add a little color to mar her perfect skin.

Normally, I clocked in via my radio and patrolled morning traffic before heading into the station. I didn't normally get an angry text from Captain, though. Something in my head told me that the fucking DA was at it again.

Throwing on my uniform, I clipped my badge and gun on to my belt before heading downstairs. After scribbling a note for Ariel, I headed out to my bike.

As I pulled into the station there were several news trucks. "What now" seemed to be my new motto in life. The second I cut the engine, there was a reporter in my face. "Deputy Christakos, what do you have to say about the accusations concerning lack of ethics on the force?" she asked as she shoved her microphone closer.

If I hadn't put my hand up to stop her, she probably would have hit me in the face with the stupid thing. I ignored the question and maneuvered around her. It was county policy for all media questions and answers to go through the sheriff and the media secretary, who would then appoint a spokesperson. She knew that. Fuck, all reporters knew that. It was the same for all departments. My morning went from lousy at having to leave a gorgeous woman in my bed to downright ludicrous when the reporter stuck out her foot to try to stop me. Restraint was an under-appreciated virtue, and I had to use every ounce of mine not to lash out at her as I headed toward the door.

"Sergeant Christakos, no comment on the allegations that you requested sexual favors from citizens in exchange for leniency in charges?"

What the fuck did she just ask? I turned to her, cameras flashed in my face, but the station door opening halted my reaction.

"Now, Christakos." Captain Getty's massive frame stood in the doorway.

"Captain. What disciplinary action can we expect against Sergeant Christakos?" the reporter asked, but Getty waved her off, refusing to answer.

"Can someone please tell me what the fuck is going on? And what did she mean about sexual favors?" Standing near the captain's desk, I seized a paperweight and proceeded to try to smash the damn thing between my hands. I had to do something to alleviate some of this fucking stress.

"I'll ask the questions," said a woman in a business suit. "I'm Corporal Grace Wickham with internal affairs, and it seems that you have pissed some people off. I need to clarify some information. You are Deputy Kayson Michael Christakos, is that correct?"

"Yes, ma'am."

"You have been with the Orange County Sheriff's Department since . . ."

This was going to be a long day. One thing most people forget was that, as law enforcement, we had access to a lot of databases. And this woman was going to try to catch me in a lie. Any lie. Whatever it was, however small, a lie was a lie and would lead to instant termination.

"I was hired while still in the academy, just over ten years ago." I had corrected. Even though I was hired while in the academy, my official start date was six months later when I graduated. Whatever her angle, I wanted to cover all bases.

"And you became a motorcycle deputy when?"

"Two years later." I kept my answers to the point.

"But on your application, you wrote that you wanted to be a motors deputy. Why the wait?"

"You have to be with the department for two years before applying." That was standard procedure, which she should have known. I had no clue where she was leading with this line of questioning.

"Impressive. Become a motorcycle deputy almost to the day that you are allowed to apply. You must have been the first," she said.

This bitch was very condescending.

"I'm not current on that information, sorry."

"And you're up for the promotion to sergeant. Head of the motors squad. Also impressive."

"Don't be. We lost a great man." I turned my head at the sight of someone escorting Piper into an adjacent office. Crap, had Brandon brought her into his bullshit?

"Eyes up here, Deputy," Corporal Wickham said. "Let me explain what exactly is going on."

"I'd appreciate that."

"In the last forty-eight hours, our office has received five complaints against you. All callers have requested to remain anonymous, so of course, we take that into account. Now, please understand that, on average, we receive about ten calls a day from people complaining about deputies. More often than not, it is after someone has received a ticket, or even out of spite from family members of inmates. To receive five complaints within two days, and all with the same accusations against the same deputy? Well, you understand, I'm sure."

No, I didn't understand. I didn't understand a single damn thing. This was bullshit.

"Before you speak, let me finish," Corporal Wickham continued. "Deputy, you have an impeccable record, and I admit five calls within two days after ten years with not one single blemish is suspicious. I still have to investigate, though. It is protocol. Unfortunately, this will also be on your record."

"What the fuck. I haven't done a damn thing. We have helmet cameras. You can see every interaction that I've made." I was pissed. I was angry that this would be in my file, and even though I would be proved innocent, it would always show that there had been an investigation.

"We know that. Don't think we haven't already pulled the videos."

"Am I done here?" I snapped.

"Sit down, Kayson," Captain Getty ordered. He used my first name, which meant he was taking on a fatherly role and I was in for a lecture. "Let IA finish."

Sure, I wanted to hear what else they were planning to do to ruin my career.

"The DA's office has also filed a complaint against you."

Fucking surprise, surprise. "That man is messed up. He is upset that I am dating his ex-girlfriend. And we have cause to believe he placed a listening device in her apartment. It's in evidence now and still has to be processed and run through forensics."

"Their complaints are a breach of ethics by law enforcement, behavior unbefitting for the line of duty, and fraternization with a subordinate. Until we can get to the bottom of this, take my advice and lie low. He is a powerful man and has set his sights on you. His office's complaint has come to our attention at the same time as the five female complaints."

"And you don't see the connection?"

"They may be separate; they might all be tied together. But we will be looking into each complaint," she said as she handed me several forms.

"One question. Did your office bother to ask these women when these events happened to make sure that I was on duty? Or even why they didn't immediately report the incident? Most people don't naturally think of calling internal affairs."

"That's two questions. Yes, we asked both. It seems that the events are all recent and that the women watch a lot of television, so they knew to get IA involved. We are having the recordings analyzed for voice modulation to see if it may be the same caller attempting to disguise her voice. We are also pulling the last six months of your calls." Corporal Wickham explained. "We aren't going to suspend you from duty, but I want you to review those forms. I will be in contact with you this week."

She left the captain's office, but I was seething. "Am I free to go?" I asked a bit sarcastically.

"You're dismissed," Captain Getty replied. "By the way. I find it convenient that the news media knew about those complaints before I did. Don't you?"

"Very fucking convenient."

I walked out of the conference room, Getty's words rolling in my brain. How would the media hear about this, unless . . . unless dickhead had given them a heads up? Captain had already figured this out. At least he was on my side. I passed by the office where Piper sat, spun, and walked back into the captain's office. "Are there complaints against Piper as well?"

"You know that I can't answer that." It was all the answer I needed to know there were.

Pulling out my phone as I headed to my bike I realized that I had missed several texts from Ariel and even a call, shit.

Ariel: Good morning.

Ariel: Everything okay?

Ariel: Something wrong?

Missed call

Immediately texting back.

Me: Sweet, sorry I couldn't answer, been in a meeting. Brandon is up to something. Please stay at the house today and lock up. Will call in a few.

Each step, I replayed my interactions with Ariel over the last few weeks. I needed to be patient with her, she didn't talk about being anti-relationship any longer, but she wasn't ready to admit she wanted more. She was just starting to open up, and I needed to tighten down for her safety without scaring her off.

AFTER PULLING out of the parking lot and away from the melee of news trucks still clamoring for a story, I drove to the nearest restaurant to pick up some lunch and tried again to call Ariel, but her phone went straight to voice mail.

ARIEL

*E*very thread of anti-relationship fiber I had left in me Kayson ripped this weekend. When I woke and found only chilly sheets next to me, I realized that I'd missed him before he left for work.

I tried texting him, and after several hours of no reply, my mind was playing tricks on me, and all sorts of unwanted thoughts started to creep in. I decided to get ready and go to the fabric store since there were several things I needed to buy.

As a seamstress slash wanna be event planner, the fabric store was my mecca. I could spend hours looking at the latest patterns and materials or buying yards of great fabric that I found on sale. There were some things that I couldn't have too much of: lace, satin, silk, beading, rhinestones, tulle, and even taffeta. As noisy as the shit was, it was still the traditional fabric for bridesmaids and prom dresses. Among the yards of fabric, I hoped to find the answers I needed. Was Kayson okay? Why hadn't he called? Scanning my phone one last time, I moved to the checkout lane, which was at least a thirty-minute wait, and dialed him, but the call clicked over to voice mail.

The second I stepped into the parking lot, an eerie feeling slicked down my spine. Whirling, I looked back into the store. There wasn't anyone there. Well, no one who appeared out of the ordinary. Twisting forward, my gut clenched when I saw him. Brandon stood near the back of the lot, leaning against his gray convertible. He raised one hand in greeting and then got back in his car and drove away.

With my eyes locked on his car as it turned out of the lot, I pulled out my phone and sprinted to my car. Once safely inside, I locked my doors, started my engine, and put my car in reverse. I held my foot on the brake while I unlocked my phone to text Stella. I wanted to call Kayson but had no clue where he was.

Fuck.

Me: I just saw Brandon while I was out shopping.

Stella: What did he say?

Me: Nothing. He just stood watching me.

Stella: Freaky.

Me: I know, right?

Stella: Want to talk about it?

Me: *Yes.*

Stella: Come over. Want me to call any of the girls?

Me: Sure.

Stella lived in an area of Orlando called Metro West. It was the "it" place to live at one time. Originally, it was a planned community for dinks, dual-income-no-kids sort of people, but grew into a place for mid-upper class families. Stella owned a townhouse in the older part. I didn't even waste time to look at the vacant home next to hers. I was too focused on getting inside where I felt secure. I walked up to Stella's door and knocked.

Several people shouted, "Come on in, door's open."

"Red or white?" Stella asked the second I rounded the corner to the kitchen.

I laughed. It was barely noon, and my posse, the Iron Orchids, had rallied together.

"I have beer as well."

"Just tea or water would be great," I replied.

"White it is." Stella handed me a glass and a plate with pizza on it. "From your text, it sounded like you needed the F's."

"F's?"

"Food, friends, and fucking. I could help with two. So, here you go." Stella waved her arm out to the group. "Now, talk."

"Where do I start?" I didn't know, so I jumped in with the shit I hadn't told anyone.

"Brandon was hiding in the vestibule to my apartment complex the other night and jumped out to propose to me."

"He what?" Stella asked. "No way. Did he have a ring? What would make that crazy motherfucker think that you'd say yes? You didn't say yes, did you?"

I rolled my eyes at the fact she would even ask such a ridiculous question. But I could tell she was trying to break the stress. When Stella was stressed, her face resembled Bubba Gump, with her lower jaw protruding with each tidbit of information I revealed.

"No clue what would make him ask. But yes, he had a ring. If I had to guess, I would say it was from Cartier with the red velvet box." I took a deep breath, counted to ten, and steeled myself for the next part. "That was the same night my apartment was broken into. Piper found one of those bugs that people plant to listen in on conversations. So, I'm staying with Kayson at his house." Things seemed to spiral downhill after that. "I'm sorry, I must sound like some old country song. I just need the dog and the doublewide trailer to make it complete, huh? I'm sorry. I'm not myself. I'm freaked. Someone is trying to scare me and doing a fucking fantastic job. What should I do?"

"You mean, what should *we* do," said Stella. "First, have you spoken to Kayson today?"

"No," I answered. "I can't reach him, tried all morning."

"I need to figure out what to do about Brandon. He's up to something, and he's scaring the daylights out of me. I think the man is seriously losing it. He's showing up everywhere, the hospital, twice now at restaurants, then today."

"I think he has a God complex, he thinks he's untouchable," Stella added. "You need to protect yourself. Ohhh, I've got it. We need to find a way to track his ass and see what he's up to." Stella opened her laptop, handed Everly a notepad, and then started typing. "Make a list."

We compiled a list of possible scenarios where Brandon might corner me.

Favorite restaurants.

Stores that he knows I like to visit.

Mutual friends—that was immediately nixed since there were none.

Everly drew a line down the paper and made a second column of places where we might find Brandon.

His office.

The sheriff station.

Outside my apartment.

And finally, Stella wanted to create a list of ways to track someone without getting caught.

Leo offered up search phrases such as "How to catch a cheating spouse" because there were bound to be hundreds of ideas listed.

Throwing my hands up in the air, I decided that it was probably best to shut up and just play monitor and only interrupt when it got ridiculous, which was that second. "No. Revolver? Have you gone crazy?"

"If you are going to get a gun, this site says to get a revolver. They're less likely to jam, and revolvers don't leave any bullet casings for evidence."

"For once the internet isn't wrong. You really should get a concealed carry license, though. I have mine and Piper can take us to the range," Leo said as if I were just going to bust a cap in someone's ass.

A part of me was frightened about where the conversation was headed and the other part was laughing at my reference to the movie *Another 48 Hrs*. I had to intervene. "Stella, are you listening to yourself? You're talking as though we're gonna shoot up something."

"Or someone," Stella interjected. "Just saying. If it means saving your life, I'll buy you the gun myself."

"Try searching how to stalk like a PI," Everly interjected.

Really? She was joining in. Great. I read over Everly's shoulder as she added binoculars, tactical flashlight, pepper spray, Taser, GPS tracker, and revolver to the list.

"I think we each should pick up one of these items for Ariel," Everly mused, tapping her pen against the notepad. "This way, we don't alert the Feds by sending everything to one address."

"We aren't buying pallets of fertilizer and alarm clocks. I think we're safe," I said as I tried to keep from chuckling.

"We are working to keep you safe and figure out who is after you. This is nothing to laugh at," Stella defended. "Let's order this stuff and plan for next Saturday. The guys are gone to the Monster Jam Trucks."

We had just marked Saturday on our calendars when Stella's front door slammed open and shut.

"Fuck me!" Piper shouted as she came in. "Turn on the fucking television."

We all stared at Piper as Stella moved and flipped to channel nine to find a reporter standing in front of the sheriff's station. "Orange County Sheriff's Department has declined comment on the current allegations." Clearly, we were catching the very end of the segment, because the screen cut to a still picture of . . .

"That's Kayson," Stella said as she grabbed my hand.

"Our inside sources say that Deputy Christakos, who has also declined comment, is currently under investigation for eliciting sexual favors from female drivers in exchange for not issuing tickets . . ."

"Fuck that bitch," Everly yelled at the television. "He can't answer her, and she knows that. His department, our department, we all have an entire media team that handles communication with the press. She's just trying to spin the public opinion."

My head ached, but not from a headache, and I caught myself rubbing the spot between my eyebrows raw as my stomach turned into an empty pit and acid roiled up the back of my throat. I was going to lose it. The mere thought of Kayson having sex with strangers sent off a jealousy vibe racing through my body.

"Stop that." Stella smacked my arm. "I've known him for about seven years, ever since Carter transferred to Orange County, and Kayson Christakos would not do something like that. There is no truth to these accusations." She searched my eyes, wanting confirmation that I believed her, trusted Kayson.

Trust.

There was that fucking word.

I nodded.

Truthfully, I knew there was no way he would do that. Hell, I was willing to have sex before he was. I just couldn't stop thinking about how I had wanted to believe the exact same thing about my dad. That everything I heard was nothing but an ugly rumor. I had been wrong then, but I trusted Stella to tell me the truth. I turned back to the television.

"In other news, Brandon Fagan with the district attorney's office has announced that he will be holding a press conference to make a statement about Erskine Sello, who is being held without bond in the Orange County jail. As many of you know, Mr. Sello is standing trial for the murder of an off-duty sheriff sergeant earlier this year. This is Haley Loles with Channel Nine News. We return you now to our regularly scheduled program already in progress."

"Motherfucker!" Stella shouted. "Way to fucking turn the fucking truth. Why not tell the public what really happened? The off-duty sergeant was walking out to his car when that fuckwad shot him. Vivian's husband had no choice but to shoot back and try to defend himself as well as the people around him. But when Deputy Haines fell, Sello came up from behind and shot him six more times point blank in the back." Stella was irate, which was completely expected.

"Funny how she didn't mention that he also shot another officer, drove over a third, and then murdered his girlfriend and their daughter," Everly added.

My head was ringing, and my friends' words seemed to fade away. All of those dreadful images flashed in front of my eyes.

God, thank you for keeping Kayson safe. Thank God that wasn't him.

My hand flew to my mouth. I was such a horrid person, people were grieving, and I was thanking God that Kayson wasn't killed by Sello. What if Kayson wasn't at the mall on Mother's Day weekend, what if he didn't walk out at that precise moment? What if he hadn't been at that fundraiser event at Harley, and what if I didn't have him to text when I heard someone breaking into my apartment?

"I need to head home." I had to be there for Kayson.

Thank God I had Kayson to rush home to. Home, Kayson's home, my home. I rushed out of Stella's house, promising to see everyone on Saturday.

I grabbed my phone, which I had left sitting in my passenger's seat, and cursed under my breath. Eight missed calls, shit, shit, shit.

Swiping my phone, I dialed Kayson, and he answered immediately.

"Please tell me that you're okay."

"I'm fine. I was at Stella's and didn't realize that I'd dropped my phone out of my purse. It's been in my car this whole time."

"Where are you now?"

"On my way home."

"Drive safe. See you soon."

Pulling into the driveway, I pressed the garage door opener, the one Kayson had put in my car so that I could park next to his truck. For a brief second, I was afraid. He'd arranged himself in the perfect position to take up the entire doorway that led from the garage to the house.

"Hi." I asked as I came to a stop in front of him. I didn't know if he was mad or scared. But he looked as if he was trying to hold his emotions together. "Kayson what's wrong?"

"What's wrong? Ariel, I've been scared to death about you. It is almost seven o'clock. It's only been a week since your apartment was broken into. Ariel, I told you, all I needed was for you to allow me to protect you. You denied me that. Don't you get it?"

"What? What do you want me to say? I woke up, I couldn't reach you, so I ran some errands. Then Brandon showed up. I freaked and went to Stella's. I'm sorry. I didn't mean to drop my phone in my car, it was an accident."

"Whoa, wait a minute. What do you mean Brandon showed up? Here?"

"No. While I was at the fabric store."

"What did he say? Tell me exactly." Kayson shoved his hands through his hair as he pulled me inside and closed the garage door.

"Nothing, which is why I was scared. He just watched me."

"I'm going to kill him. I've had it. Brandon's behind all of this bullshit, all this crap with my job. I'm going to nail his ass to a wall. What time did you see him?"

"I don't know." I opened my phone and looked at my text messages. "I texted Stella at noon. So, that was when I saw him. I contacted her immediately."

"Not me?"

"I had tried you several times by then. I thought you were busy. Or . . ."

"Or? Or what Ariel?"

"Or that was your way of telling me you were done."

Kayson let out a sigh that sounded more like a growl. "None of this would have happened had you stayed here like I asked, I told you something was up this morning."

"When did you say that?"

"In the note I left."

"What note? There wasn't a note."

"Oh yes, ma'am, there was. Same place I left it last time. On the counter, so you had to see it when you went into the kitchen."

"I looked, and there wasn't a note."

He walked over to grab the letter and show me, but I was right, there wasn't a note. He moved around to the other side, and then I saw it still on the notepad sitting next to the coffee maker.

"You obviously didn't make coffee, either." He held up the pad and showed me. "I was so furious about having to go to the station, I knew that Brandon was up to something, I must have left it there when I made my coffee." He handed me the letter. "I need to go for a walk. I'm pissed. I don't want to say something in anger that I'd regret later. You fucking freaked me out when I couldn't find you. We just had a fabulous weekend, and you'd jump to that conclusion that I was done with you?" He headed out the garage door and slammed it so hard the keys that hung on the wall rattled.

I held the note and read.

A,

Thank you for a fabulous weekend, I hate leaving you, even for work. Especially knowing that you're upstairs in my bed, naked, and exactly where you're meant to be. Don't go anywhere, please. I worry about you. I have a feeling that Brandon is up to something, got a call to report to the station instead of patrol this morning, will let you know.

Love,

K

I TRACED the words he'd written but only really focused on one: love. Was he falling in love with me or was that just an accident? Something he wrote out of habit?

I didn't know, but something about those four little letters warmed me. It also made me feel like a complete jerk for thinking that he would want me gone. He was right. We had had an amazing weekend together, and in one sentence, I ruined it.

I walked into the kitchen and searched the pantry and freezer for something to cook. I needed comfort food. I pulled out a wrapped package of frozen tilapia, grabbed the cornmeal, flour, salt, pepper, and a few potatoes. Fried fish, home fries, and hushpuppies.

I was so horrid at this relationship thing—wait, were we in a relationship? Half the world's population were men and I'd been judging them all based on the few I had known up to this point. It wasn't exactly as if I were an expert.

Was Kayson telling me that he was in love with me? Holy shit, the "L" word, it hadn't quite been a month.

I heard the door open about forty-five minutes later and saw

Kayson coming in, but I was in the zone. I had the fish defrosted, hushpuppy batter mixed, potatoes grated, and I had gone through the five stages of Ariel resolution.

Feeling hurt.

Jumping to conclusions.

Feeling guilty.

Second-guessing my decisions.

Promising to be a better person.

Of course, that last stage came with sucking up and making a Southern-style home-cooked meal, sans black-eyed peas because I didn't have time to go to the grocery story.

"Want a beer?" I asked with a hesitant smile.

"I'll get it. What're you cooking?" He removed his shoes and set them by the door.

"Southern cuisine, also known as comfort food."

"And do I get Southern cuisine for dessert as well?" Kayson's question was full of playful innuendo. Obviously, he had gone through his own transformation from anger to acceptance to let's start over while on his walk. I liked that we worked through this misunderstanding without bloodshed.

Setting out two plates, Kayson and I served ourselves and carried our plates to the table. "Want to talk about today?" I still felt guilty that I had brought the wrath of Brandon down on him.

"The DA's office is causing a lot of shit right now and making accusations, I think that IA is on my side, they know that this is all being made up," Kayson said, trying to comfort me even though he was the one going through all the bullshit.

"You know I don't think for one second that any of those accusations are true, right?" I waited until I knew that he believed me, because they were truthful. "How did the media get involved?"

"Anonymous tip, I'm assuming." Kayson raised a corner of his mouth. He and I both could guess who the anonymous person was. "But it goes beyond that. It seems that people are calling into the internal affairs office and filing complaints there as well."

"I'm so sorry. Brandon's upset that I dumped him months ago. I think somewhere in his distorted mind he thought that I'd come crawling back. He's pissed that I chose you."

"Did you?"

"Yes, I dumped him. He couldn't keep it in his pants. We only dated a few months, and I never even considered calling him again. He's jealous that we"—I pointed back and forth between us—"have been inseparable since the Harley event."

"No. I mean did you choose me?" Kayson titled his head and raised one brow, waiting for my answer.

Shoving an entire hushpuppy in my mouth, I mumbled, "Can't talk."

"Ha-ha, you're a nut. Stop blaming yourself for Brandon's actions. You aren't making him do these things to me. I believe whoever is in your life—friend or boyfriend—will have issues as long as Brandon isn't getting his way."

"Did I tell you that when Stella, Piper, and I went shopping we ran into him?"

"You didn't."

"Yup. He was insulting toward them. Rude. Like, he couldn't believe that I'd made friends." I took a swig of sweet tea and swallowed before I continued, "Why didn't you tell me about all of this going on with the DA?" I asked.

"Truthfully, I didn't know there was a connection between you two until the other night at your apartment. I just thought he was an asshole that developed a sudden distaste for Greek food," Kayson said, trying to make me smile.

"Do we know or have you heard when Brandon is planning the conference for?"

"Tomorrow. It's going to be a long day with crowd control." Kayson stood and grabbed our plates. "Sit. You cooked, I'll clean."

I watched as he moved into the kitchen and opened the dishwasher. I followed behind him and started wrapping leftovers and placing them in the refrigerator. Every time I turned around, I wondered if I would ever be enough for this man.

When the kitchen was clean, Kayson wrapped his arm around my waist and pulled me into his living room. We snuggled on the couch with me lying in front of him as he flicked through stations. When he hit a preseason football game, he paused.

"Like football?" he asked.

"Love it."

His arms tightened around me, and we watched the Packers second string get their asses beat by the Bears second string.

I was a football spiraling through the air.

Wait.

That didn't make sense.

Kayson was carrying me upstairs to bed.

KAYSON

*S*itting on the side of the bed, I zipped up my boots, hating that I had to go to work today of all days and deal with Brandon's bullshit, again. Twisting around, I pictured Ariel lying in that same position in twenty years, and the way her red hair would look waving across the pillows.

Days like today, when I knew it was going to be a clusterfuck before I even got there, I needed something to focus on, something that reminded me that life wasn't all just cleaning up one mess after another. I had a feeling Ariel had just become that thing for me. She was the reason I became a deputy. I didn't know it back then, but it was her, and I would do anything to keep her safe.

"Hey sweet, can you wake for just a second?" I whispered against her neck as I kissed her creamy back.

"Mm-hm."

"Will you do me a favor and stay home today? I'm not sure what Brandon is up to, but I suspect it is going to be a crazy day. I'll probably be late."

"Be safe." Her voice was muffled against the pillows.

"Always." I kissed her, and with one final look back at her stretched out in bed, I shut the door softly behind me.

A few minutes later, I was downstairs and on my bike reporting to shift.

All of us that worked patrol on Alpha shift and a few deputies from other shifts were called in for a briefing of today's expected events. Unfortunately, none of us had a good feeling about Brandon or what was cooking with the DA's office. The statement sent over from the state attorney's office assured us that the press conference today was focusing on Erskine Sello and his upcoming trial. Before leaving, we were grouped into teams of three, two motors and one squad car. Piper, Carter, and I paired off into one team. We were each issued extra OC spray and Piper stored two additional sets of full riot gear in her trunk. Walking out of the station, we faced a barrage of flashing cameras, and people jumped out of their cars with signs, shouting, and tossing cans.

"What the hell is this?" Carter asked.

"Brandon," Piper and I said in stereo.

"Lock up the cops," voices chanted. I was okay with the signs and with people shouting. I was even okay with them acting like idiots when they didn't know the facts, but throwing shit at me was going too far. Speaking into my radio, I informed dispatch that the first riot of the day had broken out at the edge of our parking lot, and within milliseconds, the entire area was lit up like Wrigley Field. Spotlights broke every surface, and I slid my sunglasses over my eyes.

I turned on my mic, let it make a loud squeal for a second to get their attention, and then shouted, "Listen up. Get back in your vehicles and move along. This is not a peaceful protest. Throwing cans is an assault on a deputy. You are obstructing us from our job. Get back into your vehicles. NOW!" I counted to three and didn't see anyone moving. So, I took a different approach. "Call for backup. Arrest everyone in sight for failure to follow the command of law enforcement, gathering without a permit, and obstruction." With my final words, the crowd started to disperse.

"Please don't tell me that this is foreshadowing," I said once I released the button on my mic.

"Fuck, it better not be," Carter said. "This can't all be because you're dating Ariel, can it?"

"Honestly, I have no fucking clue. The man has lost it. He has to realize that once this is over that his career is ruined."

"That's what scares me for you and her." Carter locked eyes with me as he strapped on his helmet. "People who have nothing to lose do stupid things."

Backup arrived and cleared a path for Carter and me to exit and head over to the courthouse with Piper following close behind. We still had three hours until the press conference, but media trucks were already lined up along both sides of the street. People, grown ass adults, had camped in tents overnight. The thought of citizens sleeping in this area of Orlando when I wouldn't even come there without my sidearm shocked the hell out of me.

I pulled up protest signs that had been staked in the ground but couldn't help admiring the creativity from some of the artists. Graphic drawings of a hangman's noose but with a police officer swinging and catch phrases with "Let Go Say-Low." Thank God for phonetics; I guess someone found it difficult to spell "Sello." I was just in awe of the ignorance of some people, what do they think would happen if he were let loose? He killed three cops, his girlfriend, and his two-year-old daughter. At what point does the public wake up and realize that some people are just downright evil?

"Let's find out whose signs these are and make a deal with them. If Sello is let loose, we will personally drive him to their home," Carter said.

People always support freeing criminals until we have to notify them that a sex offender has moved into their neighborhood. Or worse, knock on their door in the middle of the night to tell them that their loved one was never coming home again. Then they were outraged that law enforcement and the justice system didn't do their jobs. Funny how people only worried about someone else's rights when it wasn't hindering their own.

"I'd support an island with the survival of the fittest motto." Piper had held Vivian's hand during the funeral and saw first hand how this directly affected someone's life. "Let them build their own village so no one else gets hurt."

Following protocol, I unlatched my windshield from my bike but left it in place. When tempers were high in situations like this one, we had to expect the unexpected, and part of that was to be ready for riots. In angry mobs, our motorcycle windshields became part of our riot gear. I took sentry duty at the right front quadrant of the building, which placed me in perfect sight of the podium. Carter and Piper were stationed to my side.

By nine thirty, the place was a madhouse. There were nearly a thousand people gathered and divided. It was like going to a wedding, on the left was the groom's family, those that supported law enforcement. On the right was the bride's family, those that wanted Sello freed. Just before ten, Brandon marched down the center aisle and didn't bother trying to hide the glare he threw at me. He had a hard line set in his jaw, and if it hadn't been for that protruding vein on his forehead, I would have bought his I-got-this-in-the-bag cocky demeanor. Instead, he was fuming, and I took pleasure in the fact that I unnerved him.

Brandon was the kind of man who always wanted to prove he had more, done more, and knew more. So, when he was close to where the three of us stood, we all grinned, which made him falter on the last step.

"Deputy, I see you haven't made sergeant yet. Pity."

"Asshole, I see you haven't found a life yet. Pity," I replied.

Carter and Piper let out loud guffaws at my response.

"How's Ariel taking your unethical behavior, her trust is very fragile." Brandon scratched the side of his face, the bastard was fidgeting, he was nervous.

"Fine. She's more pissed that I have to go through it, though, I really enjoy all the support she's giving me."

Brandon turned to Carter. "Your sister is Stella, correct? She enjoys being friends with my Ariel?"

"Your Ariel?" Piper interrupted.

I felt someone's hands grab me before I decked this prick, and I turned to find Eli, a special agent with the Department of Justice, gripping my elbow.

He should have been more concerned with Carter, who was going to lose it. "Leave my sister the fuck alone."

"Believe me, I want nothing to do with your sister. I don't do white trash." With that last sentence, he looked at Piper, "Unless they are doing me." Brandon walked away without a backward glance.

"The man is losing it," I hissed.

"I just want to pull behind him once, just once. God, if you're listening, please. I know that he will find some sleezebag way to get out of the charges, but to see him in handcuffs for a little bit would be so fucking worth it," Piper prayed aloud.

"That motherfucker is up to something," Carter said as Brandon took his spot behind the podium and the crowd fell silent.

"Let me start off by thanking everyone for coming out today. I know how much stress our community has been under lately. Although I do not condone Mr. Sello's actions, I am also appalled by the way in which our law enforcement has decided to disrespect Mr. Sello's rights as a human being."

"What the fuck?" I said under my breath to Carter as I clenched my fists. "We've done nothing to Sello. Is he referring to the fact that we broke his arm tackling him?" I asked. "Jesus Christ, Sello had already killed five people. The man wasn't going down without a fight."

"All life is precious, and that is something we should never forget. After reviewing the information provided," Brandon said this last part and then went into a stare down with me. The cameras followed his line of sight, and once again, I was in the spotlight thanks to this asshole. "I have decided not to seek the death penalty in the case against Erskine Sello."

A roar ripped through the audience.

"What the fuck did he just say?" I asked.

"Oh my God," Piper stated.

"Dead man walking," Carter called. "You know some vigilante will take him out. Even though he treats us like shit and is constantly humiliating law enforcement, we are going to have to put our lives on the line to protect his sorry ass."

"I have no issue protecting people who treat us like garbage. Fuck, we do it every day. But Brandon is intentionally obstructing justice. I have a problem with that." Carter and Piper both nodded their agreement.

People cheered in support of Brandon's decision, and at the same time, a large group sneered.

"Get ready. All hell's gonna break loose." I warned as I spoke into my radio on the channel reserved for deputies at the courthouse today. Brandon returned his gaze to me then leaned back down into the microphone. "I understand your mixed emotions, believe me, I do. This has weighed heavily on me."

"Like hell it has." I was seething.

"But when you have deputies . . ." The fucker looked at me again. He didn't say my name, but he damn well made everyone think that he was referring to me. "Who care more about socializing than completing the necessary paperwork to prosecute criminals or would rather use their authority to intimidate instead of helping my office, then my hands are tied. I can only build a case based on the facts put in front of me. I'm sorry, deeply sorry for our community." Brandon waited a few seconds to give photographers ample time to capture my picture before he opened up the podium for questions.

"DA. Haley Loles here, with Channel Nine News, does your office intend to investigate the allegations of abuse of power against the deputy or deputies responsible for forcing your hand in this unprecedented announcement?"

"Yes. We have been in close contact with the Orange County Sheriff's Department and their Office of Internal Affairs," Brandon said as he smiled into the microphone.

"That is bullshit," Carter whispered from behind me. "You know damn well that IA won't discuss anything with the DA unless they believe criminal charges need to be filed. That pompous fucker."

"One more question, if I may?" Haley asked.

"Proceed." Brandon granted her as if he held all of the power.

"Is there anything that you suggest we as citizens do to help your office and protect ourselves from being victimized by those that we had wrongfully entrusted?"

"Absolutely, I encourage you to pick up your phones, go to your computers, contact the Orange County Sheriff's Office as well as the Attorney General in Tallahassee and tell them that you demand justice be done. Let them hear your complaints against these deputies," Brandon said with his open palm pointed toward where Piper, Carter, and I stood. "I'm sorry, but I am out of time." With those final words, Brandon walked off.

We couldn't do anything but stand there until someone made the first move. I could fucking feel the eyes of the camera focusing in on my badge to highlight my badge numbers and my last name. FUCK.

Brandon walked off and was back in the courthouse by ten thirty. For the next four hours, I directed traffic, arrested three women for throwing coffee on a protestor, a man for exposing himself, and issued six citations for people who refused to move their vehicles even though they were blocking traffic. If this shit occurred every day, I might seriously consider resigning. It wasn't until three o'clock that the crowd cleared enough so that the three of us could safely head back. When we got there, however, Captain Getty was waiting for us in his office along with Grace Wickham, the corporal from IA.

"Well, now, who's having fun?" Corporal Wickham asked. We just scowled. "Needless to say that the DA's office set you three up to be the scapegoats for every crazy caller out there. We've already had a call patched in from a resident in Miami, claiming that she saw the three of you beating up some kid for his lunch money. Christakos has been accused of being in the Panhandle earlier this morning, and Carter Lang, you were sighted in Tampa about twenty minutes ago. Deputy Dupont, it appears that your long lost husband saw you on the television, and he'd like you to phone home, perhaps bring some Reese's Pieces with you when you go."

"Where is the hidden camera? This must be a joke."

"Cool it, Christakos," Captain shook his head. "This isn't our first rodeo. IA knows what they're doing, and they can put two and two together," he explained. "But the three of you are on paid administrative leave effective immediately."

All three of us jumped up to argue, but Captain pushed us back into our seats.

"It is for your safety," Corporal Wickham explained. "What the DA did in a roundabout way was put a bounty on your heads. Christakos and Lang, you are on open motorcycles. DuPont every whacked out man in the state is looking to get his hands on you, consider this a paid vacation. We're doing this for safety, so stay armed."

"Wow, that's scary," Piper said.

"Yeah? That's why we're trying to keep you from being violated or worse," Grace's voice softened as she said that last part.

"How long?" I asked.

"Two weeks. For now. We'll have to see as things die down," Captain explained. "This was a safety decision, not a disciplinary one, understand the difference."

All three of us nodded.

"I need the three of you to fill out these papers and make a statement about any interactions you had with the DA's office on and off television over the last few weeks," Corporal Wickham said as she handed each of us a folder full of forms. "I need those back within forty-eight hours."

"Go home," Captain said as he looked at Piper and Carter.

Great. Just great. There had to be more.

Captain Getty closed his door after Piper, Carter, and Corporal Wickham left so that it was just the two of us.

"No shit. Why does the DA have a hard-on for you?"

Sitting in front of his desk, I propped my elbows on my knees and dropped my head into my hands. "I think he is scared that I am going to figure out that he's behind the attack on that woman from Mall at Millenia. He used to date her, but she left him. Brandon doesn't like when people don't bow at his feet." I sat up and met Captain Getty's stare. "Now, she's involved with an Orange County deputy and Fagan is freaked. He's freaked because she left him, because she's moved on, and because someone else has his toy."

"Do you have any evidence to support this theory?" Getty asked.

"No. But her apartment was broken into the other night and whoever broke in said they were only supposed to scare her. Ariel recognized the voice and those exact words. I think she had a flashback from her attack. It seems to all be linked. How he shows up at random times and random places, wherever she is. The other day he showed up outside some fabric store and just watched her."

Shaking my head at the scary thought of Brandon turning fatal attraction, which would put Ariel in even more danger, I decided he needed to be stopped.

"Is there anything you can get him on?" Captain Getty asked.

"No."

"Is there any violence, threats, anything that would help her obtain a restraining order?"

"No, not that I know of, but I'll ask."

"You seeing her tonight?"

I nodded.

"Is she safe?"

I nodded.

"You sure?" he clarified.

"She's living with me."

Captain Getty let out a long whistle. "Does Fagan know?"

"I'm assuming so. Ariel isn't at her apartment, and he knows that we're together." I waited a few seconds before I said, "I need a favor."

"Shit. Something tells me that I'm not going to like this," Captain announced. "What is it?"

"After her apartment was broken into, Piper found a bug planted in her couch cushions. Forensics has it. Can you see if they can expedite that? I've asked Eli with DOJ, but if you can help as well. I have a sinking suspicion that Brandon is tied to it."

"Will do. Now go home. Watch your back. And if you get so much as a whiff of that guy's cologne, you call me and report it." Captain opened his office door, and I was dismissed with at least two weeks of paid leave.

ARIEL

I dropped pieces of dough into the pot and covered it with the lid just as the rumble from Kayson's Harley pulled up the driveway. Today, I'd cleaned his house, paid my bills via my teeny tiny phone screen, and made dinner. But I still had been bored, all day.

"That looks delicious," Kayson said as he walked through the garage door.

"Chicken and dumplings."

"That's what smells good. I was talking about what looks good."

His words, sweet Mother of Jesus, what they did to me. How he knew just all the right things to say was beyond me. My legs went wobbly, I grabbed the counter to steady myself, chicken broth splashing everywhere. Kayson moved behind me.

"You okay?"

"Mm-hm." My words were more of a reassurance to me than they were to him.

I wanted to lean back and melt into him. Have someone to share all of my worries with, talk about my fears. I wanted someone to hold me. Fuck, I didn't want just any ole someone, I wanted him to be there for me the next day and the next. But that was a fairy tale, and even though we lived in the city of fairy tales, there was no such thing as

Prince Charming. Maybe Prince Charming for a moment, but not for a lifetime. Every time I saw Kayson smile, I imagined maybe there was a man who could be faithful and true to one woman all his life. And when he got that stupid sparkle in his eyes, I wished that woman would be me.

Looking up at Kayson, I took a hard swallow and decided that I better start talking and fast. But it was difficult forming a complete sentence, because I had a big ole frog in the back of my throat. "Watched the news today. I'm sorry. You know it's all my fault, right?" My words sounded more like a croak or that I'd been smoking three packs of cigarettes a day for the last thirty years.

"No, I don't know that." He placed a quick kiss on my temple. "Let me go change out of my uniform and lock up my gun, then we can talk."

This wasn't good. This couldn't be good. Had something happened that the news didn't cover? My heart sank. But then my brain told me to calm the fuck down. It couldn't have been that bad if he was still able to walk in and joke about how good I looked. God, when people said, "We need to talk," that was usually a bad thing. I mean, come on, he had to be tired of all the bullshit Brandon was causing, and if it weren't for me, Brandon would leave him alone.

I was losing my mind over this man. I'd forgotten everything I knew to be true about men. I was just like my mama. Lord, I'd heard enough neighbors say, "Apple doesn't fall far from the tree." I hated that saying. I fucking hated it. I needed to protect my heart, build walls like he accused me of having, he had the ability to break my heart. . ."

"Stop that," Kayson hollered from upstairs.

"Everything okay up there?" I asked back, my voice quivering.

"Everything's fine. Stop what you're doing Ariel."

"Setting the table?"

"No. I know you." I heard his feet on the stairs. "You're freaking out over what I want to talk about. Don't put walls up. I'm in." He moved in behind me and wrapped his arms around my waist. "I'm staying in."

175

He shoved his erection into my back. "And I'm never." Thrust. "Ever." Thrust. "Leaving," he whispered.

One by one, those fucking walls tumbled with each of his stupid pelvic thrusts. I was fucked. I was falling in love with this man. And just like that, in this kitchen, I'd forgotten the past thirteen years of convictions and jumped out of my fortress and into his protective arms.

I carried over two bowls of chicken and dumplings as Kayson refilled my glass and followed behind me with our drinks and the cornbread. We ate while he told me what happened behind the scenes. What the news didn't show and how Brandon's words truly affected him, Carter, and Piper.

"He's trying to get all of the kooks in the viewing area to file complaints about the three of us. He basically put us out as lambs to be slaughtered."

I was rubbing that damn spot on my forehead just between my eyebrows.

"The good news is that I have you home for two weeks." I smiled, but knew it was only half hearted. Kayson loved his job and was a natural protector. "None of this would have happened, to any of y'all had it not been for me. Well, if I'm being totally honest, it's Brandon's fault. I'm just the connecting thread."

"Stop." Kayson's hands reached for mine as he whispered, "Don't. Believe it or not, I'd go through all of this shit a million times to have you here."

My heart melted, my skin warmed, and my body turned to goo at his words.

"I've told you about my day. Tell me about yours. The house smells fabulous, looks awesome." He stood and pulled me to my feet before grabbing my waist and spinning me around.

"What are you doing?" I asked and giggled.

"Just making sure that your ass was still there. I happen to like it, and from the looks of this house, I was afraid that you worked your ass off."

"You're a hoot." Where did this man find these lines?

"Truthfully, I'm worried about my business. I need to get over to my apartment and get some sewing done or I'll never get my jobs finished. Bridezillas are not fun."

"How about this? What if tomorrow we go over to your apartment and grab whatever you need, sewing machine, fabric, you name it and bring it here. You can spread out wherever you want. Hell, you can have that extra room by my office for as long as you want it or until this shit settles down. Deal?"

If I said yes, my apartment would be practically empty, we were moving at Mach five, this man was moving me into his home room by room, first the bedroom, then the closet, then the bathroom, and now a sewing room. But I wanted this, I wanted to make him happy, if knowing I was safe made him happy, then I'd work from his house.

"Okay. But has anyone ever told you that you're like an armadillo?"

"Umm, can't say that I've been called that before."

"You know how armadillo's dig? They make holes and then build their own home right under people's houses. Nothing stops them; they just dig under the wall. That's you. You're like a friggin' armadillo."

Kayson's face glowed as he took my words for what they were, heartfelt. He'd dug his way under my walls and into my heart.

* * *

NINE O'CLOCK THE NEXT MORNING, Kayson and I were using the same boxes that he had used for my clothes to pack my sewing supplies. I never realized how much stuff I had until I filled all six boxes and still needed to grab a garbage bag for some extra fabric. I moved the lock on my Bernina sewing machine and folded it down into the hideaway style sewing table, Kayson carried it downstairs then came back up. By the time he returned, I had the drawers on both of the rolling carts taped shut and their wheels popped off. The last thing I needed was for one of those cubbies to go flying out of his truck and miles of pattern paper to litter the roads.

I separated my fabric by type of material, stacked them in boxes, and taped the box shut. One box I saved for all my needles, scissors, and cutting mats. God forbid I left any of my Gingher fabric scissors behind, some things were expensive to a seamstress, and some things were more valuable than gold. And then there were things that we were willing to do hard time over such as someone using fabric scissors to cut paper.

I grabbed the last box, which was the smallest, and filled it with all of my notes, and purchase orders. Taking one final look around, I broke out in a cold sweat when I truly took in the fact that my apartment was practically empty except for the kitchen. It seemed like forever since I had cooked or slept there, and with my entire office being moved over to Kayson's, it didn't seem as if I would be doing it again anytime soon. Slowly, okay not that slowly, this man had tunneled his way into my life. I felt his arms wrap around me.

"Is that all?" he asked.

"Think so."

"Let's go home."

Yep, his house was home. After closing the door behind me, I didn't bother to put tape on the frame since I wasn't staying there and took one last look behind me.

Kayson opened the passenger side door and helped me in, pressing the auto start on his key fob, he reached over and turned up the air before he secured my last two boxes into his truck. We held hands, his thumb rhythmically sweeping back and forth. This must be what people who take speed feel like, heart racing, endorphins pumping, and paranoia tickling their consciousness just a little. For me, it was fear that all of this was going to blow up in my face.

I had felt the absence of his hand before I took in the song that he had just turned up on the radio: "Kiss Me" by Ed Sheeran. His hand clutched mine, but he didn't weave our fingers. Instead, he encased my hand inside his and lightly squeezed. He felt it, this song, it had become our song.

When we pulled up to his house, I was shocked to see Damon and Pop there. Damon met me at the door before Kayson could get out of the truck and helped me down.

"*Kalimera koritsi*," Pop said.

I was slowly learning a few Greek words, "*Kalimera* Pop, Damon," I said as I gave each one a hug. "What are y'all doing here?"

"We have wood," Pop said.

Kayson and Damon both let out rip-roaring laughs, and Pop smacked both of them upside the head once he caught on to what they were laughing about.

"We brought supplies to make shelves. Kayson said that you were going to need shelves," Damon explained.

"Oh, you don't have to do that. There's no reason to mess up his room."

"Nonsense. You need it. We have it," Pop said and walked over to the truck with the Christakos Construction logo on it.

That was when I saw them, not shelves but cabinets. Ready-made cabinets in a gorgeous cream color that had a slightly weathered look to them. They were gorgeous. There were drawers, cabinets, shelves, and several different countertops—an entire workstation.

"What's with all of the countertops?" I asked.

"Well, we weren't sure what configuration you needed, so we brought several pieces to see if they'll fit. If these don't work, we can get something," Damon explained.

"It's up to Kayson, not me. This is Kayson's home. Whatever he wants."

All three men met me with the exact same dark, velvety chocolate eyes, but only one of them raised a single eyebrow—Kayson.

My stuff was left in Kayson's truck as the men carried the cabinets into what Kayson had called the "her office" during our tour. They moved thin cabinets next to wide cabinets, put blocks of wood down, set some cabinets on them, and then added drawers.

"If we use this countertop, it overhangs, but we can add two legs and then there's room for a garbage can," Pop added.

"She had all of this stuff spread out on her kitchen table, so she needs a large area to work," Kayson said.

"You noticed?" I asked.

He leaned over and gave me a quick kiss. "I notice everything. It's my job. But with you, I notice everything because you're so damn sexy."

"Get a room," Damon said, which earned him another slap on the back of the head from Pop.

"I'm going to go make you boys some lunch." I gave Kayson a quick kiss before pulling away.

Really, I just needed a bit of space. I found myself falling even more in love with this thoughtful, considerate man. In love? Fuck, I was in love with him. Holy shit, I was in love with Kayson. I thought if I ever admitted the "L" word that a weight would fall on me but instead it was the opposite. Like...well...being in love with Kayson was right.

In the kitchen, while I had elbow macaroni boiling, I shredded three different types of cheese. I mixed the cheese with milk, heavy cream, some white wine, and a pinch of garlic and onion into a bowl. Just before the macaroni was ready, I removed it from the water and tossed it into a pan. I covered it with the cheese concoction and popped it into the oven to bake. While it cooked, I toasted several pieces of bread and then smashed the hell out of them with some spices to make homemade breadcrumbs for the topping.

Ten minutes later, I pulled the pan out and set it on the stovetop so I could go get the boys. Just outside the door to what would soon be my sewing room, I stopped.

"How's she doing?" Pop asked between the sound of hammers thumping into the wall.

"Fine. I can't get it into her head that Brandon is dangerous."

"She's independent."

"Too fucking independent, she hates to ask for help. She feels guilty for everything going on."

"You've got two problems from what I can see," Pop said. "One, you haven't told her you're in love with her yet."

I squeezed my shirt right over where my heart was and listened to what Kayson said in return. The room was quiet.

Shit.

"Second, what if she doesn't feel the same way or can't? There are women that are too independent for a relationship. They can't accept the give and take. Can you walk away?"

My heart skipped and I wanted to walk in there and tell them that I could love Kayson. That I *did* love him. My feet carried me forward, and I pushed open the door.

"Hey, guys, ready to take a break and eat?" Okay. So, I really was a chicken shit, but at least I had a bright smile on my face.

The men scarfed down lunch. Then they obviously embraced the saying "kiss the cook," because Pop gave me a kiss on my cheek, Damon gave me a peck on the top of my head, and Kayson slid one arm around my waist and held my head with his other and dipped me while he kissed me long and deep before they returned to work.

By five o'clock, what was the sewing room was declared finished. Kayson stood outside, talking to his dad and brother, and I lay on the floor in the middle of the room tears streaming down my face. What was I doing, me, Ariel Louise Beaumont, world-class grade A men basher had fallen in love with Kayson Christakos. I had to figure out a way to show him.

I was still contemplating it when Kayson came back in and curled up next to me, his thumb wiping the tears from my cheeks.

"Sweet," he cooed.

"You call me that like it's my name." More tears fell.

"*Glika. Agape mou*," Kayson crooned into my ear.

I'd heard him speak a few Greek words to his parents but never to me.

I let my head fall to the side so I could see him, and for maybe the first time, he was just as vulnerable as I was.

"Why? Why are you so kind to me? Why me? What if you change your mind? What if I'm not enough? I've never been enough for anyone."

"It isn't that you aren't enough. It's that I'll never be able to get enough of you."

I held his face in my hands. "Why you? Mama and I weren't enough for my daddy. I wasn't enough for my mama or Brandon. What makes you so certain that I'll be enough for you?"

"Oh, my sweet, that was your father's loss. As far as Brandon? That doesn't count because he wasn't the right man for you." He gazed into my eyes. "*Glika. S'agapo.* To you, it seems like we've just met, but to me I've known you much, much longer." Then his lips were on mine, and it was a raw, hungry passion, a passion that wouldn't be doused until he was satisfied. His fingers slid through my hair and cupped the back of my head, holding me firm against him.

More than anything at that moment, I wanted to show him that I had figured out who the right man was for me. Moving my hands to his zipper, I let his cock out. I had this need to take charge. To please him, make him beg, go wild. Lowering my head to his rigid shaft, I took him in my mouth and rolled my tongue around the base of the head where he said was the most sensitive. Bobbing up and down, I sucked on him, and his groans told me that I was doing this right.

I squeezed the base of him, holding him upright while I worked my mouth up and down his length. His fingers wrapped around my hair, and I tilted my head up. He was watching me through lust-filled eyes. I wanted him to see all the words I'd been too afraid to say. I wanted him to see them so that I didn't have to verbalize them, I wasn't sure that I could.

He got my message loud and clear because I felt him, he thickened and his abs went taut.

"Oh God, Ariel. I'm gonna come."

I let out a deep moan of approval and kept sucking. I wanted it all, wanted every drop. I felt the first pulse, and I kept breathing, swallowing, as his shaft kept convulsing. I controlled this man, and it was a heady feeling. I released his cock with a *pop* and raised my head, wiping my mouth, and smiled at him. But he didn't say anything. I didn't think he could if he wanted to. He just lay there panting, trying to catch his breath.

"Did I do it right?" I asked

"Oh god. Any better, and you'd have to cover me before the coroner arrived."

He pulled me down next to him, and I rested my head on his shoulder.

"*Glika.*"

"What's that mean?" I asked.

"Sweet."

"What else did you say? You know, earlier?"

His breathing stilled for a second, and then I felt his heart speed up.

"Kayson, what did it mean? Please tell me."

Rolling onto his side, he leaned up on one elbow and tucked my hair behind my ear. "I told you I love you. You don't have to say anything. Don't let it scare you."

I shifted so I was tucked against the curve of his body.

"I'm scared," I told him as his arms wrapped tightly around me. "I think I'm in love with you, too. I'm just so scared that you'll hurt me."

His arms tightened. "I'm sure that over the years, we will hurt each other, that's normal. But not in the way you're thinking. Not in a way that can't be fixed."

He kissed me then, long and slow before scooping me into his arms and carrying me upstairs. For the next three hours, he worked at proving his love for me.

ARIEL

Saturday finally arrived, and the Iron Orchids were doing their first badass operation. Everly picked me up at Kayson's, and I piled into the back of her old Suburban. Everyone else was already inside, and we were headed to the gun range.

"Did you bring one?" Leo asked.

"Yes. Still don't know why I need it," I replied.

I was wearing my solid black boots and black jeans, but inside my purse was a long sleeve solid black shirt, per Stella's request. Piper and Stella were up to something, and that scared me. Stella was wild, but Piper was methodical.

"So, what's up?" I asked.

Just after I got into Everly's Suburban, Kayson sent me a text to tell me he and the guys were headed off to the monster truck show. It was his first time going out with the guys since he and I had met. But since I was with Piper, who promised to keep an eye on me, he agreed to go out.

I soon discovered that when Piper wasn't working, she also got bored, and that led to scary things. "I'm sick and tired of DW." The initials Stella made all of us use for Brandon, it stood for dick wad. "We need to bring him down. I'm tired of sitting on my ass and not working. No one has figured anything out yet, so we're going to try to figure out what he's up to." Piper cracked her knuckles.

"Preach it," Stella said as she raised her hands to the roof.

"First, we're going to do a little self-defense training, and then the psycho woman is taking over." Piper pointed to Stella.

"Hey, I resemble that remark." Stella opened a box, and we all peeked inside. Personally, I hoped to see kittens or puppies, but who was I kidding, this was Stella. It was full of tactical equipment, face paints, and stocking caps.

Piper rolled her eyes and pulled into the parking lot for the gun range. "We don't need any of that for the gun range. I'd like to spend time with all of you just teaching you the basics of a gun. This does not give you the right to carry one. It is just for emergency. All of you are constantly around guns, whether it is on me, or on one of the guys. If something ever happens, I want to know that you could at least fire the weapon if you got your hands on one to protect yourself."

"This is the sheriff's department gun range. The academy cadets were here today, so I asked the instructors if they would stay for just a little bit and help," Piper explained.

The instructors introduced themselves and then handed each of us a 9mm gun. Since this was defensive training, we were taught using the type of gun we were most likely to come in contact with, which made sense.

We first had to learn about proper handling of the gun, how ammunition fired, and how to load, unload, and secure a weapon before we were ever suited up with ear and eye protection.

By eight thirty, it was dark, and our arms were sore. We called it a night, and all of us agreed that we wanted to come to the range again. Once we climbed back into the Everly's Suburban, we changed into our black shirts, and then Stella took charge. She reached into the box and handed each of us a stocking cap.

"Your red hair is like a beacon."

"So says the blonde," I retorted.

Everly obviously knew where we were headed because she pulled onto the Greenbelt and headed west.

The first place we stopped was Capital Grille, one of Brandon's favorite hangouts because of the women that liked to frequent there. Stella handed each of us a walkie-talkie.

"Spread out. Someone make sure to walk through where valet park the cars, let us know if you see his gray Aston Martin convertible or him. Got your phones? Take pictures of anyone he's with. Go. Go. Go."

She instructed like we were GI Jane. But after twenty minutes, we decided it was a no-go and piled back into the Suburban. Once again, Everly and Stella were sharing a brain because she headed for Brandon's Country Club.

"Y'all, am I the only one who's concerned about six grown women walking through a posh neighborhood dressed all in black? I mean, we don't look suspicious or anything?"

"Stop being such a worry wart." Stella smacked the back of my head. "I already checked, this is unincorporated Orlando, which means that it is Orange County not OCSO."

"So? We still look like a bunch of hoodlums."

"Yes, but if we get caught we have Piper." Stella grabbed Piper's hand and held it up like she was the winner in a boxing match.

Unfortunately, because of the golf course, the gates, and the security patrol, we had to park three blocks away, only to discover that we couldn't get close enough to see anything even with Stella's tactical binoculars. The exact same binoculars I was staring through when we got busted by club security.

"I'm so sorry." Stella sobbed and leaned over throwing her head against the rent-a-cop's shoulder. "I think my husband is having an affair so we were just trying to see if he walks in with anyone." She fucking patted his chest and cried on demand until the guard asked us to kindly leave, which we did, in a hurry.

Piling back into the Suburban, Everly headed into Bay Hill.

"Tell me you know the code, please?" Stella, who was no longer crying, said.

"I think so," I said.

Everly pulled up to the resident's keypad, and I entered the code Brandon had told me months ago. When the gates opened, I clapped my hands with relief. Whatever we were doing wasn't good, and the last thing I want to do was check in with the security guard or get caught on camera.

"There are cameras. Everly's license plate will show up," I knew my eyes were wide with panic, but Stella waved the aforementioned Florida tag in my face.

"No it won't. Already took care of that."

"Have we been driving the whole time without a tag?"

"Well, not the whole time. Just since we left the country club."

"You're crazy." I laughed and shook my head in disbelief. She really was a bit crazy.

Stella grabbed two pay-as-you-go phones from the box, dialed a number with one, and the other one rang.

"Here answer this one," she said as she handed me the second phone.

"Hellooo?" I answered and realized that the call was coming in on FaceTime.

"Perfect. They're connected. I put three thousand minutes on each phone. We should be able to figure out what he's doing over the next few days. Where is DW's house?"

I gave Everly the directions, taking the route to bypass his parents' home and pointed out his house as we got close.

"Stay here." Stella reached up and turned off the dome light before opening the truck door and getting out. "Don't hang up."

"Wouldn't dream of it."

I watched as she maneuvered her way over to Brandon's home. He had a large wrought iron gate at the edge of his property, which was surrounded by hedges. I wasn't sure what she had planned. But unless he let her in, she had a remote, or she knew the code, those suckers weren't budging. The screen on the other phone bobbed along until leaves and bramble covered the picture. Then the phone turned and faced Brandon's house. I wasn't sure why we were looking at Brandon's garage and driveway, but that was where she focused the screen.

Stella came back and took the phone I was holding. From her box of tricks, she pulled out cables and what appeared to be a small black box, no joke. We had a fucking black box.

"Okay, if he finds the phone it isn't registered to a real person, and the number it dialed also isn't registered to a real person. So we are in the clear. I hooked up a recorder to the phone so we don't have to stare at the damn screen the entire time." Stella was rambling.

"Get to the point!" I nearly shouted.

"Wait," she snapped. She pulled out a roll of black electrical tape and covered the camera on the phone. Right swiping the screen, she found the mute button and pressed that.

"Has anyone ever told you that you could be scary?" I asked.

"Yep, my last few boyfriends," she replied. "Any who, now we will know when he leaves and when he gets home. I also want to know if he has any visitors."

"You think that he is already home for the night?" Vivian asked

"No clue," I said.

We were fixated on the phone screen as Everly drove us back and pulled into Sixes parking lot to drop off Vivian.

She got out and headed inside while we sat talking about what our next move was and how we could try to catch Brandon. We were so focused on our plan that we didn't notice the shadows that flashed across the windows until someone was tapping on the window. As one, we all let out a scream, proving we weren't as calm as we all pretended to be. Thankfully, it was just Carter, and I let out a sigh. I opened the backseat passenger door to get out and talk with him, but the door stopped mid-swing. I looked up to see an angry Kayson dressed in jeans and a perfectly fitted T-shirt. He looked kind of yummy when he was all puffed up like that.

"Would you care to tell me what the hell you're up to?"

I shook my head, trying not to look at Stella, who was trying to tuck all our evidence from tonight's escapades back into the box, but before she could finish, he turned on his flashlight and lit up the floorboard then swept it up and down my clothing, then to Stella's, and Leo's.

"Fuck. His damn fucking MagLite," I said between clenched teeth with a false smile spread across my face.

"What the fuck are all of you up to?" He moved the light so it wasn't directly in our eyes. "Care to tell me why you all look like Catwoman?"

"Not particularly," I said. "You're out of the monster truck show early, aren't you?"

Aiden a motorcycle deputy that I didn't know very well, asked, "Care to tell us why you traded in your Harley gear for Al's Army Supply?"

I let out a snort when Everly gave him the middle finger as our answer.

Kayson held out his hand, as if to escort me inside. Fuck. "Come, ladies." He opened the Suburban's door and the other guys followed his lead.

With his hand at my back, he led me into Sixes and then to our usual table. When we passed the badge bunnies, who I had finally learned to ignore, Gigi made a typical ass out of herself.

"Kayson, you get more gorgeous by the day."

I squeezed Kayson's hand and laughed. Some women were so desperate. Apparently, he agreed with my silent message, because he bent down and nibbled on my ear, visibly to prove a point to Gigi and me that he wasn't interested. But the bitch didn't shut up. Hell, she didn't even stay at her table, she followed us.

"Gigi, where are your friends? You might want to join them, because I don't see any at our table," Stella said, jumping to my defense.

"Actually, I just came over to speak with Ariel."

"I don't know you. I'm not sure what you'd want to talk to me about. So, let's don't and say we did."

"I just wanted to tell you that I met your boyfriend today. He's nice and super cute," Gigi said to me but kept her eyes on Kayson.

"What the hell are you playing at?"

"Nothing. I just thought you'd like to know that your boyfriend came by."

"Stop the bullshit," Kayson interrupted her. "You know damn well that Ariel and I are a couple. For Christ's sake, we're living together."

Gigi's face fell for a minute before it turned cold.

"Well, she isn't genuinely living with you, is she? She's just staying with you since someone broke into her apartment?"

"What do you know about her apartment?" Carter asked.

"Oh please, everyone knows," Gigi offered up as an excuse.

"That's it, bitch, let's go." Leo jumped in as she pushed up her sleeves. "I don't think anyone at this table would notice if I knocked the shit out of you."

"That's a lot of shit." Stella looked up and down Gigi's long lean body. "And those look like new shoes." She pointed to Leo's boots.

"Stop. All of you!" I shouted. "Gigi, I have no clue what the hell you are talking about. When you say boyfriend, I'm assuming you don't mean Kayson. Was the man about Stella's height with dirty blond hair?"

"Yep, that's the one. You know, the sharp dresser that's been on television a lot lately."

"Well, he isn't my boyfriend. So, if you see him again, you are welcome to exchange your love for the badge for a briefcase. Now that we have that settled, if you'd excuse us, I want to enjoy the evening with my friends." I turned my back to her and took a seat just as Vivian stormed toward Gigi.

"That's it, I've warned you before not to bother my customers with your attitude or your desire to go home with a badge or you'd be out of here. Get out, and don't let me see you back here until you've learned how to behave. Kayson, Carter, please escort her out."

"Shit. It's Saturday. Trash doesn't get picked up until Tuesday," Stella said wiping off her hands. "I guess she'll just have to stay out back collecting flies. Make sure to keep your legs closed, okay?"

"How do you come up with this crap so fast?" I asked Stella. "I can't think of those lines until hours later."

"Ariel, you're perfect just way you are," Kayson said as he and Carter returned to the table without Gigi.

His words were met with gag noises from the guys and *"ahhhs"* from the women.

"I'm not sure that I could handle Stella or her mouth. I think she needs a truck driver or maybe a Navy Seal, someone who's gone on missions for a long time, a long, long, long time."

Stella interrupted Kayson's laughter. "Admit it. You love me like a sister."

"Maybe like a sister that I couldn't drown, but it wasn't for lack of trying." He leaned over and gave Stella a squeeze before wrapping his arm around me.

"What can I get you?" a waitress asked, interrupting my thoughts about how delicious Kayson smelled.

"Yuengling," Kayson ordered.

"Jack and diet, please."

As soon as the server walked off, the girls and I built a wall of menus and hid behind them.

"At least we know where Brandon was tonight since he wasn't anywhere we searched," Stella whispered but her voice was drowned out by Carters.

"You do realize that making a wall of menus so that you can mouth things to each other isn't conspicuous at all, right?"

"Shut the hell up," Stella snapped.

The server returned with our drinks and everyone ordered an appetizer. This was typical of our group. On nights when we went out, no one ordered real meals, we each ordered a couple of appetizers, and they were placed in the middle of the table so we could all graze.

"Want to tell us what you were up to tonight, or should we wait until you come up with one story as to why all of you are in black." Kayson took a sip of his beer. "You ladies look like you're auditioning for the Matrix."

I was halfway through my first drink, hiding behind the wall of menus trying to come up with a plausible story to tell the guys when I wondered why was it that reflections always appeared distorted when looking through glass. At certain angles, I appeared thin, some I seemed fat, and others I was tall, or short. I was swirling my glass when I realized that my fingers were stubby, I bet a Tyrannosaurus had stubby fingers like these to go with his stubby arms.

I dropped my menu and looked over at Kayson, who was talking to Carter, but I couldn't hear anything past the buzzing in my ears. Turning my head was what I imagined it would feel like when you sloshed through quicksand: slow and sluggish. Stella was laughing. I smiled, her laugh always made me laugh. She had the best laugh, it was contagious, but I couldn't feel my lips. I tugged on them, twisted them, but nothing. My lips were attached, but I couldn't feel them.

I needed to go to the restroom, like right that moment. I stood. My movements fast and slow and clumsy all at the same time. My chair fell backward, and my knees gave out, sending me toppling to the floor.

KAYSON

"What the fuck?" Stella shouted. "Ariel, are you all right?"

I turned just as Ariel started to fall. It took me a split second to get to her, but I was too late, she had already hit the floor. I lifted her and sat her in my seat, running my hands over her arms and legs, checking over every inch. Everly and Stella elbowed me out of the way and took over. Had it been anyone else, I wouldn't have let her go. They were a first responder and a registered nurse, so I trusted them.

"She wouldn't sleep with you, so you drugged her?"

I turned to face Brandon, and my vision bled to crimson. What the fuck.

"Did you say drugged?" I asked.

I saw his face change a shade before he steeled his shoulders and put his mask back on. Drugged. That motherfucker drugged her. How else would he know what was wrong with her before we did? Not to mention he had never set foot in Sixes before. Yet, he was conveniently there the same time that Ariel was drugged. It clicked. He was fucking stalking her. This crazy motherfucker was following her and had just upped his game in desperation.

"I don't have time for you. Carter can handle this and your fucked-up, psychotic behavior, I need to take care of Ariel."

"Watch yourself, Deputy. I think you're in enough hot water as it is, don't you?" Brandon asked, trying to bait me. "Did she refuse to have sex with you in exchange for not getting a ticket?"

"I'd advise you to be quiet. At this point, anything you say or do could be considered obstruction of justice," Aiden said as he stepped between Brandon and me. "You and Carter need to stay out of this, both of you are on administrative leave. I'll handle it."

Stella was holding a bottle of water to Ariel's lips, but it didn't look like Ariel was drinking anything. From the corner of my eye, I saw Brandon stand to move toward Ariel. Aiden shifted with him, blocking his advance.

"Don't fucking move," Aiden ground out.

"Deputy. I think that I know the law better than you. Unless you have probable cause to detain me, then I believe that we're done. Oh wait, except for the fact that he is probable cause," Brandon said, pointing to me.

"Excuse me?" I asked.

"You heard me. I want to know why you drugged my girlfriend?" Brandon asked.

This time, Carter and Aiden moved swiftly to block me. This man was delusional. I was going to take his ass out.

"Sit your ass down, Fagan. First, she is not your girlfriend. Second, I have a strange feeling that you are behind her attacks and that Ariel is afraid of you—"

"Has she filed a restraining order against me?" Brandon was trying to blow smoke, redirect attention away from him. Too bad for him, everyone knew his game. "If someone was in fear, wouldn't that be their first line of action? Wouldn't that be your first suggestion?"

"Shut up and let me finish," I demanded. "Third, I was with Ariel and with all of these witnesses the entire time. Where were you? By the way, why are you here? This isn't your normal place."

"Watch your tone. Don't you think that your fellow deputies have made big enough asses of themselves lately without your help?" Brandon paused and his lips twisted into a smirk. "Oh wait, all of the unethical, atrocious behavior has been by you and your cohorts."

"Get the fuck out of my bar and never come back!" Vivian shouted, enunciating each word as tears rolled down her face. "You defended that man, that animal that killed my husband. Get out of here."

I wrapped Vivian into my arms and turned my back on Brandon to shield her.

"Vivian, take a deep breath. It's going to be okay. We'll get him out of here, but you need to let Aiden handle it."

"I want him out of here now." The tears were still flowing freely but her eyes were fierce.

"And we will. I promise." I dropped my voice so it was a whisper. "Listen. I need you to start closing out tabs and getting people out of here. I also need all the video footage from the last six hours."

She took a deep breath and pulled out of my arms. "Okay. But get him the hell out of my bar, Kayson. I don't ever want to see him in here again."

"We will."

I watched her storm to the bar, say something to the bartender, and then disappear into the back. Once I was sure she wasn't going to come back with a baseball bat, I rounded on Brandon, who was still standing there with his smug sense of entitlement.

"I've got things to do. You do not have reason to Terry stop me, and if you want to talk more, you know where to find me." His eyes cut to me. "Perhaps your friends should start watching their backs when you're around," Brandon said and walked out of the bar.

CARTER CHASED after him to give him the no trespass warning, and I was still amazed by the audacity of that man. How dare he insinuate that I would do anything to my friends, let alone anyone else.

When Carter came back inside, he was shaking his head. I would get the story later. He went over to talk with the bartender while Aiden spoke to our waitress, and I walked over to check on Ariel. She was out of it, she'd only had one drink but she was passed out as if she'd been on a drinking bender.

"I'm going to take her to ORMC and get her on a saline drip," Everly said as she positioned her shoulder under Ariel's arm.

"Let me carry her out to your car. I will come by Stella's when this mess is all cleaned up. My phone is on me, call me if you learn anything, please." I hated leaving her, but I knew she was in the capable hands of Everly and Stella. I fastened Ariel into Everly's Suburban, before heading back into Sixes.

In Vivian's office where we went through the video from today. "There. Stop and rewind forty-five seconds."

Vivian backed up the video and replayed it in slow motion. I watched as our waitress walked up to the bar and told Danny, the bartender, our drink order. Something she said caught a man's attention.

"She must have said the order was for your table, and he was listening for Ariel's drink. We all know she always orders a Jack and diet."

The man watched Danny pour my beer and then fix Ariel's Jack and diet. When the drinks were set on a tray on the bar, the man's fingers lightly skimmed the tray and turned it slowly. Once Ariel's drink was near him, he dropped something into it and moved away from the bar. Right before he walked out, he shot a look over his shoulder. Fuck. Where was he looking? I leaned closer to the screen to see if I could see anyone else, but nothing. Then the man left.

"Have you ever seen him before?" I asked Vivian.

"Never."

We asked the staff at Sixes if they had ever seen that man before, and no one recognized him. Vivian made a copy of the video for me, and I looked through the earlier feed as well. Brandon came in around four o'clock, talked with Gigi, and then left. Interesting, but not what I was looking for. The man that drugged Ariel's drink came in around six o'clock and sat in a far corner. When Ariel and I came in, he moved to the bar. Obviously, he'd been waiting for us. Brandon came in a few minutes after the man left and stood by the door. He never took a seat.

Walking back out to the main bar area "You got this?" I asked Aiden when he nodded I strode for the door.

"Hey, before you go, I want to talk to you about what Brandon said," Carter called out to my back, and I spun.

"When you followed him outside?" I asked.

"Yeah. He asked how we were going to restrain you once he and Ariel were married. And then he proceeded to enter into some fucked-up fairy world where he saw Ariel waiting for him to come home from work every night. He talked about her red hair and red lips, and then went on to tell me that she was all his. He kept reiterating that. He said that he would win because he always wins. Man, I think that dude has seriously lost it. Something isn't right up there." Carter circled his finger next to his temple.

"Thanks for the heads up." I shook his hand and turned back to the door. After I was on the way to Stella's, I picked up my cell phone and called my captain.

"Do you know what time it is?" Captain Getty answered.

"I do, sir, and I'm sorry. We had a little incident tonight at Sixes with Fagan."

I finished filling him in on the details just as I pulled into Stella's driveway. Moving the passenger seat all the way back and into a reclining position before I got out figuring that Ariel would need to sleep on the way home even though it was only a fifteen-minute drive. Everly answered the door, she looked exhausted and worn out.

"How is she?"

"We stopped by the ER, and they gave her an IV and ran her blood work for us."

"Any clue what it was?"

"Yep." Everly handed me a piece of paper from the hospital.

"What's this?"

"It's the toxicology report."

"Shit, am I reading this right? Rohypnol? Some motherfucker gave Ariel roofies?"

"Yep. Good thing is we've flushed her system and she's safe," Everly said as always, trying to find the good side to everything. "You know anyone that would want to have sex with Ariel and if they didn't succeed, leave you to hang for this crime?"

"Brandon." We both said at the same time.

I headed over to the couch, scooped Ariel into my arms, and headed for the door. Stella and Everly followed me out and opened my truck door so that I could put Ariel in the seat. The emotions in me were like a jigsaw puzzle; nothing seemed to be fitting together at the moment. I was angry, then worried, then pissed at myself, then concerned for Ariel, and then livid. The only constant emotion was my love for her.

"Thank you for taking care of her."

Everly nodded as Stella ran her hand over Ariel's hair. "Just promise me you will get that fucker. I can't even think about what would have happened if we weren't all there."

I couldn't think about that. I just couldn't. So, I promised to call her if anything else happened.

When we got home, I tucked her into bed and then ran downstairs and grabbed her a glass of water. When I crawled into bed and pulled her into my arms, her eyes fluttered open.

"You rescued me," she whispered.

"My sweet, haven't you figured that out yet? I'll always rescue you."

"I love you." Those were her last words before I heard the gentle whistling sound that she made while she slept. She loved me.

ARIEL

It took a total four days for me to start feeling like my old self. I'd slept through the first two days just getting over the funk that had seeped into my body and then the next two days were more of being a couch potato where I was groggy and did nothing except brush my teeth and eat. By the end of the week, I was on edge, Kayson had cabin fever, and I didn't have time to entertain him. I had work to do, orders to catch up on, and no time to go anywhere. Not to mention that I had just found out there was a law enforcement ball coming up, and they were currently accepting bid proposals for an event planner. I had been dying to try to find a way to break into the business and didn't want to blow this opportunity. I still needed to come up with an original idea, prepare the budget, and get it over to the committee before the deadline.

My phone rang at the same moment Kayson walked into my sewing room. I held a finger to signal one moment while I answered the phone.

"Hello?"

"Yo. Get dressed. We will pick you up at four. Piper's got a few deputies who've agreed to stay at the range and help us with our shooting practice." Stella asked, but I didn't respond. "Did you hear me? Be ready at four."

"Yes, I heard you. I didn't know that you were asking. I thought you were telling me."

"Bite me. *Ciao.*"

I hung up and looked over to Kayson. "That was Stella, it seems that Piper . . ."

"I heard. Stella talks kind of loud." The corner of his mouth lifted into a grin. "Go have fun. I was coming to tell you that Getty called, and I'm returning to work on Monday. It seems as if Brandon has gone on a sudden vacation."

"Y'all don't actually believe that, do ya?"

"Not for one second. We have deputies watching his home and his office." Kayson wrapped his arms over my shoulders and rested his chin on my head. "Carter and I are heading up to Sixes. Why don't you have the girls drop you off there and we can head home together."

"Sounds good," I agreed and returned to sewing.

At four o'clock, Kayson and I were standing in his driveway. His hands were on my waist and I was promising him for the fifth time that no, we aren't doing any Catwoman stuff.

It was only four of us tonight, Leo, Stella, Piper and myself. Everly was working, and after last week's drug incident, Vivian wanted to stay at Sixes.

Instead of taking us straight to the range like I'd expected, Piper and Finn, an officer from SWAT, lead us to a building with wall to wall mats.

"Before we practice our aim, we are going to try a few grappling techniques. These"—Piper held up two, nine millimeter handguns —"are fake guns, but are weighted as if they are loaded. I will hand you one, then I'll try to take it away from you, do not let me take it away from you."

That was how our night began–grappling, but then we moved on to things like how to use hand-to-hand combat in close situations to redirect the line of fire. With each lesson, I felt more like the badass wannabe that I had imagined when I watched my first episode of *Sons of Anarchy* than I did the helpless woman I'd somehow turned into.

By seven o'clock, my arms ached, every muscle in my body was tired, and all I wanted was a long hot bubble bath. Okay, I wasn't as badass as I thought.

"Can y'all drop me off at Sixes. Kayson is going to take me home."

"I'm starved." Stella patted her stomach. "I can freeload a meal off him as well."

Piper pulled out of the gun range and headed toward downtown.

Deciding that we needed to talk about the big ol' pink elephant in the room, well car, "Any other ideas on how to track Brandon? I hate that the rain ruined your phone contraption, it was a brilliant idea."

"Fuck no. I've been racking my brain. I can't think of anything without putting you in danger," Stella slammed her hands against the roof of Piper's car. "I still have over twenty-hours of recording, but nada, nothing interesting on a single second. No weird visitors, no coming or going at strange hours, zip. I think he knows he's being watched."

"It really was ingenious," Leo patted Stella's head as if she were dog.

"I think it is time for us to back off. Kayson's been working nonstop on this case even while on leave. He is going to figure out the connection." Piper assured me. "Until then just stay by him or with one of us." She reached into her purse. "And I didn't give this to you, technically you're supposed to have a concealed carry even for pepper spray but no one will say a word if it's used in defense."

When we pulled into Sixes and traipsed into the bar, a warm feeling of comfort washed over me. This was my tribe, my family. I had finally found them, but what I didn't find or rather see was Kayson.

"Hey, Carter? Where's Kayson?"

"Women, you can't trust 'em. One minute they're all over you and telling you they love you, and the next minute . . ." Carter finished a bottle of Yuengling and set the empty beer down on the edge of the table. "They're gone. Just like that." He tried to snap his fingers. "No word. No goodbye. Poof," he said as he held a closed hand in front of my face then opened it as if mimicking something evaporating.

I looked at Stella and asked, "What the fuck?"

"Holy fuck, he's drunk. I've never seen him drunk." Stella gave me a quizzical look as I scanned the room for Kayson.

"Hold on, I'll go see if his truck is in the parking lot." Leo got up and headed out the door.

"Poof." Carter gave me that strange hand gesture again and continued to stare at his beer.

"Carter, has Kayson been here?" I tried getting at least that much information from him.

"He's my best friend." Carter's words totally slurred. "Love. Fucking love that man. But women, don't ever give them your heart, take it from me . . ." Carter held his hand out and made that poof gesture again.

"Truck is not out there," Leo reported as she came back in. "I'm going to go ask Vivian."

I pulled out my phone and scrolled through to find his name and pressed call. It only rang once when a woman answered.

"Hello?" Her sultry voice low and out of breath, and a fist wrapped around my heart and squeezed.

"Who is this?" Stella leaned in to hear who was on the other line.

"I'm sorry, but can you call back later, Kayson's kind of busy right now." I looked at Stella and she mouthed the word, "Gigi" and I nodded.

"Gigi why do you have Kayson's phone?"

"Oh shit, Ariel? You weren't supposed to know, I shouldn't have answered."

Click.

I looked at Stella, "What the fuck."

"Not supposed to know what? Why is Gigi answering Kayson's phone?"

Carter let out a low laugh, "Don't worry, she's wasting her time. Kayson isn't interested in her. Gigi has been trying to get into his pants for years, but she wants a ring to go with that badge, and it ain't happening. Kayson won't marry them. They're just pussy until he tires of them, then poof."

"Will you stop with the mother fucking poof?" Stella grabbed her brother's hand and held it to keep him from making that stupid gesture. "What do you know about Kayson and Gigi?"

"I'm saying that Gigi's wasting her time with him. He won't marry her. He loves this one." Carter tossed a half-wave half-point at me.

"Can someone bring me a bottle of water?" Vivian ordered her crew.

"Not that it matters. He's Greek. He has to marry a Greek woman. Christine has it all planned out. You know how close that family is, he wouldn't go against her. Fuck, I think he'd have to turn his back on them or something. All four of the boys have to marry in their family's church; their mother has had the whole thing planned out since the day they were christened there. Gigi isn't Greek. She isn't marriage material. So, she'll just go . . ." He tried to raise his hand, but Stella held it firmly down on the table.

I turned and looked at my friends, completely confused.

Kayson had never said anything to me about any of this. His parents liked me, they approved of me, but from what Carter was saying, they probably didn't approve of me for their son in the long run. I thought back to when I first met his family and all of the photos lining the wall. They were all photos of beautiful sun-kissed olive toned Greeks, and I most certainly wasn't Greek.

Carter's drunk diarrhea of the mouth continued, "He just uses women. Not that I'd blame him. I've used her a few times. I'm not looking for anything serious, so I don't care. But he uses them until he finds a woman he can marry. That's what Kayson wants. Not me, I gave my heart away once, and the bitch never gave it back."

Carter kept talking, and my head kept spinning, faster and faster with each word.

I reached over and grabbed Stella's arm. "I'll be back, going to the restroom."

"Okay, let me come with you." She started to stand.

"No. Stay. I want a few moments." I held out my hand, trying to find balance. "Please. Let me try to take everything in. You see if you can't figure out what the fuck your brother is talking about, okay?"

Stella nodded. "If you aren't back here in five, I'm coming in."

I walked into the bathroom and rested my hands on either side of the sink and closed my eyes. I was happy, ten minutes ago I was fucking happy, and now I was my fucking Mama all over again. Pulling out my phone, I dialed Kayson's number once again and listened when it connected, but no one answered.

I heard background noise, was that a television? Then I heard the distinct sound of heavy breathing, sex-sounding heavy breathing, moaning, heavy-fucking-breathing.

Reaching in my pocket, I ensured my keys were there then yanked the door open and fled to the main area of the restaurant to beg Piper to take me to my apartment. I stopped when I overheard Leo reading from her phone.

"There are three obstacles that some couples may find insurmountable. A Greek must be married in the Orthodox church. Ceremonies must be performed by the priest. The bride and groom must be Eastern Orthodox."

That wasn't me. I was raised Baptist, Southern Baptist to be exact. The air in the room seemed to be sucked out by a vacuum, and I took short shallow breaths just to stay conscious .

"How—" Deep breath. "How could I be so stupid?" Without anyone seeing me, I turned and fled out the back door of Sixes, leaned over, and threw up my nonexistent dinner. Once I could stand straight again, I walked to the corner and opened my phone to the Lyft app so I could call for a car. Walking three blocks away from Sixes and away from the sympathy that I was sure to see in everyone's faces. I waited for the trademarked pink mustache car to pick me up and take me back to my apartment, my empty, bare, naked, fucking apartment.

By the time I hit the stairs to my apartment building, I was crying and had the fucking hiccups, which were racking my body. I could barely see through the tears to unlock my door, but I managed.

I unlocked my apartment door and dropped my keys when a vice like grip yanked my arm and pulled me inside. At the sound of my door shutting behind me and the gentle click followed by the clunk from the heavy deadbolt turning to lock I realized that I was fucked.

"It's about time you return home. Are you tired of playing the little slut?" Brandon's words were cold.

KAYSON

I should have known that tonight was going to be fucked up. From the moment I walked into Sixes and found Carter drunk doing some stupid "poof" hand gesture, I should have known. I sat there listening to him rant about I have no idea what and watching him pound beers. He was a fucking mess, and I had no idea why.

When my phone rang, I was relieved. Ariel would give me an excuse to leave. I fished my phone from my pocket, and my eyebrows pinched together. It wasn't Ariel.

"Deputy Christakos."

"Kayson, I need you to come into the station. We have Genevieve Christell LaRoux in interrogation. I know that you're on leave, but some of the shit she is saying, I think you should hear. It's about Brandon Fagan. Once she realizes that she's in deep shit, she'll lawyer up. I want to try and keep her talking as long as she is willing, it might help your case and bring the DA down."

"Shit. Okay. I'll be right in." I disconnected and dialed Ariel's phone but it went straight to voice mail. Of course, she was with her girls. When her recorded voice stopped talking, I left my message "Hey, sweet, we had a major breakthrough in the case against Brandon. I'm running into the station, Gigi is there and wants to talk to me. I will hurry back to Sixes, let Carter entertain you, he's on his way to one hell of a hangover. Love you."

I found Gigi and Callum, one of the most respected detectives on the force, in an interrogation room. They both turned to me as I walked in, and I sat my stuff down, ready to take notes.

"Kayson, thanks for joining us. Can I have a word with you before we begin?"

"Sure." I stood, and we headed to the office across the hallway.

"It appears, Brandon convinced her that he could help her win your heart, and in exchange, he wanted her to help him get Ariel away from you. Gigi *claims* that she was so desperate for your attention that she bought every word he said and agreed to help him."

"If she told you all of this then why did I need to come in? Obviously, she's willing to talk."

"She says there's more but will only tell you."

"Okay. Let's go find out what she has to say."

I made a move and felt Callum's arm on my shoulder. "Keep your cool, if you lose it then I'll ask you to leave."

I gave a nod and pulled the door open and took a seat across from Gigi.

"I'm sorry, Kayson, I really am. It was me and a few of the other girls that made the phone calls to internal affairs. Brandon promised that you wouldn't get in trouble. He said that he'd make sure to sweep it all under the rug."

"Can you tell us if you know this man?" Callum pulled out a photo from a folder of the guy that drugged Ariel's drink. "Look closely?"

"I've seen him before, you know at Sixes, but I don't personally know him. He was there the night Vivian made me leave."

"Did you notice who he was talking to?" Callum asked as he flipped to a clean sheet in his notebook.

"Well, um, he met with, well . . . well, he met with Brandon, but that wasn't at Sixes. That was during lunch."

"How do you know this?"

I was interested in this question because it seemed as if Brandon wasn't at work a lot anymore since he had time to follow Ariel around town.

Gigi's face turned beet red.

"Miss LaRoux, I think it's a little late to play innocent schoolgirl. How do you know that Brandon and this man met earlier in the day?" Callum waved the photo in front of her face.

"He came to Brandon's house, okay? Brandon and I are just friends."

"Friends with benefits?"

"Sometimes. We took care of each other's needs while we waited for the two of them." She pointed at me, but if she was going to say anything else, she didn't because people started moving, hustling outside the window of the room, then Finn and Porter, two guys from SWAT opened the door to our room.

"We have a possible kidnapping from Sixes," Porter said and my heart sank. "Kayson, I'm sorry, Ariel is missing."

I wrapped my hands on the edge of the table, my knuckles turning white from lack of blood because I was gripping so tightly and I stared into Gigi's eyes. "Where the fuck is she?"

"I don't know? How would I know, I've been here with you the whole time?" The tiny smile lifting the corner of her mouth made my blood boil.

"That's why you made them bring me down here. You and Brandon planned this whole thing out. You are just as sick and twisted as he is. You have two seconds to tell me where he took her. If anything happens to her, you will be tried right along with Fagan. You better start singing, you fucking canary."

"I promise, I know nothing. I was just supposed to get you away from her, I swear, that's all. Nothing else." Gigi stood and reached for me. "Kayson, listen to me. I'm in love with you."

"Don't you fucking touch me. You are under arrest for falsifying information, obstructing justice, and for acting as an accomplice to kidnapping, which is a felony. And if you know where Fagan is, I suggest you tell us, now!"

"I don't, I swear. Believe me." Callum let out a snort. "Little late to ask for anyone to believe you. I think that ship has sailed." He signaled for a deputy to come and read Gigi her rights before hauling her off to central processing.

I picked up my phone to call Ariel, only to realize I had missed two new incoming calls from her. I pressed the icon that would bring up the call information, and my heart started to jackhammer in my chest. The first one lasted a minute, and the second call, which came in five minutes later, lasted two minutes.

I yanked the door to the interrogation room open and yelled, "Stop!"

When the deputy escorting Gigi away in cuffs turned, and I met Gigi's eyes, I knew. "Where is Ariel? I know that you answered my phone and spoke to her." I could feel my blood boiling as I restrained myself from not breaking this woman's neck.

She looked down at her feet.

"Get her the fuck out of here, see if you can find out anything." I swiped my phone and searched for Piper's number.

"What?" Her curt answer took me back.

"I'm heading down there, what do we know so far?"

"Kayson this place is a madhouse. I don't think that is such a great idea."

There was a commotion in the background and then Stella was yelling. "Tell him he's a fucking asshole, this is all his fucking fault. If anything happens to her, I'm coming after him."

The sound cut off as if Piper covered the phone with her hand, and I waited, growing more impatient by the second. Finally, Piper came back on the line.

"As you can tell, tempers are flaring. I know you want to come down here, but I think it may be best if you went home. You can check to see if she's there."

"Piper what the fuck is this about? I've been at the station. We just arrested Gigi. Callum interviewed her, but she insisted they bring me in and that she had something she would only tell me. The whole thing was a plan to separate us. Now stop playing games and tell me what you fucking know."

"Okay. Hold on." She covered the phone again, but I could clearly hear her telling Stella to calm the hell down and that she didn't think I was having an affair with Gigi.

"What the fuck did you just say?" I screamed it loud enough that she heard me, and she gave me her damn attention back. I swore that I was making them all go on ADD meds. This was not the time for them to lose focus.

"Kayson, I'll explain while you drive." I listened to Piper rehash tonight's events from Sixes up until the moment that Ariel went to the restroom and never came out. "We watched the surveillance videos, she came out of the restroom, returned to the main dining area, then made a one eighty and hightailed it out the back door. I'm not sure if she saw something . . ."

"Or someone." I added for her, I disconnected from Piper and then dialed the first number I'd ever learned.

"Hello?"

"Pop, I need help, and I don't have time to give you all the details. Ariel is missing, and I need you to go to the house and check it just to make sure that she's not there."

"Okay." He hung up, and I knew at the core of my being that he would do everything that he could to help me find her.

I pulled into the Sixes parking lot and took a slow breath to take in the situation. I had to find Ariel, she was *it* for me. I picked up my phone and dialed Ariel one more time before entering the madhouse of people but it went straight to voice mail, again.

I fought back the anguish that wanted to overtake me, this couldn't be happening to Ariel, my Ariel.

Walking in, Stella's voice rang above the din, "I'm going to her apartment. What if she's there? Has anyone gone to Bayhill and checked that motherfucker's house?"

"Calm down." I placed a hand on her shoulder and jerked back as she twirled, met my eyes, and then broke down. The badass bitch wasn't so badass. "Shhh, we're gonna find her. I'll take you to her apartment."

"I'm going, too." Leo jumped up then pointed to Carter. "Someone needs to get him home, he's plastered." She shook Carter's shoulder. "See?"

"I'll watch him. You go and call me," Vivian said.

Leo, Stella, and I piled back in my truck and as I pulled out of the parking lot my phone rang, I looked down and saw it was Piper, I pressed speaker.

"You're on speaker," I answered as a way of greeting.

"I'm standing next to Aiden and a call just came across his radio about a disturbance at Ariel's complex, Coconut Bay apartments."

ARIEL

Flinging me against the wall my breath escapes me and fear rushes in.

"What have you done Ariel?"

His cool demeanor mixed with cruel words frighten me more than shouting would at that moment. My daddy was a screamer, I knew how to handle that. I had to remain calm.

"What have I done? I have no clue what you're talking about, but you're breaking and entering." Thoughts flashed through my mind, how was I going to escape. "I just came upstairs to grab a few things. I have to get back to Kayson."

He brought his face next to mine. "Well, I guess you'll be waiting a long time, since he's with Gigi. Don't play games with me, Ariel. I'm sick of your stupid little games. Do you think I've enjoyed watching you play whore to that man? When you moved here, I knew there was something different about you, then when I finally persuaded you to have sex with me, I found out . . . you were a virgin. I told you, that giving a man your virginity was special."

The thought made bile rise in my throat, and I wanted to scream at him. I wanted to demand to know why, if it was so damn special, did he treat me like I was nothing at all.

Calm.

I had to stay calm.

"Brandon, I didn't see it that way. It wasn't some prized possession, I just hadn't lived yet. My God, I'd been taking care of my mama since I was seventeen; morning, noon, and night. I'd—" My words were cut off by the force of Brandon's backhand against my cheek. Blood exploded into my mouth, and he dropped me to the floor. I fought against the tears pooling in my eyes and tried not to gag.

Then I saw it, the glint of a gun. "What are you doing Brandon? Put that away."

"Shut up. Don't make me kill you." His words pierced me and reality struck. This was what Vivian's husband must have seen, and the other officers saw when they looked at Sello. This was a man that would shoot me.

Terror had me frozen in place as Brandon brought the gun up and slammed me on the side of my head. It all happened in slow motion, every second a slow flip of a page from a picture book.

Thrumming pain echoed in my head as I came to. I could hear voices outside my apartment, and Brandon was straddling me. Leaning in he whispered, "Don't make a sound. I am at the end of my patience with you. You don't want to see me angry or what I can do to your body. If I can't have you, I will make sure that no one will ever be able to put their dick anywhere near you, do you understand me?"

I nodded at his heinous words. "Good. Now, where was I?" he asked, leaning back as his voice returned to its even staccato. "Oh yes, no one was supposed to touch you, no one. You were supposed to remain strictly mine. I didn't want a wife that people would talk about and share their stories of who else she had slept with."

Everything in my head was muddled, and I tried to catch up to what he was saying.

"But you ruined that! You ruined everything." Agitated, he clenched and unclenched his fists. "I'm willing to overlook this indiscretion of yours. I have to keep you to prove to everyone that I won, after all. Do you see all of the trouble you've caused? This is all your fault." His hand wrapped in my hair and pulled my head back, my neck bending at a harsh angle, he tugged until our eyes met. There was nothing there. His expression was dead. Cold. Heartless. No fear, no anger . . . nothing. Oh my god, he'd lost it.

"How many times have I told you, Ariel, that I always win? You have put me in a very bad position. You're going to ruin my perfect record." Brandon stood and tightened his grip so he could yank me up with him. "You were mine. You moved here, you were naive and untouched. I taught you everything. I wanted a wife that no other man had had. It's what I deserved. How do you expect me to demand respect when I can't even get my wife to respect me?"

I tried to shrink away. He fisted my hair tighter. "Why me Brandon? I'm nothing special."

"You're right, you aren't. But you're pretty and other guys want you. When you're with me, they envy me, not to mention no one else had fucked you but me. Do you know how hard it is to find a woman that isn't a whore nowadays? You ruined that. You slept with that low paid deputy. I'm going to kill him, then no one else will have had you but me. No one will be able to talk about sleeping with you or fucking you.

"Brandon listen to yourself, you're the district attorney, you're wealthy. You have a good career, you have everything. Just put the gun away and go home. I won't tell anyone, just go on with your life."

"For fuck's sake, Ariel, how podunk is that town you're from in Alabama anyway? The world doesn't work like that. You've caused all of this, you and that stupid deputy. You're going to fix it."

"Okay, I will Brandon. I will, I'll do whatever I need to do to fix it, I promise."

"Of course you will." Brandon waved the gun and directed me to take a seat at the kitchen counter. "If I'm not mistaken, that's your boyfriend on the other side of the door, and he's not alone. You're going to answer all of his questions, then tell him that you're fine, and make him believe that you never want to see him again. Are we clear?"

Shoving my hands between my clenched knees, my body taught and rigid, I took in his words and then met his eyes. "Yes, we're clear."

"Ariel, you in there?" Kayson's voice asked through the door. "Sweetheart, let's talk." I heard the doorknob jingle, but Brandon had dead bolted it. Kayson would have to kick it down. "Ariel can you please come and unlock the door for me?"

"Answer him." Brandon grabbed my jaw and squeezed, making me gasp in pain. "Make it convincing or I will open the fucking door and shoot him before he has time to pull his gun."

"Kayson. Go home." I moved my jaw, trying to regain feeling. "I don't want to talk to you."

"Ariel, just open the door for me, can you do that? Let me see you. Let me see that you're okay. Then if you still want me to leave, I will."

"Make. It. Convincing." Brandon spat on me with each word.

My voice cracked, I swallowed and forced my voice to come out steady. "I don't want to see you, Kayson." Brandon edged toward the door but still kept the gun on me. "Go home, there's nothing left for us to talk about, Gigi explained everything, no worries." My words obviously pleased Brandon because he smiled at me, a smile that might have seemed seductive if it weren't for the depravity swimming in his eyes.

"Ariel, Gigi is a lying bitch. I'm not leaving until I see you. Just open the door, let's talk this out and if you still want me to leave, I will."

Jaw clenched, Brandon scratched the side of his head with the pistol, his eyes darting from me to the door. Then Brandon shifted the gun from me and pointed it directly at the middle of the door.

Panic was making the edge of my vision go blurry. He couldn't shoot Kayson. I would rather live the rest of my life by Brandon's side than let that happen.

Kayson pounded his fist against the door, and I did the only thing I could think of.

"Kayson, just leave. *S'agapo.*"

"What shit are you playing at Ariel?" Brandon closed the distance between us and wrapped his hand around my throat, his nails digging into my skin as he squeezed.

All I could do was try to pry his hand away and get some air into my lungs. He held me there for a long minute, and right before I was positive he was going to kill me, he let go. Sagging against the counter, I tried to catch my breath. "Not playing." I wheezed. "I told him it was over. He speaks Greek."

"Don't do it again. Make sure I understand every word."

Chattering on the other side of the door was followed by a hail of pounding.

"Ariel, let us in."

"We told Kayson to go home."

"We're here. Please let us in."

"Who the fuck is out there now?" Brandon walked over to the window and looked out. Any thread of control he had on the situation was breaking.

"Stella and Leo, they are two of my friends—"

"I know who they are for fuck's sake, I've been watching you for almost five months. God, you really are fucking naive, aren't you?"

"Ariel, open this God damn door right the fuck now." Stella kicked and pounded. "Fine, I'm calling nine-one-one and telling them that I believe you've harmed yourself, and they will break this fucking door down."

"You better make her change her mind, Ariel. I will kill her. I'm not afraid. I can bury the fucking evidence, believe me, I've seen enough of this shit. The person that knows how to commit the best murder and get away with it isn't an investigator it's a prosecutor, we know all the loop holes."

"Stella don't." I took a deep breath. "Remember when we discussed DW? Well, I'm doing that now, okay? So, I'll call you tomorrow."

The force of his blow knocked me to the ground, and I cried out as pain shot through my shoulder. "You stupid slut, I told you that I'd been watching you for almost five months, that means listening." He grabbed my hair and jerked me back up with one powerful swing from his right hand my eyes were on fire and I couldn't tell if they were still in the socket. "You may have found the bug in your apartment, but I still had eyes and ears everywhere. You would be shocked

216

to find out just how easy it was for me to pay someone to break into your phone and give me access to the camera and microphone. I listened and watched."

He came and crouched next to me, and I squeezed my eyes closed. "You never went anywhere without that thing . . ."

KAYSON

*S*taying quiet as I stood on the other side of that door was one of the hardest things I'd ever done. But Porter and Finn from SWAT were lining up their team while the building was evacuated and a perimeter set up. Taking down Fagan had to be done by the book, we had to dot our i's and cross our t's, because if we didn't, he would get off on a technicality.

The hair on the back of my neck stood on end, it was that sixth sense, so to speak, that same feeling that kept many cops alive. My hand rested on the butt of my gun as the voice in Ariel's apartment turned to shouting.

"I know you're out there Christakos. This is all Ariel's fault. If she had only done as she was supposed to do, but she was too fucking stupid. Isn't that right, Ariel?"

I heard her cries of pain through the door, I felt Stella's arm on me and turned for the first time, really taking in the situation. "Go downstairs and get in my truck, now, both of you. That's an official order." The look on Leo and Stella's faces crumbled, and I understood their feelings. They loved Ariel, not in the same as I did, but they loved her. "When she gets out of there, she's going to need the both of you." They moved reluctantly toward the stairwell as SWAT took formation.

218

Brandon's shouts continued inside the apartment, he was on a tirade. "Why didn't you listen to me? After the two idiots I hired scared you, you were supposed to run to me and beg me to forgive you for leaving. You were supposed to come to me so I could protect you. But you fucked up, Ariel. You didn't do what you were supposed to do. When I told you to stay away from that deputy, you didn't. Why didn't you listen? I paid those men a lot of money for you, that makes you my property. I even offered them money a second time to bring you to me, but when they got into your apartment, you were gone. They're almost as stupid as you, too stupid to find you."

There was a scrambling sound behind the door, followed by Brandon's words, "You aren't going anywhere. I will not lose, I never lose."

Ariel's voice was muffled, but there was still the light hint of attitude in her tone. Her words rising and falling.

SWAT motioned me out of the way, and they were positioned on either side of the door, Porter signaled for Piper to talk to Ariel.

"Ariel, it's me. Will you talk to me? Are you okay?"

"Piper, I'm sorry, Piper, I'll redirect." Ariel's words were clear, but they didn't make sense, I gave Piper a puzzled look, and her mouth was ajar.

Piper turned to me and in a deadly calm monotone, "He's got a gun on her. Ariel is not restrained and believes that she is in a position to push the gun away from the door if we break in."

"How the fuck did she learn that?" I asked, my blood boiling. I wasn't sure whether to kiss Piper for teaching Ariel or to shout at her, because now Ariel believed that she could save herself and handle a mad man with a gun. I was ready to call Asher, a sniper on the force.

"Finn and I taught her the move yesterday."

Finn had his gun at the high-ready and held up his right hand with three fingers as Porter held the entry ram. Three other SWAT members were close by, ready to take point and flanks after the door gave.

Piper and I held our guns bladed, ready to lift and fire if needed as Finn dropped the count to two.

Then one.

As if in slow motion, Porter pulled back the ram, and as he let it fly, he shouted, "Now."

The door burst open, a shot rang out, and Finn moved in with several team members behind him.

The seconds I had to stay in the hall felt more like hours, and as soon as someone shouted the all clear, I was through the door.

Ariel was standing with her legs spread wide, taking deep heaving breaths. Our eyes locked, and tears ran down her cheeks.

A gun was being unloaded and tagged as evidence.

Porter had Brandon handcuffed and was escorting him out of my way.

I closed the distance between us and swept her into my arms. Blood oozed from the corner of Ariel's mouth, and the apple of her cheek was blooming dark purple, which was so stark against her ghost white skin. I wasn't thinking when I crushed my mouth down on hers, so when she flinched away from me, my heart dropped.

"Sorry." Her voice was so small as her hand came up to cup my cheek. "My lip hurts."

My anger at what Brandon had done to her consumed me, and the only thing stopping me from going after him was the smell of honeysuckle and oranges from her shampoo. Having Ariel in my arms was the only thing keeping me from killing him. Ever so gently, I traced my fingers along the side of her mouth, wiping away the blood that trickled, and she winced.

"You're going to have puffy lips," I whispered. "And one hell of a headache."

The paramedics rushed in, I held Ariel in my arms, her back to Brandon so that she didn't have to see him again, I waited until Porter pushed him through the door and out to his new future behind bars before handing her over to be examined.

Stella and Leo rushed through the door, and I heard Aiden holler, "Stop" as he followed in behind them. Stella was trying to thump Brandon on the head with her thumb and middle finger while Leo was sticking out her foot and tripping him.

"Ariel, Ariel," They shouted, running to her.

"How are you? What did the bastard do to you?" Stella slid in next to the paramedic talking to Ariel.

A warm feeling slid over me. I forgot about the last few hours, I forgot that there was ever a time I didn't know her. It had always been her, and I knew it would always be.

"I'm taking Ethel and Lucy home," Piper said as she wrapped a hand around an arm of each of the girls.

"You rescued me," Ariel whispered as she reached for my hand.

"Sweet, how many times do I have to tell you? Always. I will always rescue you."

I settled onto the couch while Ariel gave her statement and the paramedics examined her cuts and started an IV.

LISTENING to her chronicle the events that led up to tonight was like watching a television show. I hadn't known that he had proposed to her, which would be something we would talk about later. When she started talking about how Brandon ambushed her inside her apartment, I had to focus on my breathing so I wouldn't change my mind and go after him.

"He was already inside when I got here. I had just come through my door, and he grabbed me. When I turned, I saw him. He was just staring at me, and his eyes were glassy and red like he hadn't slept in days." Tremors ran down her body. "It wasn't me; it had never been me as a person. It was so much more." Ariel wiped away more tears as Aiden handed her a tissue.

I stood and moved back over to her, but she recoiled, and the fear that was in her eyes just a few seconds ago was replaced with hurt and anger.

"Well, Miss Beaumont, I think I have all I need for now. I will call you to come in if we need more," Callum said.

"We're going to take her to ORMC. You coming with us?" The paramedic asked.

"No," Ariel answered for me.

"Yes."

"No."

"Deputy, I'm sorry but if she doesn't want you to come then we're going to have to go without you."

I watched them wheel her out and stood frozen, she had left, and I didn't even have time to psychoanalyze what the hell had just happened because my phone rang and dinged at the same time, interrupting my moment of pity. Pulling it off my belt, I looked at the name before answering.

"Deputy Christakos."

"Christakos, I suggest that you remain in Miss Beaumont's apartment until you receive further notice. The governor and attorney general just landed via helicopter, and we are motorcading them to you," Captain Getty announced.

"Yes, sir. I will wait for your call."

Hanging up, I looked at the text. It was Callum telling me that Ariel's apartment complex was full of news trucks.

What little there was left in Ariel's apartment, I decided to pack up, whether she liked it or not, she was moving in with me. I was on my third box of kitchen shit when my phone dinged.

Captain: *ETA three minutes.*

Me: *Roger*

I HEADED out of her apartment and then down the stairs. Lights from cameras lit up as soon as my face appeared through the glass in the entryway door. I waited inside until I heard the telltale screams of the sirens and then the *woop, woop* of the cavalry warning people to move so they could get by. A group of men got out of a department van and removed a podium. I waited until I saw Captain, the governor, and the attorney general peel out of the vehicles before I opened the door and hustled over to the officials.

Cameras flashed and microphones were stuffed into my face, but I had been trained not to say a word.

Everyone quieted as a press secretary started talking.

"Let me begin by asking you to hold all questions until the end, at which time we will open the floor for some Q&A. Today, you will hear from Governor Richard and Captain Mark Getty with the Orange County Sheriff's Department. We'll begin with Governor Richard," the press secretary announced and walked off.

The governor took his spot behind the podium, but he didn't smile like normal as he greeted the crowd with a curt, "It's a sad day when we have to defend our deputies from those that were elected to support them. District Attorney Fagan has been removed from office to protect our citizens due to his personal choices over the last several weeks. Former State District Attorney Fagan was not protecting the people, supporting law enforcement, or the laws governed by the state of Florida. As such, until a new district state attorney can be elected, we will be appointing an interim state attorney to step in and handle the case workload, especially those facing heinous charges such as Erskine Sello. Along with Attorney General Conte, who will be assisting and lending attorneys from her office so that our justice system can continue to provide each person with a speedy trial as according to the law." Governor Richard had a grave look on his face as he met the eye of Haley Loles from Channel Nine News. Obviously, there was no love lost between those two.

Captain Getty took the podium next, and he was his typical, straightforward self.

"The problem with this is that we had a man that abused his power, we had a media circus, and unfortunately, we had an innocent woman held hostage." Captain focused his gaze on Haley Loles, the reporter was taking a verbal beating today. "Sergeant Kayson Christakos is one of our finest. He is honest and devotes his life to keeping the streets of Orange County safe. It is a shame when one man can inflict so much damage before being stopped. Thank you to those who stood by us, supported us, and defended the truth." Captain Getty didn't say it, but I could hear the silent *and to the rest of you, go fuck yourselves.*

Getty finished, and the press secretary opened the mic for questions. Unfortunately, the questions were about Ariel and me.

I looked over at the captain, and he gave the nod to answer if I wanted. Reporters raised hands, shouted questions, and vied for the lead to speak first. Haley was among them, but I'd be damned if I would acknowledge her. She wasn't getting one more second of my time.

"How did you and Miss Beaumont meet?"

"I rescued her."

There were oohs and ahhs.

"What's next for the two of you?"

"If you'll excuse me, but the woman I intend to marry is in the hospital, and although I understand your need for answers right now, she needs me more."

I turned to the press secretary and gave him the signal that I was done and then looked at Captain Getty to see if I was excused, and with his nod, I was out.

I climbed into my truck, started the engine, and headed to get my girl.

ARIEL

*C*urling up into a ball, the first teardrops fell, proving that I was broken, not in body but heart. How serendipitous, meeting Kayson and saying goodbye to him both revolved around me ending up in a hospital.

"Miss Beaumont?" I leaned up to see a middle age man in a white lab coat at the foot of the emergency room bed. "Your CT scans look good, we're going to let you go. Take it easy for the next few days, use ibuprofen for the pain and swelling, and if your symptoms worsen or if you experience any difficulty breathing, please come back. I will send a nurse in to get you discharged."

Closing my eyes, I waited for the nurse. Home. What did I have at home? Fuck, I needed to call a cab.

"You ready to go home?" The perky nurse asked me. "Hold out your arm, and I will get that IV needle out." She secured a cotton ball and some medical tape around my arm and then laid a stack of papers on my lap. "Here are your instructions to follow for the next few days."

"Thanks." My soul matched my appearance, battered and bruised.

I dressed in the clothes that I had arrived in, they were splattered with blood, but at least they weren't open in the back like the hospital gown. After slipping on my boots, I picked up my papers and walked out of the ER toward the curb and dug in my purse to find my phone.

A shiny black pickup truck pulled up to the curb and a gorgeous man got out. "What are you doing here?"

"I'm here to rescue you."

"Kayson, I can call a cab. I'm not in the mood. I feel like shit, and I look like I've been through a gristmill."

His hand moved to my face, his thumb lightly swiping my tears. "You look beautiful. Let me help you. Let's talk on the way, if you don't like what I have to say, then I will drop you off at your apartment and run home to start packing up your stuff. Okay?" I nodded. He held out his hand and helped me up into his truck then closed the door. "I want to talk about all the misunderstandings yesterday with Gigi answering my phone."

"Does it matter? It's not like we can be together anyway. I was just temporary. I gave you my heart. Kayson . . . I fell in love with you." He pulled his truck into a parking lot. "What are you doing?"

"I want to see your face. What did you just say?"

"It doesn't matter."

"It matters to me. What did you just say, Ariel?"

"I fell in love with you. There, are you happy now? I fucking fell in love with you and you crushed me. I called you when Carter was going off with bullshit about you using me until you found the right Greek girl to marry, and I get fucking Gigi on the phone. I called back and listened to several minutes of her orgasmic shouting of your name."

"I'm going to remember that you just told me that you loved me, not that you think you're in love with me but that you *are*. So, with that, I'm going to keep my cool because I've been waiting for those words. Last night, I was at the station watching them interrogate Gigi, and I made the mistake of laying my shit down on the table and leaving the room to talk with the detective. While he was bringing me up to speed, you must have called, I didn't hear the phone ring, and she answered it. I didn't realize this until after we had her in hand-cuffs and discovered you were missing. Finally, Carter? He was shit-faced. He has no clue what the fuck he was saying."

"But Leo looked it up on her phone, I'm Baptist."

"Fine, then we'll be Baptist. I don't care, I only want you."

"But your parents. Your church."

"Ariel in the Greek church anyone may convert to Greek Ortho-dox. Before someone converts they must meet with the Priest and attend religion classes but there isn't much more."

"That's it? No drinking sheep's blood?" I gave him my cheekiest of grins.

He put the truck in gear and headed back toward my apartment. "I'm in love with you. I think that I fell in love with you the first night I locked eyes on you. I wanted to be your warrior, your rescuer, and your lover all at the same time."

"You are, you did. You're my hero."

"I've never felt anything like that in my life, and I feel it every single day that you agree to be in my world. I once told you that I needed to protect you—I did that. Brandon won't hurt you again. Now my needs have changed, and I need you to trust me, and I need you to talk to me."

There were several moments of silence before he broke it. "Well, at least I knew that answer."

I wasn't sure where to start but if I didn't say something I was going to lose him. "Because of that man, my daddy, I made a decision that eventually killed my mama."

"I don't know what happened, but that can't be your fault. Anything he did lies solely on him."

"No. This was my fault. My daddy was a whoremongering fool, at least that was what all of our neighbors called him. One day I'd had enough. I told Mama that either she left him or I was leaving. I had it all arranged. I was moving in with my best friend."

"What did your mama say to that?"

"Nothing. I told her that she wasn't ever going to be enough for

Daddy, and I wasn't enough for her. Then she . . . collapsed. That was her first stroke."

"That wasn't your fault, sweet."

"It was my fault. Mama was fine putting up with Daddy's crap, I wasn't. Me. I couldn't take it anymore. Instead of keeping my mouth shut I heaped more stress onto her. Stress causes strokes. Mama was willing to put up with all of his bullshit, but he hightailed it out of dodge as soon as we learned that she would move a little slower and might always have a slur to her speech. Mama had her second stroke three years later, and her final stroke well, that was when I left."

"Oh, sweet, you have to stop blaming yourself for this. Your dad was a jerk, I'm sorry. Your mother stood by him and at the first sign of trouble he left and left you to carry all of that weight. That is not how a real man handles his family. You had every right to decide your limit, what you could or couldn't take, that was yours. Your mother's stroke tells me that she had a lot more stress than you realized. Look at Pop, that is the kind of man I want to be. The kind I want to be for you."

Kayson's words melted me and that night when I crawled into bed, our bed, I was emotionally drained, but Kayson promised to fill me. His warm hand slid up my body, the backs of his fingers brushing against my tender skin as he slid the silk of my nightgown up. He peppered my flesh with kisses, his nighttime whiskers long enough to tickle with each peck he placed on my bare skin.

"I love you, Kayson. I'm sorry. So sorry. When Brandon pulled out that gun and I was listening to his words, all I thought was I wasn't enough for my mama, and I may not be enough for most people, but I was going to be enough to save you and my friends at that moment. It made me want to fight. I'd just learned how to redirect a gun, and I figured if you were in the hallway, Piper, Leo, and Stella were out there, too. I had to make sure that the gun didn't go off and shoot me or someone coming in through the door."

"Ariel. You are more than enough, but as I told you before, I will never have enough of your kisses." He pecked my lips. "The taste of you." He licked my nipples. "Or that sweet pussy of yours," he said as he moved between my legs.

"Tonight isn't going to be rough, or fast. It is going to be slow and deep, right here," he said, tapping my bare entrance. "And deep here." He touched his chest and then mine, right where our hearts were.

EPILOGUE

ARIEL

*R*unning upstairs, I changed my outfit. I had thirty minutes to get ready before Kayson got home from work and we headed to Sixes for our Christmas party. It had been a little over two months since Brandon's arrest and life was smoothing out.

Tonight I was wearing my typical attire of jeans and cowboy boots. But, I'd found a fabulous T-shirt that showed a plate of cookies and the words: I put out for Santa. Needless to say, I had gotten Kayson a red T-Shirt with one of those Hello name tag stickers screen printed on it. Kayson's shirt read: Hello, My Name Is Santa.

I felt Kayson's arms wrap around me as he kissed my neck. "We need to get going if we're going to make it on time." He tugged my hand and pulled me out of the house and helped me up into his truck.

On the way to Sixes we talked about Greek lessons, I had one week left and then I could officially be chrismated as Greek Orthodox.

We walked into our favorite hangout and it was Stella's voice that we heard first, not a big shocker. "Oh my God, I fucking love those shirts. I thought mine was awesome, but you so have me beat." Stella was wearing a shirt with a giant candy cane that read: I'm twisted. "How are the plans for the charity ball coming along? I am so excited for you." Stella and I looked over at Carter when she asked about the ball.

We weren't positive about his whole "poof" girls disappear thing, but we believed it had something to do with Kayson's cousin Sophie. We'd soon find out since she was moving back to Orlando in a few months. Stella and I were anxiously awaiting the drama.

"Good. I've got everything in order. I'm just excited that I won the bid to be the event planner. As you know Sophie's agreed to be one of the women auctioned off at the event." I shifted my eyes toward Carter, his knuckles were white from gripping his bottle of Yuengling so tight. I met Stella's smirk.

That night as we said goodbye to everyone and walked to the truck, a weird deja vu feeling came over me. Not really deja vu since it hadn't happened yet but "future-ja-vu" if there was such a thing. Kayson helped me into his truck, and I saw us doing this exact same thing but in my future memory, I guess that was what people called a premonition. He had a mischievous look on his face as he asked, "What time does the babysitter have to be home, want to go make out somewhere?"

Before he shut the truck door, I wrapped my arms around his neck and pulled him close. "I love you."

"Then marry me."

I was taken aback by his words then figured he was just giving me the line from my favorite movie *Sweet Home Alabama*. "What you wanna marry me for anyhow?"

"So we can have more nights like this." Kayson pulled out a ring that was tied with a piece of ribbon. "This was *YiaYia's*, my grand-mother's."

I looked down at the band etched into a filigree pattern resembling lace in the vintage style ring, a large center diamond surrounded by tiny diamonds. My heart pounding, and my head spinning. I came to Orlando alone, no family, destined to spend my life all by myself. This gorgeous Greek god standing in front of me rescued me, he gave me his family, and I never wanted to be without him.

"If I say yes . . ." A smile spread across Kayson's face. "Does that mean I can kiss you anytime I want?"

Kayson didn't answer me until we got home.

"Mm-hm." He rolled so I was caged under him and slid his hand down so he could pop the elastic on the top of my panties. "Take these off."

I nodded, tossed the fabric on the floor, and smiled as he kissed his way down my body.

He leaned on his forearms and dropped a hand between my thighs. I moaned when he slid one finger then two inside me. He took his time, hitting all the right spots until he had me writhing beneath him. He kept pressing, petting, massaging, his thumb rubbing my clit at the same time. The stubble on his face prickled my skin as he dragged his cheek up my stomach to rest on my chest. With his mouth positioned perfectly he took in one nipple, gently between his teeth and tugged.

I felt the muscles in my legs tighten, my toes curl, and my feet point as my body ached for its warm release. A few more flicks inside with his come-to-me finger movement and an explosion washed over my body as I shouted his name over and over in a soft chant.

"That's one," he said, looking down at me smiling.

"One? One what?" I panted, the glow from my orgasm coating my skin with a thin layer of sweat.

"One orgasm. You have two more to go before I'm letting you up."

Kayson dipped his head, teasing as he drew long licks along my folds before kissing the inside of my thighs. Then with a hand on the inside of each thigh, he spread me open and sucked my second orgasm from me.

"That's two," he whispered.

While the vibes still rippled through me, Kayson positioned himself at my opening.

"Let me get a condom," he said, leaning toward his nightstand.

Squeezing his forearms to stop him, "No. Just you," I whispered.

Slowly, he lowered himself over me, bracketing my body between his strong arms so we were chest to chest, my legs wrapped around his hips. When he pushed into me, I wanted to cry. The man was so gentle as he worked himself into me. Lines of restraint pulsed in his neck, arms, and along his forehead.

"Don't, baby. Don't hold back. I want you, all of you," I said into the crook of his neck, and it was all he needed.

With one powerful thrust, he was seated, balls deep, and his face looked euphoric. He held himself still for a moment before he started moving, his hips lifting and then driving him deeper inside me. I'd never imagined having three orgasms back to back, but I could feel the throbbing, aching need build inside me.

"I'm so fucking in love with you." His words matched his rhythm.

"I love you. I love you."

"Sweet, please tell me you're close?" he asked. "Because I'm coming,"

I nodded. "Yes, yes," I assured him.

He pulled back his hips once more and drove deeper than ever, and I felt it, each spurt of his release as it splashed inside me. His guttural moans weren't words. They were sounds of pure bliss. Ecstasy. It was a sound that rocked my world.

"Will you tell me again?" I'd asked Kayson that question nearly every night before falling asleep.

"I'll never get enough of you."

The End

ACKNOWLEDGMENTS

- Editing by AW Editing
- Proofreading by Tandy Proofreads
- Proofreading by Lisa Guertin
- Cover Design by Najla Qamber Designs

First let me start by thanking you for taking the time to read Enough, the first book in the Iron Orchids of Florida series.

Let me grab a drink before I get started.

I would like to thank Ashley for catching all the clashing of past tense and present tense in my draft.

-drink one part caramel vodka with two parts RumChatta.

Thank you Next Step PR and all of the bloggers for supporting me and this book.

-finish first drink, start on second.

Thank you Ashley for catching all my spelling errors. Sorry that I tend to favour the British spelling which is fucking funny since I'm not British.

-finish second drink, start on raspberry vodka with pineapple juice.

Thank you Tina for running our fabulous Iron Orchids group on Facebook, being a kickass assistant, as well as being a fabulous friend.

-finish third drink and cuddle bottle of vodka like it is my new best friend.

Thank you Ashley for catching all my introductory participle dohickies.

-hiccup.

To my awesome Stiletto's because we would never be flip flops.

And finally to Leslie, JJ, and Natasha: you three are the bomb.

POOF.

MEET DANIELLE

Danielle Norman is a Harley riding romance writer that lives in Florida. Most days she can be found in blue jeans, cowboy boots, and sporting her favorite set of pearls (she wears them as a way to balance her trucker mouth with the lady her mama tried to raise). She begins her mornings at six by heading into her office that she refers to as "The Duchess Suite."

"I've never wanted to be queen; they have rules and stricture. But read a historical book about aristocracy, and it is always the duchess that is causing mayhem."

* * *

www.daniellenorman.com
Dn@daniellenorman.com

- Website: www.daniellenorman.com
- Twitter: @1daniellenorman
- Facebook fan page: @authordaniellenorman
- Instagram: @1daniellenorman
- Amazon Author Page @daniellenorman
- Goodreads @daniellenorman
- Bookbub: @daniellenorman
- Book + Main: @daniellenorman
- Official Iron Orchids Reading Group : on facebook
- Newsletter: http://eepurl.com/cVmu39

Enough Playlist - Ariel & Kayson

- Sweet Home Alabama- Lynyrd Skynyd
- Kiss Me- Ed Sheeran
- Stronger- Kelly Clarkson
- Marvin Gaye- Charlie Puth
- Womaizer- Britney Spears
- My Next Thirty Years- Tim McGraw
- Maria S'agapo- Yiamas Music
- Bringing In the Sheaves- Patti Page
- Dancing Queen- Abba
- Say You Won't Let Go- James Arthur
- Just Can't Get Enough- Depeche Mode

Purchase Now

Available on Audilbe, iTunes, and Amazon.

Read by Stella Bloom and Jonathan Ash

ALMOST

Chapter One
   Sophie

The siren wailed, I looked into my rearview mirror just as the sheriff's car closed in behind me and flipped on its lights. Shit. I slowed and drove just past the turnoff to my subdivision, the last thing I needed was someone seeing me get pulled over. Glancing at the clock on the giant center gauge in my MINI Cooper, it was barely past midnight, but it was officially my birthday. I put my car in park and waited for his approach. Looking around I had this sinking feeling in my stomach, that sense of apprehension that something was about to happen. This part of the road was deserted with no streetlights. For a second, I seriously considered calling Carter; he was a deputy, after all. Then I remembered that he wasn't working this area tonight, so he wouldn't be much help.

Damn it, Sophie, you should've stayed in a well-lit area. I was bitching myself out about my bad decision, knowing full well that it was too little too late. My mental lecture was interrupted by the man's

249

voice that came across a PA system. "Turn off the engine and step out of your car."

My legs went numb, I threw my head back against the headrest and tried to take this all in as I fumbled to unbuckle my seatbelt. Oh, my God. This wasn't right. It couldn't be. Something was wrong. This wasn't normal protocol. Unclasping my seatbelt was one of those things I did without thinking, but tonight it took every bit of brainpower just to find the damn button. Free from the restraint, I slid out from my vehicle.

"Close the door. Place your hands on your head and face away from me," the steely voice ordered across the PA.

The beat of my heart increased, and I was positive that at any moment it was going to explode. I'd seen cops do things like that in movies just before they hauled the person off to jail. Only, I hadn't done anything. There had to be some mistake. As I stood waiting in the dark with only the flickering lights behind me, eeriness seemed to surround me, and I started to panic at the thought that the man who just ordered me out of my car might not be an actual cop. Maybe he was a serial killer. I'd read about stuff like that happening, where some guy stole a car and then pulled over innocent people just to rape them or chop them up. I silently pleaded for God to please not let anything happen to me. I'd do anything—I'd be a better person, I'd start volunteering more, I'd go to church every week—if only I didn't end up in jail or dead.

Feet crunched on the gravel shoulder of the road as the officer got closer. My body was electrified with the combination of fear and anticipation. Would he handcuff me? Taser me?

In an instant, his hands were on me, spinning me around until I was face to face with Officer Carter Lang. "Happy eighteenth birthday, Sophie," he whispered as he pulled a small wrapped box from his pocket . . .

Another voice came across a PA system, this one waking me up. "Ladies and gentleman, please return your seats and tray tables to their upright position as we prepare for our descent into the Orlando International Airport."

Apparently, I'd slept the entire flight from California. Pressing my hands against the armrests, I took several rapid breaths. That damn flight attendant. That motherfucking flight attendant. My dream was just getting to the good part. I rocked in my seat, remembering Carter's smooth hand as he slid it into my—

The plane jerked as it touched down, braking to a speed slow enough to roll to the gate. I waited for the chime that signaled it was safe to remove my seatbelt before standing and grabbing my overhead bag. I stood in the aisle fidgeting, shifting my weight from leg to leg waiting for the slow-as-fuck attendants to open the damn plane door.

I couldn't believe myself, that dream, even after ten years, he still filled my every fucking fantasy.

Maneuvering my way off the plane, I headed for the tram that would take me to the main concourse. People raced by me, I never understood why people ran, and scrunched in, climbing over each other as if this were the very last tram of the fucking day. Trying to keep my carry-on close against me, some asshat jumped in just as the doors were closing, causing the surrounding people to stumble. As everyone righted themselves and held on, the doors closed and we moved. A buzzing sound echoed around us filling the small acoustic car.

Buzzzzzzzz.

Heads turned as we all tried to find the culprit. A slow burn crept up my cheeks for whoever's bag was going off, I could only imagine the humiliation boiling inside of them at this very moment. I mean, come on, it was obviously a vibrator. A quick glance around lets me know that clearly, I wasn't the only one who thought so by the number of people grinning. Men in business suits were smirking and women were snickering.

A little boy near me knelt down to the front of my suitcase before looking up at me. And in his little boy voice that was too loud for such a small space said, "Lady, your bag is humming." I froze as all heads turned to stare at me. What? There was no way. I didn't travel with a vibrator, there was no way in hell I was having a TSA agent find something like that in my bag.

"Can't be mine." I dismissed the kid hoping that he'd go away.

"It's your bag." He placed his hand on my suitcase. "Mommy come feel, it's her bag."

Everyone watched me as I wracked my brain for what in the fuck could be vibrating, and the realization hit, my toothbrush. My motherfucking Crest Spinbrush toothbrush.

"Oh shit, it's my toothbrush."

"Surrre." I heard one man say as others laughed at his comment.

I shot daggers at him. "No, I'm serious. It really is, it has to be." Just as I was bending to unzip my bag and pull it out, the monorail came to a stop and people started to file off. In a last-ditch effort, I finally got my hand on the vibrating culprit and pulled it out, waving it in the air as if it were the baton for the relay at the motherfucking Olympics. But unfortunately, most people had moved on, leaving me as the lone survivor in the security area. I was sure there was some agent watching me on camera waving my toothbrush and wondering what the hell I was doing. Turning it off and then shoving it back in my bag, I swore to never travel with a vibrating toothbrush again.

I walked out of the secure area and headed toward ground transportation. Opening my phone, I sent a text to my cousin Ian to let him know that I was there. When I headed through the sliding doors, the squawking honk of a horn had me smiling at the silver sports car pulling up to the curb.

Made in the USA
Lexington, KY
22 February 2018